# I, SAID THE FLY

**A gripping crime thriller**

**'The D.I. and The Assassin' Series – Book 1**

**JAY JONES**

*\*Winner of the 2022 Page Turner Crime Genre Award*
*(under its working title 'The Assassin Who Loved Me')*

1st edition 2024

ISBN: 978-1-7384433-0-7 eBook

ISBN: 978-1-7384433-1-4 Paperback

www.jayjonesbooks.com

*To George*

.

# PART I

**Dreams and nightmares**

# PROLOGUE

*Who saw them die?*
*I, said the Fly,*
*With my little eye,*
*I saw them die.*[1]

H igh on the wall, the gravid housefly buzzed softly, her iridescent, multifaceted eyes glued to the corpses.

She spread her gossamer wings and skimmed down to the lifeless forms. Flexible proboscises extended to suck up the blood oozing from the victim's hand.

Soon her rivals—especially those metallic green blowflies who could smell death from miles away—would become aware of the corpses and they would find their way in through even the minutest of apertures.

But she was here first and had first dibs. Right now, she was the only diner at this lavish feast.

---

1. Paraphrased from of the nursery rhyme *Who Killed Cock Robin.*

The fly's primal instincts recognized the opportunity. This was a perfect environment. Warm, moist, with an abundance of food. A godsent head start for her progeny.

Her abdomen quivered, aching for release. She had over 300 eggs inside her, fertilized by the sperm she'd stored in her body from the encounter with her mate during the last unseasonably warm weather.

Squeezing her ovipositor, the fly crawled and hopped upwards to the corpse's head. The saliva on the cadaver's chin guided her and the partially open mouth drew her in.

Shuddering with relief, she relaxed, extended her ovipositor and in a timeless ritual, released the eggs. One by one, the first clutch of 90 tiny white eggs slithered out of the thin, delicate appendage.

Exhausted, the fly rested. Two minutes later, out she scrambled and hopped into the second corpse's mouth.

She hunkered down in the still moist warmth while her contractions released another 120 eggs.

Drained, she slinked off to her hiding place on top of the wardrobe. She'd lay more in a day or two, but for now, she needed to rest. For now, her job was done.

Soon, her eggs will hatch into creamy white maggots. And those writhing, legless dancers will thrive in their macabre nursery.

# 1

# CATHY

## Monday 23 July

*C lang*!

Although she knew it was coming, was expecting it, her heart jumped within her ribcage. Shivers wracked her frame. The *clang* of the steel door reverberated inside her skull long after the metallic echo died away. Shutting her in. Caging her.

She crouched on the narrow bed in the far corner of the cell. Knees to her chest, she papered herself to the wall. Tried to blend in; to become invisible.

There is a special hell reserved for police officers and she was in it.

They say hindsight is a wonderful thing. But cringing in the Met's cell, knowing what she now knew, could she – would she – have done anything differently on that Friday evening back in March?

Outside these walls, this cage, the sun would be shining on another hot, bright summer's day in late July. Just like the one she'd enjoyed yesterday, walking through the streets and parks of London, enjoying the spectacular views of the city bathed in the summer sunshine. Dinner at the Shard, then cocktails tucked into an intimate corner of the Gong Bar high in the night sky. A perfect day followed by a perfect evening.

Her world had changed overnight. Never in a million years did she expect to have the words that she had declaimed to many others, recited back to her.

*Detective Inspector Catherine Collins, you are under arrest on suspicion of...*

# 2

# STANLEY

## Thursday 22 March

This was his special place, this rubbish-bin storeroom, tucked into the back of the apartment block, the Naylands. Stanley drew his long coat tighter about him and huddled into the corner of the alcove, waiting for his alcohol-addled consciousness to catch up.

*It's dark, so it must still be night.*

He wished he could lie down and go back to sleep, but his full bladder persuaded him otherwise. He rose, steadied himself against the wall and peeked out.

Nothing to see except the eerie shapes of bushes and shrubs. Nothing to hear except the passing traffic and rustle of wind through the hedges.

He edged out, searching the night for any sign of Grozdan Horvat or any of his friends. Stanley suspected they would look for him especially hard tonight, knowing he had collected his weekly army pension. But they had yet to discover this hiding place where the ripe, fetid smell was no worse than his own body odour. He was safe here, at least until they found it.

Keeping to the shadows and out of sight of anyone looking out of their window, he limped to the tall hedge and relieved himself.

He turned to head back and froze, squinting into the darkness.

*There. Was that a shadow by the building?*

He squinted harder. Fear squeezed his heart. A resident or a visitor would have simply walked up the path, used their fob to unlock the door or buzzed one of the shiny buttons on the wall by the entrance.

*It's Grozdan, He's here, stalking me.*

Stanley trembled and held his breath, afraid the hunter would hear his frantic heartbeats. He stayed rooted to the spot until the cold leeching into his bones set him shivering. There was nothing, no one out there. Neither a whisper nor an unnatural shadow disturbed the hazy March night.

Like scum, logic floated lazily to the surface of Stanley's pickled brain. *Can't be Grozdan.* That evil bully had neither the patience nor the stealth to stalk anyone. Big and loud, he would barge in, pushing, shoving. Grozdan was all about instant gratification.

Reassured, Stanley crept back to his hiding place, but sleep eluded him. Something was not right. A flicker of instinct, a vestige of the rigorous training of his former career that had somehow survived a decade and more of his determined efforts to drown it in alcohol and drugs, gnawed at him. It kept him awake and vigilant for a long time. If he had a watch, it would tell him it was 2.20 a.m., and that he had been awake for almost an hour.

Still nothing. Stanley relaxed, knelt down, straightened the pieces of cardboard that served as his bed and the backpack that was his pillow.

His head snapped around. This time, he was sure. He had not imagined the faint rustle in the bushes or the scrape of grit on the tarmacked drive leading to his alcove. A security light flashed on. Something had crossed the range of its motion sensor. Heart thumping, Stanley cowered in the corner, shrinking himself into the smallest potential target.

*Meow.* Soft fur and a warm body brushed against his hands.

'Oh, you silly bugger! You scared the shit out of me.'

With a whoosh of breath, Stanley laughed, leaned forward, gathered up the big ginger stray and nuzzled him.

Purring like a motorbike revving up, the cat dropped something into his lap.

'What the—?'

A dead mouse. The cat had brought him a present. Despite his repugnance, Stanley's heart swelled. A lump caught in his throat. He couldn't remember the last time anyone had given him a gift. He stroked the matted fur and kissed the top of the tomcat's head.

'Thank you, Tommy. That's very kind. But I'm not hungry right now. I'll save it for later.'

With the cat watching his every move, he picked up the tiny rodent by its tail and set it carefully to one side. He would pop it into the bin after Tommy left in the morning. But for now, he could go back to sleep holding the warm furry body close, its soothing purrs lulling his tormented mind, keeping his nightmares at bay.

With a sigh, he lay down on the cardboard, the cat tucked into the crook of his shoulder.

Suddenly, the cat growled and leapt away. Back arched, it hissed at the shadow looming outside the alcove. Then, crouching low, it fled past the intruder's legs.

Stanley sprang to his feet, shielded his eyes from the blinding torchlight shining straight into his face.

He heard a sharp hiss of indrawn breath from behind the light, then it swept down his body and around his hiding place. The silhouette came closer. A glint of light flashed on the edge of steel in the intruder's hand and Stanley knew this was the end.

The shadow stood immobile, undecided, the knife and torch at chest height. Stanley made out a lithe shape dressed in dark camouflage. He gasped in recognition at the flash of silver-grey from the eye slits in the balaclava.

But the person he thought this was – had once been – was dead. Long dead.

The ghost had returned.

Stanley felt the tip of the knife pierce the skin beneath his grey stubble. He relaxed. He didn't mind dying, waited for the pain, knowing it would be a quick release.

The ghost stared into Stanley's eyes, put a gloved index finger to a balaclava-covered mouth.

*Shhh.*

'I promise,' murmured Stanley. He wouldn't scream or cry out. His head tilted back further as the pressure of the knife increased. Eyes squeezed shut, he waited.

The knife withdrew. The ghost backed away.

'No!' whispered Stanley. 'Come back! Do it! Finish it, please.'

But the ghost had already disappeared.

# 3

# CATHY

## Saturday 31 March

*S od it!* She huffed, creeping her car down the middle of the street. But the sight of the blue flashing lights taking up all parking spots along Harold Road was reassuring.

All along the drive to this place, DI Cathy Collins had wondered if it was a prank. The message, supposedly from her boss, asked her to attend a crime scene in one of the residential block of flats along this road. But she wouldn't put it past that infantile lot at the station to send a newly promoted detective inspector to a non-existent crime scene. It was just the sort of thing to keep them amused for weeks.

She found an empty spot on a parallel street, parked her car and walked back to Harold Road. Even as she showed her shiny new warrant card to the uniformed officer manning the blue-and-white tape at the ungated entrance to the four-storeyed block of flats, a grain of doubt still lingered whether all this could be an elaborate hoax.

*But surely, even DI Paul Hayes wouldn't go that far? And talk of devils...*

'Ah, there you are, Detective Inspector Collins.'

Dressed in white coveralls, Paul stepped out of the double-door building entrance to meet her halfway along the drive. 'I hope you didn't have a big breakfast this morning. It's ripe in there. Hang on, I'll be right back.'

Cathy frowned as he trudged down the drive. Normally, the 42-year-old stocky, brown-eyed DI was annoyingly energetic and raring to go, bouncing on legs that were ready to race off, with or without him. But not this morning. He was pale and shaky, his vitality and liveliness leeched away.

He was soon back with a set of crime-scene protective wear for her and bounced impatiently on the balls of his feet while she climbed into it. He held out a small jar of strong menthol-scented ointment and a sick bag. Although DI Paul Hayes could be a right shithead most times, he did have the odd redeeming quality.

Cathy noticed the bag tucked under his arm.

'That bad, is it?'

'Oh yes. The two bodies have been in there for almost two weeks and are still pretty bloated. The windows are shut, and the place swarming with flies and maggots. They've been feasting on the stuff oozing from every orifice and the smell, it's—'

'OK, stop! I'll go see for myself. You needn't come with me.'

'Oh yes, I do. I wouldn't want to miss you seeing it for the world!' He grinned. 'Besides, the boss would want me to make sure you're OK.'

*That's probably true.* The DCI had drafted her into this case to work alongside Paul. *Mentoring*, they called it, although who was mentoring who was not clear.

At any other time, she would've been over the moon to be assigned as a joint investigating officer but wished it hadn't been today. A text from Mick last night asking if he could see her this weekend had her insides churning like a giddy teenager's. She'd barely slept. Had spent most of the night doing her nails, face and hair, waxing and tweezing, tidying up the house. Doing all the things she tended to ignore or postpone.

To her delight, when she'd called Mick to break the news that she'd be working, he'd replied that as he and Tom Cassidy, his friend and business partner, were already en route to Southampton, he would come anyway, hoping to catch whatever time they could together. Although her best friend Andrea Brown had said nothing, it didn't surprise Cathy to learn that Tom Cassidy was coming too. Those two had really hit it off.

And in her excitement, Cathy had skipped breakfast. A good thing, it now seemed.

'I'm not a rookie. I have seen bodies before, you know,' she said. 'Remember that young man washed up ashore last year? That was bad.'

'Oh god, yeah!' Paul groaned.

Despite the liberal application of the menthol-scented ointment, the smell of putrefaction grew worse as they climbed up the carpeted stairs to the fourth floor. Masks on, they breathed through their mouths. A constant buzz filled the background, almost as loud as the voices behind the closed front door.

The police officer stationed outside looked pale and wobbly, but checked their credentials and logged the details before stepping aside.

All the neighbouring front doors were firmly shut. The police presence had initially drawn the inquisitive neighbours outside, but the odour from Flat 401 soon sent them scurrying back indoors to focus on keeping the disgusting smell and flies out of their own homes.

Cathy did a quick calculation: 8 flats on each floor × 4 floors = 32 D2Ds, door-to-doors, in just this building.

A plastic makeshift curtain hung immediately behind the front door, which opened into a little hallway with a shoe rack and hooks above for coats. To prevent the flies from escaping into the stairwell, another thick plastic sheet covered the internal entrance to the flat. The whole place would have to be fumigated when the CSIs were done with it.

With no great faith in her ability to withstand the sight or smell, Cathy held her sick bag at the ready and in they went, treading carefully along the paths laid out by the crime scene officers around areas of key evidence to avoid cross contamination.

Under normal conditions, and without the million or so little black beasties buzzing around, this would have been a good flat, located as it was in a good neighbourhood, close to the city centre and Southampton's St John's Hospital. It was a functional place, the layout simple. Past the little foyer, the open-plan living room had a comfortable three-seater sofa and two armchairs, all upholstered in a dark-grey leatherette material, facing a large-screen TV. The glass coffee table was piled high with books and magazines. In front of the kitchen area was a rectangular dining table with empty computer-docking stations at either end, complete with monitors, keyboards and mice. Cathy assumed, rightly as it happened, that the three doors on the opposite wall led to the two bedrooms with a shared bathroom in the middle.

Desperate but still unwilling to draw a lungful of the foul-smelling air, Cathy panted in short gasps. The pungent air made her eyes stream even before they'd got to the corpses.

Paul led the way to the bedroom on the far left, dodging the white-clad crime-scene officers who seemed to be everywhere, but were in fact moving in a carefully choreographed pattern, intent on their assigned tasks. He waved for her to go on in.

Dolly Qing, the assistant pathologist, looked up and her eyes crinkled almost shut behind frameless spectacles. 'Hey, Cathy. Congratulations! We should celebrate your promotion. How about one evening next week?'

'Sounds good. Let's do that. Call me when you're free.' She kept her gaze on her friend. Anything to avoid having to look at what lay on the bed.

Dolly gave a thumbs-up and returned to her task. Cathy's eyes automatically followed the pathologist's hands as she placed them on either side of a victim's head, carefully tilting it upward.

'Oh shit!'

Dolly reared back and let go, but it was too late. The skin on the victim's face split and slipped aside like a ruptured mask, exposing the putrid ivory streaked deep red and purple mass beneath.

⁂

D I Paul Hayes guffawed as Cathy rushed past with her mask down, the sick bag clamped to her mouth. Sweat drenched her clothes and ran down her temples.

Cathy's *mentor* went in for a look, but was soon back beside her, leaning over the kitchen sink. Behind them, one of the crime-scene officers tittered. The two DIs glanced at each other and straightened. They were letting their side down badly.

One of the kinder CSIs tapped Cathy's shoulder and pointed to the large black rubbish bag where their own waste went, separate from the crime-scene evidence.

'Don't worry about Remi. His barf bag's in there too.'

They returned to the bedroom where the path team was preparing to move the bodies.

'Sorry about that. I wasn't expecting that skin slippage,' said Dolly. 'Anyway, we'll soon be out of your way.'

With arms wrapped tightly around her waist and nails pinching hard into her sides, Cathy forced herself to look at the two victims. The pain helped to keep nausea and dizziness at bay. This was something she had to do to bring their killers to justice. Their pale, greyish, marbled skin, still bloated in places, was shiny and wet. Even as she watched, fluid still oozed out of their mouths and nose. She gagged but persevered.

They were of identical build, but with the skin on one of their faces peeled away, it was difficult to tell whether they looked alike too. If the photos in the living room were anything to go by, and these were indeed the same young men depicted in them, then yes, they would have looked alike too.

More than brothers.

Identical twins.

Both were dressed in pyjama shorts and t-shirts and lay side by side.

*Had they been sleeping together or did their killer move them?*

Cathy asked the question.

'The bed in the other room's been slept in and looks well used, so no, I don't believe they were sleeping together. I suspect this was all their killer's work.'

'What can you tell us about them?'

'You know, the chief doesn't like us saying anything until we've taken a proper look. "No speculating," he says.' Dolly turned around, saw her two colleagues had left to fetch body bags and stretchers. 'But then he should have been here, shouldn't he? Not buggered off to golf the moment he heard about the smell and the flies. Made me come instead. Said the experience would be good for me.'

Cathy's eyebrows shot up. *Really? Dolly and the chief pathologist?* She would almost certainly hear all about it at their little get-together next week.

'Two IC1 males, likely to be brothers, maybe even twins, in their late twenties to early thirties. They've been dead for over a week, nearer ten days. Both show signs of having been restrained and gagged. That one had his little finger chopped off.' She held up a plastic bag with what looked like a large, pale slug.

Cathy groaned but held herself together.

'That took place in the kitchen, at the dining table. There's blood on the floor. They were then killed. But I can't confirm anything at this point. Ah, there you are.'

Four men garbed in white coveralls arrived with two stretchers and body bags.

'And now we have to work out how to get these poor souls down four flights of stairs without too much damage.'

That was definitely something Cathy did not want to see and from the speed at which he turned and scooted out of the bedroom, it seemed that neither did her colleague.

They went past the bathroom in the middle to check the other bedroom. It was marginally smaller, with furniture identical to the other. A thick book titled *Clinical Medicine* lay open beside the pillow. The sheet and duvet were in disarray, as though they'd been dragged off the bed. A pair of jeans, socks, a black t-shirt and jumper lay on the floor, and the wardrobe held all the normal clothes and shoes they expected to see, along with three sets of suits in garment bags.

*So, Dolly was right. They had their own rooms, and, on the night they were killed, had slept in their own beds.* Cathy paused, glanced at the rumpled bedding. *They started the night in their own beds,* she corrected herself. *Until the killer got here.*

Their next stop was the kitchen area to look for the blood stains Dolly had mentioned. Had it not been for the markers pinpointing to them, the detectives would have struggled to locate the reddish brown drops on the deep burgundy carpet or the dark surface of the kitchen table. Cathy counted seven drops on the floor, plus a smear on the dining table, the surface of which bore a deep score ingrained with blood. Scuff marks on the carpet showed signs of struggle.

'Where are their laptops? Are they in their rooms?' she asked.

'No, ma'am. We didn't find any,' said a CSI. 'We've looked everywhere, but they don't appear to be anywhere in the flat. Their empty laptop bags are in their rooms, so it looks like they had them here at some point. We couldn't find their mobile phones either. Oh, sorry. I have to ask you to move. We'd like to finish photographing this area now.'

'I think we'll leave you to it and come back when you're done,' said Paul. 'C'mon, Cathy. Let's go have a chat with the guy who found them.'

Her phone buzzed with a text message. Mick had arrived and was at his hotel. The same one as before, Bluebell Inn. Room 9 this time. Cathy's heart thudded so loudly she was sure Paul could hear it. Her entire being turned to fire at the memory of her first visit there just over a week ago.

# 4

# MICK

## Early February

The rhythmic thuds of Mick's trainers pounding the streets of London were the only sound splintering the silence at this time of night. It was actually 2.14 a.m., so technically it was morning already, but that implied sunshine and warmth, neither of which was present under the cold, dark cloud-filled February sky. The pub-crawlers had long skulked off to bed, the homeless hunkered down in shapeless mounds in nooks and crannies that offered even the least bit of shelter. Only the rats and urban foxes roamed the streets, rummaging boldly through bins and bags awaiting collection.

They called it the 'dead of night' when all souls – those whose consciences were at ease and those without one – were tucked up in bed. People whose memories did not shapeshift into nightmares and wrench them out of their restless sleep to pound the streets. He had the worst ones caged, locked up in a strongbox, but occasionally, they still escaped and returned to torment him with images, emotions and sensations as vivid and real as they had been eight years before.

## Eight years ago

T he boat rocked gently as it drifted, the sun warm on his face and chest. Mick smiled, tried to open his eyes to the blue above.

The boat shuddered, lurched violently, dipped deeply to each side, turned turtle and plunged him into cold reality.

Mick tried again to lift his heavy eyelids. His eyeballs scurried around their sockets, seeking freedom, seeking light. He licked cracked lips with a dry tongue. Thirsty, so very thirsty.

*Where am I?*

He could not recall, but every bone in his body knew that wherever he was, it was not a good place to be.

It took an effort to remember he needed a hand to scrub at his eyelids, to peel them open. To look, to see where he was.

But where were his hands?

Behind him.

His brain clamoured for attention, reminded him he was in pain, but he ignored it. He told it to shut up and work out how to get home instead.

*Home was a place. No, it was a time before this. Stop! Now was not the place to think about it.*

Sensations trickled through and suddenly, every single part, every single cell in his body screamed. The pain threatened to overwhelm him.

*Ignore it! Focus!*

In this battle of wills, SAS Captain Michael O'Neal needed to win, if only to survive.

Mick tried to ignore the stench of sweat, urine, faeces and stale food. There was no one else in here, so it must be his own excretions. That had to be better than sitting in someone else's waste, right?

But his treacherous mind was not done with him yet. First, it booted forward a memory, the image of one of his captors laughing as he unzipped his trousers. Next it pushed the sensations to the forefront, the warmth of urine flooding his face even as he jerked his head, holding his breath, eyes and mouth squeezed shut. Then the pressure and pain as his captors held his head still as they prised his mouth open.

A scream of fury arose from the pit of his stomach. But his survival instinct was brighter and swifter. It leapt forward, clamped his jaws shut, locking the bellow behind sealed lips.

*Breathe. Think. What happened? How'd I get here?*

Memory crash-landed and ejected its passengers all at once. Mick remembered the *bang,* the explosion that had rocked the jeep when the bazooka hit. The blinding flash. Bodies somersaulting, spraying red rain. Then voices. The sharp stab of a boot in the ribs, being lifted and thrown roughly into a vehicle. Passing out.

He remembered waking up cold many, many times. Remembered the slaps to his face, the punches to his chest and stomach. Three, or was it four, men shouting. He'd fought back and knew he had hurt them. That was when they'd used the needle and syringe.

He could not, would not, let them use the needle again.

How long had he been here? Days? Weeks? The door to the storeroom of recollections of what had happened during that time, what his captors had done to him, tried to swing open, but he thumped it shut.

Mick drew in several deep breaths and took stock. Wrists cuffed together behind the straight back of the metal chair. He stretch-tested them. Bound tight, the plastic zip ties pinched the skin. He tried lifting his hands and gasped in surprise to find that he could. They had not cuffed him to the chair.

Ankles cuffed together, but again, not to the chair. He wondered why. Realized it was so they could move him quickly if they needed to.

Mick pushed himself up off the chair, linked his fingers, leaned forwards then sideways, twisted his arms over his head and rotated his shoulders to bring his wrists to the front. He had not tried this trick in a long while and it hurt, but no more than the rest of him.

He rubbed scabbed eyelids, picked at them with his fingernails and prised them open. Everything remained black. He saw no more with his eyes open than shut.

Panic banged at his chest until reason whispered that he was in the dark. He blinked, squinted, made out the squarish shape of the small windowless room, his chair the only furniture.

Voices outside approached the door. He sat, bare feet planted firmly on the earthen floor, hunched over, let his head droop, pulled his shoulders back so that his arms appeared to be still cuffed behind the chair.

Now they were inside. He watched through slitted eyes. Three of them, chatting in Dari. No sign of rush or alarm in their tones. Mick listened hard. He knew enough of both Dari and Pashto, learnt during the months of this posting to Afghanistan, to understand.

They were going to move him, to hand him over to another group, to *another command*. Early tomorrow morning.

They came closer. One set a kerosene lamp on the floor, one carried what looked like a bucket. All three had rifles slung over their shoulders. They fanned out, stood shoulder to shoulder, one on each side, the third with the bucket positioned directly in front of him.

'Shame, we have to give him up. I was enjoying him,' said the one with the bucket.

Mick knew who he would kill first.

As the two on either side leaned forward, reached out to grasp his shoulders to straighten him up, Mick exploded.

He caught their necks within the confines of his cuffed arms, crashing their heads into each other, unbalancing them. He volleyed the metal bucket upwards with his cupped hands, heard the *crunch* when it hit the third man full in the face, breaking his nose and several front teeth as he toppled backwards under the weight of water and metal.

Mick grabbed the rifle from the man nearest to him and smashed the butt hard against the side of his head. The one on the left lifted his gun to his shoulder, but Mick brought his weapon around in a full swing, felt the vibration up to his shoulder when it connected with his captor's jaw. He closed his eyes to avoid the blood spray and bone splinters. The man collapsed in a heap, cradling his skewed chin, now hanging beneath his ear.

The bucket man tried to sit up, to align his rifle. There were others in the camp outside. Mick could not risk alerting them to the sound of a shot. Using the rifle like a baseball bat once more, he targeted the head and watched the bucket man's neck snap as he hit a home run.

Now he had time. The bucket man was not going anywhere, ever, and the other two were too busy trying to hold their faces together.

Mick dropped the rifle, shuffled up behind each man and with an efficient twist, broke their necks. He found a sheathed combat knife in one man's pocket and cut himself free.

Clothes. He needed clothes. Assessed their sizes. Recognized the boots and socks on the man on the right. A simple choice, then. Mick undressed the man, donned his clothes, reclaimed his boots and socks.

He stripped off their ammunition belts, chuckled at the two hand grenades in the bucket man's pockets, then dragged the bodies out of sight and dumped them in the shitting corner of the room.

He checked their rifles. All were fully loaded. Slung two across his back and turned towards the door.

His brain, too, had been busy. It had cobbled together the tiny pieces of the jigsaw – images, conversations, impressions – and concluded that this camp was almost certainly a small command.

*Probably not more than a dozen men at the most. Should be easy-peasy,* it assured him.

The liar.

Mick picked up the third rifle and slipped outside.

# 5

## CATHY

**Saturday 31 March**

Hands clasped around his head, Terry Dawson sat hunched over the steering wheel beside a police constable. He raised an ashen face when DI Paul Hayes rapped on the car window.

Luckily for the detectives, the first attending officer (FAO) sent to the scene had been an experienced one. He had assessed the situation correctly and done everything by the book. After a quick glimpse of the corpses told him that CPR would be pointless, he had warned the paramedics. Described the state of the bodies so they'd be prepared to issue the necessary Recognition of Life Extinct forms. They certainly would not be trying to resuscitate the victims. He blocked further public access to the flat, requested his superiors for backup, and informed CID. He also held on to Terry Dawson, who had reported finding the bodies.

The police constable vacated the passenger seat and while Paul walked around to take his place, Cathy slipped into the back seat, sliding across to the other side so she could watch Terry Dawson's face. It never ceased to surprise her how young so many employees in the estate agency and property management sector were, yet they all had an air of supreme self-confidence and spoke with authority on their subject.

Terry Dawson, 29, who looked about 22, was the primary contact for the leaseholders of the apartment block.

'My company, Wallis & White, is a firm of chartered surveyors, but we also provide block-management services for both commercial and residential freeholders. That means we look after all the maintenance and repairs for the building and the grounds. I look after this building, the Naylands, and six others. The leaseholders contact me if there are any issues,' he told them.

'So, what made you come out on a Saturday morning?'

'I'd been getting a few calls and emails from some of the residents complaining about a smell from Flat 401, but it didn't sound urgent, so I left it. Thought it was probably a blocked drain. I planned to come here sometime next week. Then last night, I got a call from Mrs Harman in Flat 404. She's also a director of the freehold company, Naylands Limited.'

From the change in his tone, Cathy guessed Mrs Harman was not a lady to be easily ignored.

'Mrs Harman said that the smell was unbearable and if I didn't get there immediately, she was going to call the police and have them break down the door. I calmed her down and promised to come this morning, which I did. And then when I opened the door—' He shivered.

'I know this is difficult, but can you tell us exactly what you saw? What time did you get here?'

At Cathy's question, Dawson twisted in his seat to face her.

'About 9.45 a.m. I parked here, and as soon as I entered the building, I saw what Mrs Harman meant about the smell. It was bad and got worse as I reached the fourth floor. I'd already emailed, phoned and texted both the Dwyers several times during the past few days, but got no reply. Under the lease terms, we can enter if there's a good reason. I have keys to the flat but have never had to use it before. Anyway, I rang the bell and knocked several times just in case they were in. I could hear buzzing and thought it must be their TV. There was no answer, so I went in.'

He hunched his shoulders and shuddered at the memory. The detectives waited while he composed himself. He drew in a deep breath and continued.

'Luckily, I'd shut the front door behind me, otherwise all those flies would've been in the stairwell. The smell made me feel sick, so I held my nose. I wondered if the tenants had been dissecting something in the flat. They're, er, were doctors after all.'

'And then?'

Dawson gulped and gazed off into the distance. 'Except for the flies, everything looked OK in the living room. There was a pizza box and four empty lager cans on the coffee table. The kitchen and dining area looked normal, but most of the flies seemed to be in the bedroom nearest the kitchen. So I went in there. That's when I saw them. It was horrible!' He gagged and panted hard.

'Take your time, Terry.'

The young man turned towards the open window, took a few deep breaths.

'At first, I couldn't make sense of what I was seeing, and then when I did, I'm afraid I turned and threw up in the kitchen sink. After that, I couldn't stay in there any longer, so I got out and sat on the stairs for a while and then I called the police.'

'What can you tell us about the two victims?'

'Not much, really. I only know their names: Derek and Dillion Dwyer. I understand they're both junior doctors at Southampton St. John's. This is a popular place for people working at the hospital. The Dwyers rent the flat from Brenda Knight and have lived here for three years. The owner, Mrs Knight, lives in London and we handle all the rental and maintenance issues for her. I know the two Dwyers keep odd hours because of their shift work, but I've not had any complaints about them.'

'Are there any security cameras in the building?' asked Paul.

Dawson shook his head. 'No, there was talk of installing one by the main door into the building, but in the end, the residents agreed it wasn't particularly useful or necessary. The argument at the time was that to access the flats, one must first pass through the building entrance doors. That's double the security of a house. And there are motion-sensor security lights. But I expect after this, the residents will see things differently.'

'How does the entry to the building and the flats work?'

'Every leaseholder has one of these.' He held up a small black clicker fob. 'It unlocks the entry door to the building. And then they have keys to their individual flats.'

'Is the main door always locked? How do post and parcels get delivered?' asked Cathy.

'The local Royal Mail sorting office has a fob like this to access the main entrance, but it only works between 7 a.m. and 4 p.m. All other delivery companies have to buzz one of the flats to be let into the building.'

'Does the panel record the entry and exit times for each fob?'

'No, it doesn't. Three or maybe four years ago at their annual general meeting, the residents discussed upgrading the system, but in the end, they voted to stay with the existing one.'

*We need to check out those locks and work out how easy it was to gain access to the building.* Cathy made a note in her pocketbook, adding to a growing list of To Dos.

'Have you had any problems with unlawful entry or vandalism?'

'No, never. Touch wood.' He tapped his head. 'And certainly nothing like this. What happened to them? Who did that?'

'We've only just begun investigating, Terry. We need you to come to the station today for a formal statement while it's fresh in your mind. Can you do that?'

He nodded.

They thanked him, got out, and watched him pull slowly away. Dolly and her team had already left with the corpses, but the crime-scene officers were still about gathering forensic evidence as Cathy and Paul headed towards the building entrance to check the locks.

# 6

# MICK

## Late February

The carpet muted his footfalls as he ran up the stairs: 59, 60, 61 ... Without slowing, Mick crouched low, reached out, placed his hands past the 62nd step, launched himself into a roll and sprang upright to stand with his back wedged into a corner of the landing just outside Flat 4C on the fourth floor.

*So far so good.* All looked well in his home in the red-brick building – Inglewood Mansions – in West Hampstead, London.

Mick tapped the stopwatch button on his wristwatch, wiped the sweat off his brows, and squinted at his wrist.

*Damn! One second slower than last week.*

*If only there were ten more treads, it'd be just like Rocky Balboa's 72 steps up to the Philadelphia Museum of Art.* And a terrific way to crown his bi-weekly half-marathon. But unlike his boyhood hero, Mick had no interest in running 30-plus miles. He preferred speed.

*But you can't outrun a bullet.*

He touched the puckered scar of the entry wound beneath his sweatshirt just above his heart and flexed his left shoulder against the dull ache.

He stared intently at the front door before unlocking it, then slipped inside, relocked and set the safety chain. Exchanging his damp trainers for a clean, dry pair, he moved into the open-plan living room to complete ten minutes of stretches.

Mick walked into the spare bedroom he'd converted into a home gym. Professional-quality cross trainer, rowing machine, bench press and punching bags lined the perimeter of the room with its mirrored wall and a large-screen TV.

Enlarged photos lined another wall, all images of the same girl from infancy to her early twenties. His daughter, Ayesha, who called someone else Dad.

He stopped to stare at one full-facial shot. A present from Leila on their daughter's 21st birthday.

It was like looking into a mirror and seeing a female version of himself. Dark-brown hair springing from a wide forehead above dark-lashed grey eyes, high cheekbones, wide mouth, square jaws. Mick did not consider himself good-looking, but Ayesha was beautiful.

Mouth twisting in a wry smile, his gaze rested on the earliest photo. Ayesha, just days old.

Twenty-one years ago, he was offered £100,000 by Leila's father to keep out of her life and to relinquish all claims on the child.

*'Take the money, Mick. Daddy can afford it. Invest it. Buy yourself a house or something,'* Leila had said.

*'But we could get married. I'll look after you and the, I mean, our baby,'* his 18-year-old self had protested.

*'No Mick. It wouldn't last. We'd end up hating each other.'*

Leila had been wise even then. Neither his protests nor pleadings budged her.

*'I'm going to marry Amir. I love him. And don't worry about the baby. He or she'll be fine. I'll make sure of it.'*

Eventually, Mick had accepted the money and promised never to have any contact with his unborn daughter or to reveal his relationship to her. He had kept his word.

But with a good set of telephoto lens and his friend cum business partner, Tom Cassidy's computer skills, he'd kept track of her.

Leila, too, had flitted in and out of his existence. Although her visits grew increasingly infrequent with the passing years, she kept him posted on events that mattered in Ayesha's life.

Mick straddled the bench press, adjusted the weights, lay back, tensed as he strained to lift: 18, 19, 20 ...

His day's workout ended with a half-hour session of Pilates.

Strolling to the kitchen area at the other end of the room, he assembled his breakfast of porridge oats, eggs, half a pint of fresh orange juice and coffee. A glance at his watch brought a smile to his lips as the second hand crept up to 6.45 a.m. *Perfect.*

An hour later, the flat tidy and spotlessly clean, Mick locked up and took the tube and trains to his workplace at the limousine-hire firm in Kingston upon Thames.

'Hey, Tom,' said Mick, walking into the office he shared with his boss-cum-friend-cum-business-partner ex-SAS Major (Retired) Tom Cassidy.

Tom turned away from his bank of four computer screens and grinned at the sight of his puppy, CJ, cradled in Mick's arms while his friend tried unsuccessfully to dodge the little dog's over-enthusiastic tongue.

'You all set? Your suit's cleaned and ready in the back room. What time's your lady friend arriving?' he asked, watching Mick set the puppy down in her basket, where she collapsed with a dramatic huff and fell instantly asleep.

'Quarter-past twelve. And she isn't my lady friend.'

'Sure, she is. She asked specifically for you. You lucky dog.' Tom's laughter boomed in the small office.

Mick's heartbeat picked up a pace, but his face remained blank, eyes narrowed.

'And don't you give me your death stare, my boy, or I'll have you down on the floor doing 200 push-ups.' Tom's grin faded. 'You don't have to take the job if you don't want to, Mick. I can swap you with someone else and tell the client that you're not available.'

Mick's eyes lowered. 'Nah, it's OK. I don't mind. I can handle it.'

Tom laughed, then grunted. 'Now, Michael O'Neal, don't you go falling for that lady. You can bet she has a chauffeur at every airport.'

'It's just a job.'

Tom studied Mick's impassive face. 'Just a job, eh? Good. Keep it that way.'

But Mick was not so sure. He too hoped he was not losing his heart to Missy, the super-rich, spoilt pop star, twelve years his senior, with a razor-sharp brain, ethics of a shark and morals of an alley cat.

'It's just a job,' he repeated.

*For an ex-SAS Captain, now a part-time chauffeur, occasional gigolo, and full-time assassin for hire.*

# 7

# CATHY

## Sunday 1 April

'So, what do we know so far?'

Eighteen people made up of detectives, technical and support staff crammed into the incident room at 8 in the morning to review the information collated since the discovery of the bodies in Flat 401 in the Naylands the previous day.

DIs Cathy Collins and Paul Hayes stood at the head of the rectangular room in front of the array of boards and flip charts. Paul nodded to Cathy to kick off the briefing.

Caught off balance, she hesitated. Normally, the man loved the sound of his own voice and would have led the briefing. She quirked an eyebrow.

*He's really buying into this mentoring malarky. Or maybe it's because the DCI's here watching and listening.*

Like her, their boss, Detective Chief Inspector Mathew Holt, too, had worked at the Met, and he'd joined the Solent

Constabulary four or five years ago. Cathy had learnt that from day one, he'd worked the beat with both uniformed and plainclothes officers to more than earn their respect, and had built a close-knit, efficient team around him. At seventeen months into the job, she was a far more recent transplant. Practically a newbie.

She stepped forward. 'Two bodies suspected to be that of 29-year-old Derek Dwyer and Dillion Dwyer, identical twin brothers. They've been dead for ten days, time of death in the very early hours of Thursday, 22 March. However, we have yet to confirm their identity. Although we found various ID documents in the flat – photographs, their wallets, bank cards, the lot – we can't at this stage say that it is definitely them. The corpses are badly decomposed, and maggots did a lot of damage. But Dolly is still attempting to get fingerprints for us. They'll make a cast with silicone putty, photograph it, and compare it to other fingerprints discovered in the flat. We've already checked those against IDENT1 and PNC. They are not on any of our databases.'

'What about DNA identification?' someone asked.

'It's being done. We should get the results tomorrow, which will confirm whether the two victims are related and indeed if they are identical twins. If they are, then we can safely assume they are the Dwyer brothers.'

'What if it's not the Dwyers at all? Maybe, for some as yet unknown reason, the brothers needed to disappear but didn't want anyone to know they'd gone. So they lured the two victims into their flat, killed them and took off,' said DC Salim Khan. The 30-year-old with thick, dark, curly hair was blessed with a vibrant, cheerful personality and an overactive imagination.

'Don't be silly,' scoffed DC Ian Shepherd, the team's IT wiz. The quiet, bespectacled 31-year-old with a perpetually worried frown, and Salim were best friends, although this was far from apparent from their constant bickering. 'Everyone knows we can check familial DNA and would soon realize if they weren't the Dwyer brothers.'

Salim deflated, but Cathy could see the cogs spinning in his head, trying to churn out a derisive comeback.

'There's a high probability that the victims are the Dwyer twins,' she said hastily. 'The DNA results may show that they're brothers, even twins, but to establish that they are the Dwyer twins, we'd need to test for a familial match. They have no siblings, and their parents are on a Caribbean cruise. We've contacted them asking if they've heard from their sons and that's got them worried enough to cut short their trip and head home. When they get here, and if the twins haven't turned up by then, we can get their DNA for comparison.'

She paused and flicked a glance at the DCI, who was watching her like a cat ready to pounce.

'Until we're sure, we can't name them or release their identities,' she added, before continuing. 'The two brothers were last seen on the Wednesday 21st March when they did a shift at the hospital. They're both junior doctors there. They got home around 7.10 p.m. on Wednesday, ordered pizzas and chips at 7.20, which were delivered to their flat just before 8. The pizza-delivery man said that the person who answered the door and tipped him £2 was definitely one of the men who lived there. He's delivered to them many times before. They haven't been seen or heard from since. They were due to be at work at 6.00 a.m. the next day, and when they didn't show up for their shift, the hospital tried to phone them, but got no answer. Their managers phoned and sent text messages for the next seven days. But because their rotas are so diverse, no one realized they were missing. They've been short-staffed at the hospital and the managers were more annoyed than concerned.'

'What about friends or girlfriends?'

'Ian and Salim checked, but although they dated on and off, neither appears to have anyone steady at the moment. It seems they generally kept to themselves. Their colleagues and friends said they were pleasant enough and joined in, but were a bit odd, although no one could say exactly why they thought so.'

'I talked to the staff and managers at the hospital,' said DC David Plummer, who would be the FLO, the family liaison officer, for the Dwyer parents when they arrived. Always calm and soft-spoken, David was easy to talk to and confide in. 'According to them, both men were very bright, worked hard and seemed to enjoy their jobs. They asked to be rostered together as often as possible, and as they were willing to do night shifts, the schedule manager tried to accommodate them when she could, in totally different wards, of course. There've been no complaints about their work from staff or patients.'

'Anything from the neighbours? Larry?' asked Paul, stepping forward and Cathy guessed her time in the limelight was over.

DC Larry Ives, a big, jowly and paunchy 38-year-old who looked like everyone's idea of a jolly uncle, sat up. 'We've spoken to all except the resident in Flat 306, a Parnell Walker. He's in insurance and away at a conference for a week. All the residents said almost the same thing. They noticed a smell which got steadily worse and some of them contacted the managing agent. It got so bad that the resident in Flat 404, a Mrs Harman, told the managing agent she would call the emergency services and get them to break in. The thought of the hassle and cost of replacing the door got the agent to come out to the flat, and he found them.'

He flicked through his notes. 'Mrs Harman mentioned something interesting, though. Apparently, about four or five months ago, there seemed to be some kind of problem between Mr Walker of Flat 306 and the Dwyer twins. She didn't know what it was about, but one evening, she saw Mr Walker march up to Flat 401 and bang on the door. He barged in as soon as the door was open and started shouting, but she couldn't make out what he was saying. When he came out about half an hour later, he was calm. She heard him say "Sorry" before he walked back down the stairs to his flat. We'll follow it up with Parnell Walker as soon as he returns.'

'Good,' said Paul. 'Could've been something minor, like parking in the wrong spot. That always causes friction between residents. But we need to know. Cathy'll go with you to interview Walker.'

Her curiosity piqued. That was the most interesting thread so far. She smiled and exchanged a thumbs-up with Larry.

'Did any of the residents see either men during the last two weeks?' asked Paul.

'Not that anyone remembers, but no one noticed their absence either,' said Larry. 'One of the residents said she passed one of them on the stairs. He was going down, she up. That was the Tuesday before they died, she thinks, but she isn't sure. They said hello to each other. She couldn't say which brother it was. Apparently, people often get them mixed up. When they're together, their differences are obvious to people who know them, but separately, it's harder to tell. The couple in the next-door flat heard and smelled the pizza being delivered that Wednesday evening about 8.00 p.m. and ended up ordering one themselves. All the people we spoke to said that the brothers worked long hours and seemed to just come home and crash. They sometimes had friends over but weren't loud or noisy and didn't give any cause for complaints. Their car is still parked in their space at the back. It's quite dusty and doesn't appear to have been used for a while.'

'Although their wallets, debit and credit cards were still in the flat, their mobile phones and laptops are missing,' Cathy said. 'Ian, anything from cell-site, internet or social-media activity?'

'Nothing. Dillon's phone was last used to order pizza at 7.20 p.m. on Wednesday. Their phones were last active at 1.50 a.m. on Thursday, 22 March and stayed active for 38 minutes. No incoming or outgoing calls or texts at that time. Cell site puts the phones within the range of their flat, so we presume they were used inside. Both were then shut down and have been dead since. Absolutely no activity. Same thing with their social-media accounts. They both posted likes and brief messages on their mum's Facebook photos on Wednesday, but thereafter, nothing at all. We're waiting on access to their email and personal data. Without their phones and laptops, it will take time to figure out what email and social-media accounts they had.'

'What about their credit or debit-card activities, Ian?'

'Dillion's was the latest payment when he used his card to pay for the pizza. Their banking arrangement is odd for siblings. They have a joint account from which they pay the rent, service charges, council tax, gas, water and electricity. Which makes sense, as that's shared equally between them. Although they each have separate accounts, they hardly ever use them. Both salaries go into the joint account and all their expenses, even personal ones, are paid from it.'

'I should be so lucky,' said Larry. 'My salary certainly goes into our so-called joint account, but I never get to take anything out of it without the missus' say-so.'

Everyone laughed. Larry might be big and bluff, but there was no doubt who ruled the roost in the Ives household.

'What kind of personal expenses?' Cathy was curious. It seemed an odd arrangement for two brothers. Even many married couples used separate accounts to pay for personal stuff, presents for each other and family, and so on, and then contributed into a joint account to pay household bills. Like she and her husband had done during their married life. Even now, they contributed equally towards their daughter's expenses.

That reminded Cathy she needed to get in touch with her ex-husband to discuss their daughter's birthday present. Ticket to a pop concert with her friends. Which was fine. *But no way am I going to let her go without one of us there.* Cathy was not looking forward to her daughter's arguments nor the looming tantrums.

Ian's voice dragged her attention back to the briefing. 'Well, on 18 December, Derek's card was used to pay for a meal for two at an Italian restaurant and Dillion's for two cinema tickets and snacks at around the same time. Which means they weren't together. But the card payments were settled from the same account. On 10 January, Dillion's shopping in Boots included condoms, again paid out of the joint account. That's really personal, right?'

*It certainly was, although his brother could have asked him to buy some for him too, I suppose, especially as they both appear to have been dating around that time.*

'We need to find out who they were seeing,' said DI Hayes. 'David, would you do that and then talk to their dates? At this stage, we won't presume their dates' gender.'

Cathy shot a glance at Paul. He was pretty good at this, and David was a perfect choice. The twins' dates would be lining up to confide in him.

'What's this about signs of them having been restrained and one of their fingers chopped off?' asked the DCI.

Cathy bit her lip as the image of the slug-like section of a pinkie in the clear plastic evidence bag jumped into her mind. There had still been a few maggots squirming on that pale severed digit. She shook her head to dislodge the picture of Dolly shaking the bag in front of her face.

'We're still waiting for full forensic details, sir, but Dolly said that both victims appear to have what looks like marks of restraints on their ankles, wrists and necks. One corpse is missing a section of the little finger on his left hand. It was neatly severed at the top joint and left on the table, where Dolly found it. There's a deep score on the dining table where it was done and blood on the carpet. The chairs have scuff marks where the victims' hands and feet were tied and along the top bar of the chair, which Dolly thinks may have been used to anchor a noose to keep them immobile.'

'Tortured and then killed?'

'Looks like it, sir.'

'And do we know how they were killed yet?' DCI Matthew Holt asked, his diction clear and precise.

*He really has a lovely voice.* Cathy glanced at the tall, slim man, leaning forward in his chair, his dark-grey eyes fixed on the information on the boards. Far from traditionally handsome, he was charismatic and genuinely liked. At 37, he was young for a DCI, but already had a string of successes to his name.

'No, not yet, sir. Dolly's promised to schedule the PM for tomorrow afternoon.'

'So, the twins had something the killer, or killers, wanted. Could it be gang-related?'

No one had an answer.

'Have we established whether it was just one, or more than one killer?'

'Not yet, sir. The killer or killers left no trace at all,' said Cathy.

'I want a tight lid on this. Nothing about torture or any of the injuries to the media.'

'Yes, sir.' Everyone present knew the media would hound them, particularly the top brass, who would get most of the flak, which in turn would flow down to the lower ranks.

'As their phones and laptops were taken, there must be something in them that their killer wanted. Something they saw. Maybe photos? Something they'd heard and recorded?' mused Paul. 'From what we've gathered about their routine, it seems to have been pretty much work, go home, eat, sleep and back to work. So, it could be something they came across in their daily life, most likely at work. Did they then try to blackmail someone?'

The DCI nodded approvingly. 'Good questions, Paul. I notice no one has mentioned narcotics. Could they have been dealing?'

'There's been no evidence of that, sir. Nothing in the flat anyway. Of course, we're still waiting for toxicology results.'

'Ian, Salim, have you checked HOLMES 2 and the PNC?'

The two men had spent several hours trawling the Police National Computer (PNC) and the Home Office Large Major Enquiry System (HOLMES 2) databases, searching for even the most tenuous of similarities or links to their case.

'We checked and found no similarities to other homicides on HOLMES 2 and neither of the Dwyer twins are on PNC,' said Salim.

The DCI sighed. 'Start putting together a complete picture of their lives. Every single day for the last three months. We might need to go further back, but start with that. Find out where they went, who they saw, talked to, who they met. It's unlikely to have been something online or in the media, as others could've seen it too. The victims may have witnessed or overheard something at the hospital where they spent most of their time. Check all patients and staff. I'd better warn the Super that this will need to be scaled up.'

'Sir, we just got a message from Forensics,' said Ian, whose laptop screen gave a whole new meaning to multi-tasking. 'They found a shoe print in a border in the back garden. Apparently, no gardener's been in for the whole of March. It's a stable print, as if someone stood there for a while, and it's several days old. It could've been made on the day of the murder, maybe even by the killer.'

Everyone sat up. Things were beginning to look up. Cathy wished they'd also found half a cigarette butt like they did in the old days, complete with fingerprints and DNA. But with fewer tobacco smokers these days, chances were that any dogend they found would be of the more exotic variety. *Still, a footprint's better than nothing.*

'Excellent. Let's get in some professional help to speed this up. Cathy, see if Professor Andrea Brown is available. She's good and cheaper than the other podiatrists on our list of experts.'

Delighted, Cathy nodded, although she wouldn't be repeating the last part of the DCI's comment to Andrea and risk having her friend hike up her fees. *Plus, it'd give us a chance to catch up and to talk about Mick and Tom. I can't believe it's only ten days since we met them...*

# 8

# CATHY

## Friday 23 March

With the police station only a nine-minute drive away, Cathy had arrived early and sat in her Peugeot estate in the Red Lion pub car park, reading her emails. She even answered a few before her friend, Professor Andrea Brown's red BMW pulled up beside her.

Cathy took her time getting out. From experience, she knew it would take Andrea at least five minutes to exit the car. She had to collect her scattered belongings, fluff up her hair, freshen her lipstick, add another layer of mascara and undo the top button of her blouse. Just in case they met someone interesting.

Like her car, there was nothing subtle about Andrea, but Cathy knew she had the biggest heart in the universe, and although they'd known each other for only five years, Andrea, an expert podiatrist with a footwear fetish, was beyond doubt, her best friend.

The days were getting longer, but the sky was a grey shroud as the two women made their way to the pub with their umbrellas still furled. Andrea tottered in her knee-high, four-inch-stiletto-heeled designer boots as they ambled along the well-lit paths.

'One of these days, you're going to break an ankle in those ridiculous things,' said Cathy.

'You say that every time we meet.'

'You'd think an expert podiatrist, and a professor at that, would know better.'

'And you say that every time, too.' Andrea laughed.

'Oh, look,' she squealed a moment later, grabbing Cathy's arm and pointing towards a small grassy area of the pub's car park with its lone oak tree cordoned off by a low fence.

The man beneath the bright light of the tall lamp post appeared to be in his mid to late forties. Cathy would later learn that he was fifty-six. Of medium height, he was broad-shouldered, squarely built and heavyset, but even from here, they could see that little of it was flab. He stared into the distance, as though he had nothing to do with the thing at the end of the lead in his hand. The scrap on four little legs rolling at his feet.

Andrea dragged an unwilling Cathy towards the odd pair. The man turned bright blue eyes on them.

Was that a flash of recognition? But Cathy couldn't recall meeting him before. Then the man's gaze landed on Andrea and stayed there as a smile lit his craggy face.

'Ooh, isn't she beautiful?' Andrea crooned, bending down to pet the creature that had bounced over to her and latched on to the fringes of her skirt.

'May I?' she asked him.

'Be my guest, but watch out. She has sharp teeth.'

Andrea picked up the puppy, which immediately nuzzled into her neck and chewed on the collar of her jacket.

'She's adorable! What's her name? How old is she?'

Cathy slanted a sharp glare at her friend, who was in full flirt mode, but neither she nor the stranger paid her the slightest attention.

'Her name's CJ, short for Calamity Jane, and she's twelve weeks old.' The man glared at the puppy, who had fallen asleep cuddled into Andrea's ample bosom. 'That's not really helping, ma'am. I'm trying to teach her to poo on command,' he said with great dignity.

Even Cathy had to laugh at that.

'I'm Tom, Tom Cassidy. Why don't you ladies go inside and let us buy you a drink or two? My partner is waiting inside. My business partner, I mean,' he assured Andrea hastily, who peeked at him through thick fake lashes with a cheeky grin as she handed over the dozing pup.

'Size nine and half, Dr. Martens. Strong, sensible, dependable,' said Andrea smugly, as Cathy hurried her into the pub.

Unsure whether her friend was talking about the man or his boots, Cathy groaned. She could see where this was going. Unless he was already married or gay, Tom Cassidy would soon be another entry in her friend's little black book.

'You need to be careful who—' she started.

'Did you know there are at least 632 Red Lion pubs across the UK?' Andrea asked, deftly changing the topic before Cathy could launch into her well-rehearsed 'stranger-danger' lecture.

She scoffed and gave up, but no way was she going to leave Andrea alone with the man, no matter how charming he was.

The usual after-office crowd clustered around the bar, with most of the tables occupied by families or work groups. Her glance landed on the lone man sitting on a swivel stool at one end, leaning back against the wall, nursing a half-empty pint glass of Guinness.

Despite his posture and casual wear of jeans, white polo shirt, a black leather jacket draped across his legs, he seemed alert. Poised to spring. She automatically clocked his description: late thirties to early forties, height about five-ten, lean, broad-shouldered with dark hair springing back from a wide forehead and a chiselled profile.

Even as she willed her reluctant gaze away, Cathy saw him tense. His head lifted and grey eyes glinting silver in the glow of the pub's chandelier swivelled towards her. Their gazes clashed and held. Her legs turned to jelly as a blaze of heat flooded through her. She froze. Andrea gripped her upper arm and shook her.

'Oh my gosh, Cathy, stop staring at him like that! You look like you want to devour him!'

Cathy drew a deep, wobbly breath. This was stupid. She wasn't a giddy teenager. She was a sensible, 41-year-old divorcee with a 14-year-old daughter, who'd worked her way up the ranks to her recent title of Detective Inspector with the Solent Constabulary. Not easy in a male-dominated institution. She was respected, maybe even a little liked by some. She was quiet, reserved. Uptight, as her ex used to say. She didn't make friends easily, but those she did were for life.

What she, DI Cathy Collins, was not and never had been, was a hussy, who made it a habit to stare brazenly at handsome strangers. Yet here she was, behaving like one.

'Oh, god, he is beautiful,' Cathy groaned as he slowly got to his feet, his eyes still locked on hers.

'He is that,' agreed Andrea. 'Not my type, but I can't see many women saying no to him. Girl, he could be an axe murderer or an assassin for all you know!'

'I don't care,' muttered Cathy, trembling.

'Hmm, size ten. Serious runner's shoes. Good athlete too. Great balance.'

'Ah, there you are, ladies. Please, join us,' said a voice behind them. Tom Cassidy with the puppy hidden inside his coat – they could see the gentle rise and fall of the fabric as it slept – had arrived and led them towards the man at the bar.

'This is my friend and business partner, Mick O'Neal.'

Cathy thought she would pass out when his hand clasped hers, afraid the heat flooding her would set the place ablaze. She was conscious of his gaze, his nearness, even though he sat a respectable distance away from her. Neither of them said much that evening. Andrea and Tom did all the talking. She learnt neither men were married. They had both served in the military, were retired SAS officers, but now ran a limousine service from Kingston upon Thames, catering to celebrities and the rich. They were here to expand their business to the well-heeled embarking on cruises from Southampton.

Her hour's break long spent, Cathy stood up, pulling a reluctant Andrea to her feet. She knew her friend wanted to stay, but she would not leave her alone with two unknown men. Andrea and Tom exchanged phone numbers. The men said they were returning home the following morning.

'I hope we meet again,' said Mick, taking Cathy's hand gently in both of his.

She thought her heart would break. Her fingers made a fist over the little piece of paper he slipped inside, but did not open it until she reached her desk at Southampton City Police Headquarters.

Written in a bold, no-frills handwriting on a scrap of napkin were the words: Room 12, Bluebell Inn.

She lasted until 1.00 a.m. before she found herself outside his room. She raised her hand to knock, but dropped it before it reached the door, twisted aside and leaned against the wall, tears streaming down her face.

What the hell am I doing?

The door clicked open. He stepped out. He must have been waiting, must have known she would come. She straightened and turned.

For a moment they stood eye to eye, then hungry mouth to mouth as he drew her into the room and kicked the door shut behind them with his heel.

# 9

# MICK

## Eight years ago

*You have three rifles, enough ammo, and two grenades. Even you should be able to take down a dozen of these insurgents.*

But Mick didn't buy into his own motivational talk. Instead, he was convinced his brain was trying to get him killed.

*What choice do you have?*

He drew in a deep breath, crouched and trotted noiselessly out of the semi-open door. Slipping to the side of the building, he scanned the area. As he suspected, the camp was a small one. A couple of fires blazed at one end, lantern lights waved and flickered as men moved around the site. From the strings of electric wire and bare bulbs hanging around it, the large tent in the middle appeared to have the only electricity supply in the place, probably running off a generator.

The aroma of singed naan bread and kebabs filled the cool night air. Mick's stomach growled and saliva leaked down the corner of his mouth. He swallowed hard, could not remember when he had last eaten. He steadied himself against the wall as a wave of dizziness hit him. Breathed through the mouth to keep out the pungent smells that threatened to overwhelm his thoughts and elevate food as his first priority. Food would have to remain a luxury for now and take a back seat. Way back.

A series of loud clanging and shouts startled him. He ducked down and stayed still, his pulse racing. *Had they discovered his absence?* Several voices joined the shouts. They sounded happy. Cheerful.

*It's dinnertime. That was a 'Come and get it' call.*

He watched from the shadows as figures converged from various directions towards the tent. Like his own base, it must have multiple purposes and served as a mess tent during mealtimes. He counted more than the dozen men his lying brain had promised him: Fourteen plus the two cooks. A quick calculation told him he had twenty minutes max.

*Not everyone will go to eat,* he reminded himself.

True. The sentries would still be at their posts, only relieved and fed after this lot finished. But it should be OK. They would be watching for intruders coming from outside and should, at least in theory, have their backs to the camp. He could sneak around the edges, get away from the camp, hide, and wait for daylight.

*You won't hide for long, not if they have dogs.*

And right on cue, *woof, woof* sounded from the north edge of the site.

Mick listened hard. Two dogs. Medium-sized, or so he hoped.

By now, there was no one outside. No one that he could see, anyway. Images projected on the tent walls. Like marionettes in a shadow-play, the men reeled and weaved their way up and down, before settling down to eat, their voices loud and boisterous.

Keeping to the perimeter, hugging the gloom, Mick slung his rifle over his shoulder and dashed swiftly towards the empty cooking fire. The flames were low, left to die. The cooks were in the tent too, serving the men. He halted out of range of the embers with their glowing yellow-orange hearts and squinted at the cooking utensils. To the left of the firepit, he found what he was looking for. A bucket of scraps.

He crept up to it and rummaged through the mess for bones and sinew discarded as too tough for human consumption. The odour emanating from the bucket was a welcome relief. It dried his mouth and tightened his stomach in revulsion. He picked up a tin bowl from a stack, scooped up two large bones and as much meat scrap as he could find and edged back into the shadows.

The barks grew louder as he drew nearer to the two dogs straining at their ropes hitched to a tent peg in the bare earth.

Mick heaved a sigh of relief. They were indeed two medium-sized mongrels, not German Shepherds, Rottweilers, Dobermanns or one of the other breeds of specially trained guard dogs. Their tails swished, rocking their bodies. They could smell the raw meat and knew they were going to be fed. Best of all, they did not appear to care who fed them. They scented no fear or threat from this stranger. They did not mind in the least that he was unwashed and stank.

'Here, boys,' he said in Dari, throwing a scrap each in front of them. The dogs wolfed them down. He stepped up closer, threw another piece to each animal, stepping ever nearer. He let them sniff his hand, murmuring soothingly all the while before giving them another chunk. This time, they fed from his hand. When he reached out to stroke their heads, the wary animals skittered away, cringing and whimpering. Mick stayed still, waited. They did not stay away long. The dogs slunk forward, whining, risking a beating for the food and maybe, just maybe, even a pat or a stroke.

He stroked their heads, knelt and divided the remaining scraps and the large bones equally between them. They pounced on the food. It was probably their entire week's ration in one go. Tails wagging and grunting with delight, they bit, chewed and swallowed, keeping close to the man who had not kicked or beaten them even once. Not yet anyway.

Mick reached into his pocket and brought out the combat knife he had taken from one of his captors. He put an arm around one of the dogs. Startled, it turned to face him.

'Shh, it's OK,' he murmured. Two heartbeats later, reassured, it returned its attention to the food, stretching its neck as it gnawed on the bone. Mick tensed, reached out with the unsheathed knife, drew it deeply across the scrawny throat. With barely a whimper, the animal collapsed. He turned his attention to its companion.

Less than a minute later, Mick rose to his feet, blinked furiously to clear the hot tears and watched the final twitches of the two animals. His conscience offered no consolation or justification. No condemning admonitions either. It was hiding in shame.

He had less than ten minutes left. He raised his eyes to the tent as he pulled the two hand grenades from his pocket.

Ignoring the taste of salty tears and blood oozing from a bitten lip, Mick strode towards the tent. For a start, that lot would pay for the dogs.

# 10

# CATHY

## Monday 02 April

The crime-scene investigators had not only been thorough, but they had also been quick with their report on the shoe print found on the grounds of the Naylands. Left foot, UK size eleven. Just the one shoe print. Sadly, and despite a fingertip search of the area, there was no sign of the providential cigarette butt or a joint.

Whoever waited there had stood on the edge of the border and his or her – Cathy and her team had not ruled out a female killer at this stage – right foot had been on the hard landscaping, leaving no usable impression. Semi-obscured beneath a fine layer of dust and earth, the overhang of the bush had largely protected the lone shoe print. It was several days old. The CSIs had done a good job of photographing it before taking a cast.

The print could, of course, belong to the gardener, but there was no reason for him to go there, especially as he wouldn't be paid to do so. A team of police officers had already asked at every flat and checked shoe sizes. Four of the residents took UK size eleven, and much to their annoyance, the police had brought back all their shoes as evidence.

To Cathy's delight, her friend, Prof. Andrea Brown, was not off on one of her lecture tours and was pleased to be asked to help with her expertise. She would probably even have waived her fee, but neither women felt inclined to tell that to the DCI. It would also give them a chance to sneak in a bite of lunch and catch up on news of Mick and Tom.

'I'd like to see the footprint in situ,' said Andrea when Cathy phoned her. 'Can we meet at the Naylands?'

They agreed to meet at eleven, which for Cathy invariably meant waiting for a further ten minutes for her friend to arrive. Without the police and emergency vehicles, there were several vacant spaces along Harold Road. She pulled into one within sight of the Naylands' entrance and remained in her car, scrolling through reports.

A short, sharp hoot alerted her to Andrea's arrival. The red BMW eased past and pulled into a gap further along the road. Two minutes later, Cathy got out to be enveloped in a hug by Andrea on the pavement outside the Naylands.

'This is great. Who'd have thought we'd be working together again?' said Andrea.

The pair had first met when Cathy was still a detective sergeant in London and Andrea had been called in as an expert to help with a footprint found at a crime scene. Although of a similar age, in their early forties, they were chalk and cheese in almost everything, from their appearance, personalities, and attire to mindset and philosophy. But their acquaintance quickly developed into a firm friendship, and they made it a point to meet for a girls' evening out at least once every couple of months.

Cathy briefed Andrea on the footprint forensic report as she led the way into the well-maintained grounds surrounding the building. A faint musical jangle stopped her in her tracks.

'What on earth's that?'

'It's lovely, isn't it?' said Andrea.

'Oh, for god's sake!' Cathy shook her head in despair. The woman had tiny bells on the edge of her skirt.

'There it is.' Cathy pointed to a taped-off section.

They ducked under the blue and white police cordon around a flower bed surrounding a big, attractive variegated shrub clipped to a cone-shape, which the forensic report identified as a *Pittosporum Tenuifolium.*

Although lightly covered by dust and fallen leaves since the CSIs had cleared it of debris, the footprint still stood out on the dark brown earth. Andrea squatted on the hard landscaping surrounding the border.

'As forensics may have already told you, it's a Treaders.' She pointed to the impression of a stick figure runner breasting the finish line that was the brand's logo. She stood up and peered at it from various angles.

'Something doesn't feel right. The imprint's too even. Almost as if someone placed their foot here deliberately. Is this the only print you found?'

'This is it. The crime scene guys did a fingertip search but found nothing else.'

'Hmm. Then maybe I'm just being paranoid. Maybe all he did was to move quickly away when he realized the ground was soft and didn't want to get his boots too muddy. Do they know when it was made?'

'Probably around eight to ten days ago. That's close enough to be of interest but not enough to tie it to the date, let alone the time of death.'

'That's a shame. But I'm sure something will turn up and you, my girl, will solve this case.'

Cathy smiled at her friend's faith in her and crossed her fingers. It was early days yet. She pulled her coat tighter around her while Andrea took photographs from various angles.

'Hurry up,' she said.

The sky had darkened and heralded the impending rain with a test run of a light drizzle.

'Done. Let's get out of here. I'll meet you at the Station. Conference room on the third floor, is it?'

Thirty minutes later, Cathy hurried into the conference room where the detectives, as well as staff from the IT department, three admin staff, and an analyst sat hunched over their laptops while waiting for the forensic podiatrist.

*Where's she got to now? I needn't have rushed. She's late as usual.* With a sigh, Cathy settled down to tick off a few easy wins on her *To Do* list.

Andrea bustled in seven minutes later, full of apologies. She moved up to the head of the rectangular table, already set up with a projector and connections for a laptop.

Stood side by side, they made an unlikely pair and the contrast between them could not have been starker. Cathy was tall, taller than many men. All bones and angles. She kept her dark, almost-black hair short in a pixie, easy to wash 'n' go cut. Whereas even in her high heels, the top of Andrea's head barely reached her friend's chin. Soft, plump, buxom with bright red hair escaping in tendrils around her face, Andrea appeared colour blind in her choice of clothes, but her bohemian style suited her character and personality. Cathy's idea of dressing up was to add a pretty scarf or a necklace to her standard wear of tapered trousers, close-necked tops, jackets and low-heeled shoes and occasionally, a pair of earrings and a touch of lipstick.

The enormous computer monitor on the wall showed the tread pattern retrieved from the crime scene. The cast had picked up the impressed print perfectly and showed the manufacturer's distinctive embossed stick figure trademark clearly.

'That's an excellent cast,' said Andrea. 'It's a boot print, not a shoe. No points for guessing the brand. Whoever wore those boots probably didn't realize he was standing in clayey soil.'

'He?' repeated DC Ian Shepherd. 'Could it not be a woman, professor?'

The others tittered, but Andrea regarded him thoughtfully. 'It's possible, but given the size and the style, I would say it is unlikely.' She paused and looked down at Cathy's feet, which the latter hastily tucked under her chair.

'Even someone tall like Detective Collins here doesn't take size eleven.' She grinned.

Cathy glared at Andrea. *Now every detective in here will try to find out my shoe size. They might even run a book on it,* she fumed.

Ignoring her, Andrea addressed her audience. 'As you guessed from the mark, it is a Treaders brand from their Confidence range and sold as men's boots for £90 a pair. That's in their lower price bracket and compared to their range of shoes and trainers, their selection of boots is more limited. To me, that suggests vanity, but not someone rich. There are way more expensive boots out there, but I think the person chose to buy a brand name, but at an affordable price. The tread pattern looks new and shows no wear, so it's a fairly recent acquisition.'

The detectives already knew that there was no way to tell exactly when the boot print had been left, except that it hadn't been recently. It could have been a few days earlier and had nothing whatsoever to do with the crime. No way to tell whether the wearer was a witness to the killings, or even the perpetrator. In any case, they needed to find him. Or her, however, remote the possibility. Cathy made a note to ask Forensics whether there were any trace elements trapped between the distinctive treads that could help.

'As to the wearer,' said Andrea, 'the pressure along the print appears very even, which would indicate that he has good balance and is probably athletic.'

She paused to study the tread pattern on the monitor. 'As these are popular boots, I would have to go with a wide age range. Most likely mid-twenties to mid-forties. I would say he is between 170 and 180 centimetres tall. That's 5 ft 7 in to 6 ft in old money. I'm sorry I can't be more accurate. He could be taller, say, a tall man with small feet. But given his stance, I'm inclined to go with the top of that height range. As you know, shoe size is more or less proportional to a person's height.'

Andrea paused and looked at her audience. 'Unfortunately for you, Valentine's Day was less than seven weeks ago, and these boots were a popular buy.'

'Well, go on, tell me all. How's it going with Mick? Must be good. You've a glow about you.' Andrea leaned forward, peering short-sightedly at Cathy with a knowing grin.

The pair had nabbed a corner seat for a quick lunch in the station's café by the big glass windows overlooking an attractive courtyard.

'Don't be silly,' scoffed Cathy, but couldn't prevent the rush of heat to her face. She hastily ducked her head to bite into a burger.

'How's it going with you and Tom? He seems nice, but isn't he too old for you? You normally date younger men,' she said, hoping to get Andrea off the topic.

'Nice try, Detective Inspector, but it won't work. We're not changing the subject. Anyway, it's not true about Tom. He isn't too old. He's only 56. Only thirteen years older than me. And he doesn't look it, does he? He's very fit.' She giggled, drawing curious eyes to them.

*Bingo!* Cathy shushed her and leaned back with a smirk. Andrea would be useless under questioning. She'd cave right away and blurt everything out. She sighed as her friend, who had, as usual, ordered a salad, nicked more of her chips.

'Tom's really nice, very gentle. You wouldn't think so, would you? What with him being an ex-SAS major and all. He doesn't like to talk about that part of his life, but I looked it up. The SAS get involved in some really scary stuff and I bet those two certainly have. But Tom's as normal as anything. Oh, and I love their dog. Calamity Jane's adorable.'

'*Their* dog? I thought she belonged to Tom.'

'I think she does, although Tom insists she belongs to both of them, and Mick pretends he has nothing to do with her. But Cath, you should see your Mick with her. When we were waiting for you the other day, he sat still for a whole hour with that pup on his lap because he didn't want to wake her. I swear he didn't move a muscle for fear of disturbing her. They look and act tough, but I think they're real softies underneath.'

Cathy swallowed the lump in her throat. Having known Mick for such a short time, she was avid for any information she could get. He wasn't the most garrulous person in the world and had a quiet way of turning conversations away from himself.

*I could, of course, surreptitiously check him out on the police system. I'd probably get a load of information about him, but that'd be wrong. Besides, I might get caught.*

'Tom really cares for Mick, you know,' said Andrea. 'Almost like a son. He was asking me all about you. He told me a little about Mick, too. You know, he was captured while he was in Afghanistan and held prisoner for nearly ten days before he managed to escape. Then he got shot and almost died, but Tom and his squad found him in time. Tom didn't say, but I think Mick suffers from PTSD.'

'I didn't know that, but it explains a lot. And his scars. Even in the short time we've been together, I noticed he has trouble sleeping. Last night, I woke up and found him sitting up sweating and shivering. He said it was nothing and asked if I minded if he went out for a run. Apparently, that's what he does. Goes running in the middle of the night.'

*Running to escape his nightmares. Nightmares, just like mine,* thought Cathy. *Only, I sleep better knowing mine is safely behind bars.*

Cathy's nightmare was Travis Ferrell, a 19-year-old stalker, who had the temerity to kidnap her three years earlier. He'd held her prisoner in a disused shop for two days, almost killing her with injections of a mix of his own antipsychotics and ketamine. In one of her more lucid moments, Cathy had persuaded him to release her hands, which were turning blue. When she became semi-comatose, he'd panicked and called for an ambulance. While waiting for it to arrive, Cathy had regained consciousness. With superhuman effort, she'd gathered enough of her wits and strength together and clocked him a hard one with a length of solid timber lying in the corner behind her. Then she had arrested him and used his phone to call for the police.

Luckily, Travis was not a hardened criminal. To this day, Cathy wondered whether he wanted a mother or a lover. *Probably both, the poor sod.*

After that unpleasant experience, her family, particularly her daughter, had insisted she get out of London and move closer to Winchester, where they lived. Although not particularly traumatized or even afraid of her abductor – in truth, Cathy felt rather sorry for Travis Ferrell – she had complied and was fortunate enough to find a job with the Solent Constabulary.

*And now here we are, Mick and I, two damaged people who found each other.*

'Oh, Cath. Do be careful,' said Andrea. 'Have a fling by all means, but don't go falling in love with him. It'll only end in heartbreak.'

# 11

## MICK

**Eight years ago**

Every millisecond counted. Mick sprinted away from the tent. It was probably the fastest 50-metre dash of his life. Even so, he felt the thudding boom of the detonations deep in his chest as the shockwave lifted him off his feet.

Twisting mid-air, he landed face-down on the rocky, barren earth, palms and forearms shielding his face, taking the brunt of the fall. He cried out in pain, his voice drowned by the echoes of the boom and the screams from the tent. It bloody hurt, but not as much as it would have done had he landed on his back. Not with a rifle slung across it. He quickly squeezed his ears shut with the heels of his hands and braced himself for the second detonation. A second later, the repercussion lifted him almost a foot off the ground and slammed him back, the sonic rumble shuddering through the earth beneath him.

Shaking his head to clear the cobwebs, he sat up. The tent was in shreds, a bizarre shadow-play in progress under the lone light bulb that had somehow survived the blast. Mick could not hear a thing. The hollow boom still echoed deep in his head, but his eyes worked fine. Blinking, he watched the shadows stagger and totter. A few lay still. A couple of men crawled slowly along the dry ground. Others sat still, hunched over.

He needed to find cover, somewhere from where he could pick off the guards as they came in. The hut where he had been held captive seemed to be the best bet. Built on a slight elevation, its wall would protect his back. He quashed the reluctance and repugnance churning in his guts at the thought of returning to his prison, picked up his rifles and ran the short distance towards it.

No time to waste. The two grenades in a confined space, albeit just a tent, would certainly have had a devastating impact, but not necessarily immobilized everyone inside. Some of those who had been on the fringes of the tent and escaped the worst of the shrapnel would soon shake off their confusion and come looking for him.

There were also the sentries to contend with. They would abandon their posts and come running to investigate.

And there they were, running in from different directions as though the loader at a film shoot had just clacked the clapperboard and yelled 'Action'.

Mick lined up the rifles, laid them within reach. All three were fully loaded. He'd checked. He raised the rifle, took aim, fired. Watched the first man stumble. Another shot. A second Afghan flung his arms out as he fell back. A third shot brought down yet another, who doubled over clutching his stomach.

For a camp this size, he estimated they would post guards at five locations, at the tips of a five-point star. He had taken three down, two more to go. But they had ducked down and were staying out of his firing line. Mick lowered the gun, raised his head and squinted. He knew where they were, he just needed to get closer.

But his estimate and assumption of the star-shaped surveillance points were wrong. So wrong.

Following his capture, the group, probably expecting trouble, or simply because they were a cautious bunch, had posted six guards around the perimeter, not five. Mick had also failed to take into account the fellow who had left his dinner to take a leak.

The bullet took Mick right in the chest, slammed him back hard against the brick wall, holding him against it like a butterfly pinned to a spreading board. The rifle slipped out of his hands as he slid along the wall and down to the hard concrete. He gasped, the pain like nothing he had ever experienced before.

Mick heard the voices first before he felt the sharp pain of a boot in his ribs. His body jumped and flopped like a dying fish at each kick. Two men, their faces in shadows, were yelling at him. One, with a rifle aimed at his face, shouted incoherently. The second man's hand gripped the shoulder of the former, trying to pull him away, all the while chattering loudly and pointing in the opposite direction.

He felt his heart slowing and his breath getting more laboured. He stared at the silhouettes looming over him, wished there was more light so he could see their faces.

Wished he could watch them watch him die. See who these men were beneath their turbans. Observe the expression in their eyes above their face coverings.

He wondered what ideals and motives lay inside those heads.

Heads that bloomed and exploded even as he watched.

Shots rang out around him. Boots hit hard ground.

A hand gripped his shoulder. 'Mick?'

'You took your bloody time, major,' he wheezed.

He heard the whirling *thwok-thwok-thwok* of approaching Apache choppers.

'Yeah, well. Thought you'd be able to sort this out on your own, boy. Didn't expect to have to come looking for you. Anyway, stop lying there like a dummy. We need to get moving.'

The aerial sounds grew louder and changed to a reverberating *thith-thith-thith* as the helicopters drew closer. This camp too would soon be obliterated, like the dozen others in the ten days that his squad had been searching for him.

'Sorry, major, don't think I can,' he whispered.

The last thing he heard as his head fell back was a string of expletives.

He smiled. No one could swear quite like Major Tom Cassidy.

# 12

## CATHY

**Monday 02 April**

'What are you grinning at?' asked DI Paul Hayes.

'Us four. The way we're standing in the four corners of the lift,' said Cathy.

She, Paul and DCs Larry Ives and David Plummer, were in St John's hospital's service lift sinking down to the mortuary in basement level 2, on their way to attend the post-mortems on the two bodies found in Flat 401 in the Naylands.

Her companions, being the perfect gentlemen, had waved her in first. Which, she had noticed, was something neither Mick nor Tom did. Neither allowed her nor Andrea to enter or exit any room before one of them. They did it in style, of course, stepped forward, ostensibly to hold a door open, but their gaze roved constantly, checking for danger. *Not like these three, whose focus was usually on their phones.*

On entering the lift, Cathy had immediately slipped into the left corner by the door while the others took up station in the other three corners, each acting without conscious thought.

By the time the four detectives tried to work out what, if anything, this meant, the big cage shuddered to a halt and a ping alerted their arrival at LG2. They filed silently along the stark, white-walled, dark-grey-floored corridors to the forensic pathology rooms, or 'Frankenstein's Lab', as Dolly Qing called it.

Cathy shivered and rubbed her upper arms. It was cold down here, and silent except for the hum, hiss and whirl of machines and ventilator fans.

Paul pointed to the left along a tiled corridor. Unconsciously, they were using sign language to communicate with each other as if their voices would wake the dead.

But Dolly had no such qualms. 'Hey, guys, come on in. Hiya, Cath. Good to see you again! Bit better here than at the flat, huh? Larry, you OK? You're a lovely shade of green, and I haven't even started yet!'

All this shot out like bullets from an automatic rifle in a loud, cheerful, high-pitched voice.

With the media pressuring the top brass and the public demanding that the killer, or killers, be behind bars already, the superintendent had approved the budget for the lab's overtime and additional expertise to speed up the results. Both post-mortems were being done simultaneously, and Dolly split the four into two groups.

'Cathy, you and Larry come with me. Paul, you and Dave are next door. You guys can compare notes afterwards. We'll try to get you the results and reports as soon as we can.'

*Bet I get the corpse with the chopped finger,* thought Cathy.

The 99.99% DNA similarity between them confirmed that the two victims were monozygotic twins, and there was little doubt that they were the Dwyers. While a familial DNA match to their parents would remove any vestige of doubt, the team didn't need it, but the parents had insisted. They simply would not believe or accept that the corpses were their sons.

The distraught couple, who had insisted on seeing their offspring, were still recovering from the shock. Cathy and her team did, however, get one further piece of information from them, which helped to identify which twin was which. Derek Dwyer had broken his collarbone when he was 14.

The corpse on the metal table in front of Cathy not only had a chopped finger but also a callus on his collarbone. She and Larry were looking at Derek Dwyer as Dolly Qing began her grisly job with professional relish.

Two hours later, exhausted and emotionally drained, the four detectives returned to the welcome bustle of the station to congregate in the incident room and compare notes. DCs Salim Khan and Ian Shepherd joined them to help update the police system databases and logs.

'The pathologists estimate the time of death as the early hours of Thursday 22 March. Best guess between 2 and 5 a.m. That's the closest they are willing to give as the TOD,' said Cathy. 'Larry and I attended the autopsy of Derek Dwyer. His identity's confirmed by a callus on his collarbone. His blood toxicology showed he'd been chloroformed. There is evidence that the killer used a stun gun on him. Once on the back of the neck and once on his shoulder. He had restraint marks around his ankles and wrists from plastic double-flex disposable cable ties. There are ligature marks around his neck, with traces showing that the perpetrator used a common blue-and-white polyester washing line. It looks as though in addition to the plastic ties on Derek's hands and feet, the killer used a rope around his neck and tied it to the back of the chair, so he would effectively strangle himself if he moved. The little finger on his left hand was severed at the top joint. It was a clean, almost surgical cut right through the middle of the distal interphalangeal joint.'

'He was tortured?' asked DC Ian Shepherd, looking up from tapping notes into the computer, his fingers flying so fast over the keys that Cathy could not follow the individual movements.

'Looks that way. They had something their killer wanted. All this suggests he was made to talk.' She turned to Paul and David. 'What about your victim?'

'That makes the second victim Dillion,' said Paul. 'Except for the lopped-off finger and the callused collarbone, everything is almost identical to Derek. Chloroform, restraints on ankles and wrists, and ligature around neck. Their killer hadn't been gentle. The ties and rope had scored deep into the flesh. He had three burn marks on the skin, two on his left shoulder and one on the back of his neck.'

'What did the killer want from them? Information or a physical object? Were they dealing drugs and tried to cheat the supplier?'

'No evidence to suggest that. They're not on the Drug Squad's radar or on any of their lists. In order to be a successful dealer, you need an active social life and come into contact with lots of potential buyers. These two men had hardly any social life, especially in the last four months. They had a heavy workload at the hospital, put in long hours there. Not only did they have regular assignments to submit, but their exams were also coming up in a couple of months. I'm inclining towards something other than drugs.'

'Was it just one killer or were there more?' asked David.

'Don't know,' said Cathy. 'There's nothing to suggest that there was more than one. If there were two or more, there would've been a higher chance of one of them leaving some evidence, but we found nothing. Which suggests it was one killer, or two very careful murderers.'

'Their phones and laptops are missing, aren't they? So, whatever was on them could be the motive. Did they back up to the cloud? Ian?' asked Paul.

'I'm still going through that, but so far, it's all research and notes for their assignments, backup of their old dissertations, some photos of family, friends and girlfriends, but I found nothing that could warrant getting them killed.'

'Maybe it's in code, buried within the dissertations,' suggested DC Salim Khan.

Ian looked aghast. 'But some of those are over 10,000 words long and there are dozens of them.' If looks could kill, Salim would be on Dolly's slab right now.

'That's a really good point, Salim,' said Paul. 'If you go through all of Dillion's notes, research material and assignments, Ian can do the same with Derek's. We'd like the results by ... shall we say, end of the week?'

Cathy and Paul laughed at the pair's horror-stricken expressions.

'How did they die? How were they killed?' asked Ian.

Cathy had been dreading that question, not wanting to think about it. There had been so much hate in that room, which made her think the murders were very personal. Emotional, rather than for monetary gain, information, secret codes or any sort of conspiracy.

'Please remember, this is speculation. We've no way of proving that this is what happened. A likely scenario of events is that the twins were asleep in their own rooms when the killer entered the flat. He used chloroform to subdue each one, brought them into the dining room, sat them in the chairs, tied their wrists and ankles with plastic ties and used lengths of rope to restrain their necks. He then forced them to talk using stun guns and by chopping off one of their fingers, perhaps to show he really meant business. After he – or *they*, if we are going with more than one – finished questioning them, he rendered them unconscious again, either chemically or with a stun gun. We're still waiting for forensics to tell us. The perpetrator or perpetrators then took them into the bedroom where we found them.'

Cathy stopped, swallowing hard, trying to block the images playing inside her head. She, like the rest of the team, had seen the results of heinous crimes, the atrocities inflicted by some on others, but for some reason, the cold, calm, calculated way in which this killer had executed his victims, made her shiver.

It spoke of rage and hate, yet every move, every step, had been precise, disciplined. The perpetrator had exercised total self-control, not allowing his emotions to overcome or overrule his actions. Or to make any mistake. The two young men had seriously wronged someone.

'As we know, both men were strangled using ligatures when they were on that bed. The pathologist found it odd that there was no upward pressure on the garrottes. For example, if the victim was face-down with the strangler choking him from behind. The pressure on both victims seems to have been applied sideways, as though the killer lay down in bed with them.'

'God, that's horrible. Why would he do that?'

'He didn't. Although that was a possibility, it seemed unlikely. Dolly came up with another theory, which she tried on mannequins. But she stressed about a dozen times at least, that this is only a theory, and she has no evidence that's how it was done. According to her, the killer tied two nooses on a single length of rope similar to the ligatures used in the living room. He put a noose around each of the brothers' necks, keeping them as close together as possible, probably back to back. Then he pushed them apart, effectively tightening the rope around their necks. And he kept pushing them apart until they choked to death.'

She stopped abruptly when she saw everyone staring at her hands. Used to signing ever since her daughter had lost her hearing, the aftermath of a meningitis infection at the age of six, Cathy had unconsciously acted out the scene in British Sign Language. She quickly tucked her hands behind her back.

'You could say that, in effect, the two brothers killed each other.'

# 13

## CATHY

**Tuesday 03 April**

'There, see that?' The young constable pointed at the CCTV footage from Naylands' peripheral cameras.

Her colleague leaned to peer at the fuzzy, frozen image. 'It looks like someone's trying hard not to be seen. Could it be the killer?'

The young women exchanged a horrified yet delighted stare.

They rewound the video, slowed it down, and replayed the captured footage. A tallish, hump-backed figure, wearing what appeared to be a long overcoat, crept and sidled along the far edge of the road, keeping to the shadows and stopping occasionally to look around him. They were sure it was a 'him'. As he fidgeted with something on his shoulder, the two young PCs realized the man was carrying a backpack and wasn't actually hump-backed.

They tracked the direction of his movements on to another camera, this one closer to the Naylands. The man's progress was slower now and more cautious. Often, he was barely visible as he slipped into the shadows of hedges and boundary walls.

'Ma'am, I think we've found something. It could be the killer.' The constable reached out a hand but stopped short of actually grabbing hold of Cathy.

'Come and see this, please.'

Cathy followed her and watched as her colleague carefully rewound the recording to replay it at half-speed. Within two minutes of focussing on the jerky, slow-motion images, she pressed her fingertips to her temples, convinced she was developing a migraine. Ten more seconds later, Cathy was ready to give up and tell them to copy and send her the clip, when she too spotted the mystery figure.

Like a triple-headed entity, the three of them leaned towards the screen to follow the figure's slow progress across several cameras and through three different streets onto Harold Road. They picked him up again on a camera close to the Naylands. He seemed to be more vigilant, checking his surroundings before moving forward. Then they lost him completely within about forty yards of the building.

With her heart pounding so loud, she could barely hear herself think, let alone speak, Cathy managed a 'Well done' to the PC.

'Do you think that's the killer?' asked the young woman, her eyes shining with excitement.

'I don't know, but it's certainly someone we need to know a lot more about. Have the tech guys enhance the images and let's verify it's not a resident. It seems unlikely, seeing how he's creeping about at that time of the night.'

Cathy instructed them to carry on monitoring the footage to see when he showed up again. She expected him to. Around 3.00 a.m., after killing the doctors.

Three hours later, they reran an enhanced version of the CCTV capture. Although they still couldn't see his face, his figure was clearer in a couple of shots. Cathy hoped it was clear enough for them to work with. Something about him seemed oddly familiar, especially the long overcoat, but she couldn't quite grasp it.

It certainly wasn't a resident of the Naylands. Was it someone from one of the neighbouring buildings? It may have nothing to do with the Dwyer twins' murders. It could be an assignation, a secret lovers' tryst making a cuckold of some poor sod. But Cathy didn't think so.

She turned to DI Paul Hayes for help.

'Paul, do you recognize him?'

'Hmm, I think so. Who is it?'

Cathy rolled her eyes. 'That's what I'm asking,' she said and explained how the PC had spotted it. 'There's something familiar about him, but I can't recall who it is.'

Paul perked up and leaned in to watch the enhanced clips.

'I know who that is,' he said. 'That's—'

Her cogwheels clicked in simultaneously.

'Stanley!' they said together.

Her heart plummeted.

Ex-Corporal, retired, James Benjamin Stanley, to give him his full name and title, was a 62-year-old homeless war veteran and, for years, had been a familiar sight on Southampton streets. A friendly, cheerful alcoholic. One of society's misfits.

'No way is Stanley our killer. No way could he have done that to those doctors,' said Cathy.

'I agree. If Stanley killed anyone, it'd be by accident. I doubt he has the mental capacity left to plan and carry out those murders.'

'So, what's he doing, creeping about like that at near enough midnight?'

'Let's ask him,' said Paul. 'I'll get Uniform to pick him up.'

# 14

# STANLEY

**Tuesday 03 April**

S hadows lengthened as the sun inched closer to a horizon obscured by buildings tall and short, but daylight still clung to the edges of the skyline in a lingering embrace, whispering last goodbyes. With a rucksack holding the bulk of his worldly goods slung across his back, Stanley staggered along the pavement. Over his shoulder was a large tote bag with his most valued possessions – a fan-folded sheet of corrugated cardboard, which when opened out, was large enough for him to sleep on, a thick sheet of plastic to protect the cardboard and a Mylar space blanket that an emergency worker had given him. These he guarded and kept hidden. These he would fight for.

He weaved along the pavement of Southampton High Street, muttering under his breath, a constant litany of words that made sense to no one but him. The sparse evening crowd parted as people stepped out of his way, most turning their eyes away after a quick glance. Stanley clutched a newspaper-wrapped bottle from which he took surreptitious gulps when he thought no one was watching.

For the last two days, or rather nights, Stanley had not been a happy man. That's not to say that he was happy on other days or nights, but he had been especially unhappy over these few days, ever since the police had descended on the Naylands. His block of flats. He hadn't been able to get anywhere near it since Saturday, which meant that he'd had to look for other places to sleep. That wasn't easy. Even looking for one had been hard and had got him into trouble: the first occupied by a rutting couple, who'd screamed abuse, the woman kicking out at him, all without stopping their activity. He ran away from the second corner when one of Grozdan's friends grinned up at him. He had barely settled down in a third likely spot when its usual occupant had turned up and kicked him hard in the kidneys.

Stanley stumbled along the side streets of Southampton, lurching tiredly from one place to another before finally spotting a relatively sheltered corner under the ledge of a small convenience storefront. But the owner was still there, locking up when he arrived, and Stanley started to retreat. The man turned to face him, jerked his head at the empty porch, and walked away.

It was not an ideal spot to kip in, not with the streetlight directly in front and two bright shop lights overhead. He'd be illuminated like a Christmas tree, visible to all and sundry, especially to any passing police patrols who would wake him up and get him to move on. But he was so tired. It'd have to do, for tonight at least.

It was still dark, with dawn just breaking over the horizon when the store owner returned the following morning. The clang of the metal shutter rolling up jerked Stanley out of a restless sleep. Without a word, the man ducked inside, pulling the shutter down behind him.

Probably stock-taking or doing his books, thought Stanley, lying down again. He reckoned he could sleep for another hour before he needed to clear out. He awoke before the hour was up and sat up to find a brown paper bag by his makeshift bed. Inside was a tall disposable container of the most delicious-smelling coffee, a large ham-and-cheese bap, and two granola bars.

There wasn't much Stanley could do for the shopkeeper in return, but he made sure the forecourt was spotless before he left. He picked up every piece of litter and scrap and left no trace whatsoever of his overnight presence there.

That had been over ten hours ago. Despite the alcohol sloshing inside, his stomach rumbled, reminding him he had eaten nothing since the shopkeeper's generous breakfast. Stanley ducked into an alleyway, checked to make sure that no one was watching, before slipping his hand down his trouser front to bring out a tattered wallet. His money, all £20 of it, was in small-denomination coins and notes, none larger than £5, and scattered in small bundles around his person. He quickly counted and gathered £5, replaced his wallet, chucked his empty bottle into the alley, and returned to the main road, heading towards the nearest fast-food site.

Half an hour later, gripping a polystyrene box of double burger and chips, Stanley hurried along, looking for a quiet place to sit and eat, well away from those who would snatch it away. Maybe the parks? They would be relatively deserted now, with most residents and visitors either at home or in restaurants enjoying their evening meal. It was a nice evening, and he would be warm in his long quilted coat.

He veered off the main road and slipped into Palmerston Park – one of the five that made up the 21 hectares of green space in the heart of Southampton City.

Stanley spied a bench and hurried towards it, but stopped short when he saw someone was already sitting on it. Grunting in annoyance, he prepared to move on when he recognized the occupant.

'Hiya, Rafi. All right, mate?'

Startled, the grizzled, rangy man looked up and his teeth gleamed white on his dark face.

'Hey, Stanley. Bin a while, man. What you got there?'

Stanley opened his food box and breathed in deeply.

'I got the same. Look.' Rafi laughed and held out a half-eaten double burger and a dozen or so skinny chips remaining in his box. They ate in companionable silence for a while.

'You won't believe who I saw the other day,' said Stanley.

'Who?'

'The ghost. Yeah, the ghost.'

'You saw a ghost? You serious, man? What shit you on now to be hallucinating like that?'

'Not a ghost, Rafi. The ghost. You know, from when we were in Iraq and the SAS squad was with us for those weeks. That ghost.'

Rafi stared at him wide-eyed while he digested the information.

'Nah, not possible. You musta bin dreaming, man. That ghost is dead. Has bin dead for years.'

'No, I swear. He was there. But don't tell anyone. I promised I wouldn't say a word. Oh, God! I shouldn't have told you. Now he'll come back and kill me. Swear you won't tell anyone. Swear it, Rafi.'

In his agitation, Stanley had grabbed Rafi by his coat collar and was shaking him.

'Stop it! Calm down, man. I won't say a word. Who'd I tell, anyway? There's only the two of us left from the old days.'

Stanley calmed down and sat staring into space for a while. 'Yeah, just us two. But now I know the ghost is around, I feel better. That Grozdan and his gang have been hounding me. They got most of my pension last three times and now I'm too scared to go get any more.'

'Yeah, me too. I'm thinkin' of leaving. Maybe go to Portsmouth or somewhere else.'

Stanley shook his head. 'Won't do you any good. There'll be another Grozdan there. Maybe even worse than this one.'

'True. Maybe we should stick together, see if we can find others to join. What you think?'

'That's brilliant, man! You always were the clever one. Yeah, let's talk to some others. Maybe we could ask—'

But Rafi was staring at something behind Stanley, the whites of his eyes gleaming bright in the growing dark. He hastily gathered up his belongings and scurried off deeper into the park.

'Wha—? Wait! Where you going? What's the matter?'

'Hello, Stanley. Thought we'd find you here,' said a voice behind him.

T he half-eaten meal fell to the ground as Stanley leapt up to face the two grinning, uniformed police officers. He stared in dismay at the spilled food, wondering how much he could salvage.

'I'll just get this and be on my way. I wasn't going to sleep on the bench, officer, I promise.'

He got down on one knee, picked up the polystyrene box and began to collect bits of his dinner that were relatively unscathed; pieces not totally covered in mud and grit.

'You can't eat that, mate!' said one officer, the shock clear in his voice.

'Stanley, leave that and get up, please.' The second officer leaned forward, gripped Stanley's arm, and forced him to rise. Removing the food box from the despairing man's hand, he walked to a nearby litter bin and tossed it in.

'Look, Stanley mate. We need you to accompany us to the station. Our detectives have some questions for you. We'll make sure you get a hot meal.'

'But why? I haven't done anything.'

'We just want to ask you some questions.'

'What about?'

'Let's go to the station, shall we? You're not under arrest or in any trouble, as far as we know. But you could be a witness and they need to ask you some questions. We'd like you to come with us voluntarily, Stanley. For an interview. Sooner we get there, sooner you can have that hot meal and drink.'

It was a long wait before that promise was finally fulfilled.

First, he had to wait for a solicitor, who explained that as he was there voluntarily, he could leave anytime. Stanley thought about that for a long while. In the park with Rafi, he had smelled the rain in the air. His little hidey-hole in the

Naylands was still out of bounds and the overhang of the convenience store was too shallow to keep him from getting wet, whereas this place was warm and out of reach of Grozdan. He had been here before, brought in when he had been 'drunk and disorderly' as they called it, put into a warm cell to sleep it off and even given breakfast before they asked him to leave. Stanley decided to stay.

They asked if he would agree to them collecting evidence from him. 'For elimination purposes,' they said. His eyes had widened in shock at that word, but his solicitor had explained. That didn't sound bad.

'Sure,' he said, 'and, please, can I sleep here tonight?'

Mrs Aslam, the lady who said she was his solicitor, and the custody sergeant had a chat with the two officers who'd brought him in. He saw them and the sergeant give her some money.

'I'm sorry, Stanley, the sergeant says you can't sleep here. But he'll refer you and we'll get you a room at Dickson House for the night.' She waved the notes in her fist.

The photograph session was followed by being prodded, poked and swabbed. Then they took all his clothes, even the ones he had been wearing, and gave him a tracksuit instead. The soft warm material felt weird against his skin, more used to the stiff, crusted texture of his own clothes. They seemed particularly interested in his boots and despite his feeble protests, they took them away. The sneakers on his feet felt as if he were walking around barefooted. They promised to return everything. He didn't believe them.

Now, finally replete with the promised hot food, which included soup, dessert and a coffee, Stanley sat waiting in the interview room with Mrs Aslam beside him.

They'd told him again that he was being interviewed under caution. Try as he might, he couldn't think of a single reason why the police would want to question him, but suspected he might have done something that his pickled brain could not recall.

* * * * *

There were two of them.

One was a tall, slim lady dressed in a navy suit and a light blue sweater that he was sure would feel soft between his fingers. Her shiny black hair fell in a wispy fringe over a wide, smooth brow. Cut in a short page-boy style, it emphasized the long delicate lines of her neck. Warm brown eyes beneath thick, shapely brows stared unwaveringly at him. She stated her name in a clear, crisp voice. Detective Inspector Cathy Collins.

A name even he could remember and a face he would find hard to forget.

The other was a big, friendly looking bloke who looked like he'd slept in his clothes and treated Stanley like an old friend. Called him 'mate'. He said his name was Larry something. Hives? No, Ives. That was it. Like that place in Cornwall. St Ives, where he'd once gone on holiday with his wife, now a long-time ex, and a little boy who might have been his son. He couldn't remember. It really was a long time ago.

Larry St Ives had introduced himself as a detective constable and told Stanley to call him Larry. But he wasn't fooled. Stanley knew they were going to find out whatever it was he had done and then lock him up.

Would that be so bad? He would be safe from Grozdan and his gang but, like he'd told Rafi, *that coward, who was supposed to be my friend but who'd run at the first sight of the police*, there would be other, probably worse Grozdans in prison.

'We'd like to ask you about that block of flats, the Naylands, on Harold Road. We know you sleep in the alcove in the bin store round the side.'

Oh, no! They'd found his hiding place. Now he had nowhere safe. He tried to deny it.

'We have CCTV showing you going in there each night and out again the following morning, plus you've left enough evidence there for us to prove it was you, Stanley.'

He slumped in his seat.

'Can you tell us everything you saw, heard and did on the evening and night of Wednesday, 21 March? That's thirteen days ago.'

Stanley's jaw dropped. Were they kidding? Surely, they didn't think he would remember something from so long ago! He could barely remember this morning.

'I don't know. I don't remember!' he said. His voice, raised in agitation, had them straighten in their seats.

A pat on his arm made him turn.

'Shh, it's OK, Stanley,' said Mrs Aslam. She turned to the two officers. 'Detectives, I suggest you consider your witness and his circumstances carefully before you continue. If you want any answers, that is. Otherwise, I shall have no option but to advise my client to refuse to answer.'

That certainly told them off. Stanley saw a flush of colour on the inspector's face and Happy Larry's smile disappeared. After a long pause, DI Collins leaned forward.

'I'm sorry, Stanley. I know it is a long time ago, but we really hope you'll try to remember everything that night. It's very important. Now, let's see if we can refresh your memory. On that Wednesday, there was a protest by the staff and residents of that care home on London Road. We know you were in the area at the time.'

He shook his head. 'I don't remember.'

'OK. How about that accident on Hughes Road, the two-car collision in the afternoon? The police were there for ages and moved everyone on. They said you were on a bench.'

Something stirred in the mush that was his brain. He recalled the bang. It had frightened him even though it hadn't sounded like an explosion, more like a clash of metal, but it was at the top of the road, and he couldn't see what it was. Yes, he remembered that. And that nice policeman with the turban who usually left him alone had asked him to move on.

'Ah, I see that's helped. So, can you tell us everything you did after that, Stanley?'

He frowned, but other than walking away as he'd been told, he couldn't remember anything.

The two detectives exchanged glances, and Stanley worried they would be angry with him. But angry was OK. It was scary, but he could deal with it and the pain that usually followed. At least it wasn't the screams, the wails of terror and the howls of anguish as people scrabbled in the rubble, looking for their loved ones...

'That evening, the Salvation Army served a special meal donated by that family whose sons were murdered in the park last year.' Happy Larry's voice chased off the clamour building up in his head. 'We're told all the food came from an Indian restaurant in town. The Moti Mahal. That it was delicious. They served two or three kinds of chicken and lamb dishes.

We have a list here: tandoori chicken, lamb saag, chicken tikka masala, naan bread, and vegetable biryani. Gosh, Stanley, you've got to remember that mate! Just reading this is making me drool.'

The cogs turned and clicked. That was the night he'd seen the ghost.

He sat up straighter, a smile lighting his face.

'I remember that. It was the best meal I've had in years. It reminded me of the street markets in Bagdad, those lovely smells...'

'Well done, Stanley. That's excellent!'

He blinked. She really was beautiful when she smiled.

'Now, can you try to tell us everything you did from the time you finished that meal?'

He closed his eyes. 'There was so much food, I couldn't finish it all. I saved the rest for my breakfast, and I went to that off-licence on Albert Street. I'd still got the money from my pension, so he let me in to buy a bottle.'

His eyes were still closed, so he didn't see the nods of satisfaction nor the detectives tick something off a list in their folders.

'Go on, Stanley mate, you're doing great.'

'I went into an alley. I think it was the one off the Greens. Sat and had my drink. I don't remember for how long, but I was sleepy, and it was dark, so I got up and went to my building.'

'Which building?'

'You know, the one you said. The Naylands. I have to wait until it is dark an' make sure no one's about before I go in, otherwise they'll know I sleep there and catch me. You won't tell, will you? Please don't tell.'

'We won't, Stanley, don't worry. No one except us knows you sleep there.'

He nodded. Maybe it would be OK after all.

'Go on, tell us what happened then.'

'It was all quiet, so I went in along the hedges and into my hidey-hole. And I fell asleep.'

'Did you see anyone at all? Or hear anything when you went in?'

'No, not then, not when I went in.' Stanley stopped, his mouth open in an O of horror. He hadn't meant to say that. He held his breath, hoping they hadn't noticed. But they pounced.

'Not when you went in. You saw and heard something later?'

He stayed silent, small tremors building inside him.

'Come on, Stanley, you need to tell us. It's really important.' DI Collins' voice, soft and low, calmed him.

'I woke up to, you know, take a leak behind the hedge, and I thought I saw someone near the building. I waited, but I didn't see anything, so I went back inside and fell asleep. Something woke me up again, and that's when I saw—'

'Go on, Stanley, tell us.'

'I saw someone outside the alcove leaving the building.'

'Who was it? Can you describe the person?'

'It was the g—'

'Who, Stanley? Who did you see?' Both detectives leaned forward eagerly, and Mrs Aslam too had turned around to stare at him.

'It was ... I'd had a couple of drinks, and it was dark, you see. But I'm sure it was ...'

'Go on.'

# I, SAID THE FLY

'I'm sure it was that Grozdan and his friend, Marek, that evil skinny one who grins all the time.'

# 15

# MICK

## Thursday 05 April

Mick picked up the Daily Telegraph from Tom's desk, neatly folded it in quarters, and scanned the headlines. The murder of the two junior doctors had made the bottom half of the front page of the national newspaper.

With no pickups until early afternoon, the two men were lounging in Tom Cassidy's office, going through their week's schedule and rostering.

Tom studied Mick's face. 'Ah, you're reading about the twin doctors. That's in almost all newspapers.'

'Yep. It was on the BBC morning news too.' He glanced at Tom's computer screen. 'Is that a police report?'

'Yes, of course. What else?'

Mick had long ceased to wonder how Tom got his information, or rather, from whom. His mantra was, 'It's who you know, not...' Although his boss had discovered the power of the internet later than most, he had taken to it like duck to water. That, combined with his network of contacts, gave them an edge over their rivals.

Mick sat back as Tom read snippets and summarized them aloud from the reports on his computer screens.

'The police have finally released the names of the victims. 29-year-old identical twins, Derek and Dillion Dwyer. The morning newspaper called it a senseless crime. The victims were popular, well-liked, and had no involvement with drugs. They were simply two hard-working junior doctors dedicated to helping others. Lives cut short in their prime.'

Mick crossed his arms and flexed his neck. 'It happens. Perhaps they were in the wrong place at the wrong time. It's called kismet, their predetermined fate or destiny. Or maybe it was karma, the consequence of their own actions.'

'Kismet? Karma? What're you on about? Where's all that come from?'

'That was something a doctor said to me after we blitzed that site in Operation Sand Cat. The one we were told housed militants, but the Iraqis claimed was a family gathering? That there were women and children there?'

'Look, Mick, that could have been propaganda to make us look bad. Our command had good intelligence, and we simply did our job. Ours not to reason why, etcetera, etcetera.'

'Maybe we should have. Questioned why, I mean.'

'Yeah, right. I can see us doing that. I suppose we should have gone and knocked politely on their door. Asked if there were any militants hiding in there as we were going to bomb that place to hell. No, lad. If what they said was true, why wouldn't they let our medical team go in to verify? We had a job to do. We did it. That's why we were there.'

He didn't voice his thoughts then or now that both versions could be true. The hiding place contained militants, as well as women and children. Militants too had families.

'Don't dwell on it. I don't. Those and our other missions are a thing of the past. Another life. We have more pressing matters to consider now.' Tom's worried glance probed Mick's expressionless face and haunted eyes.

With a shudder, Mick shook off his melancholy and nodded at Tom's computer screen. 'What else does it say?'

Tom scrolled through the pathology report. Particularly Dr Dolly Qing's experiment with the mannequins and her conclusions about how the Dwyer twins were killed. Despite the dry, unembellished wording littered liberally with medical terms, it made gory reading. He decided not to mention it to Mick. The man had enough nightmares chasing him already.

'The police now have Dwyer parents' DNA test results, which confirms that the victims are indeed their twin sons, Derek and Dillion. CID also found a witness, a homeless man who had been sheltering in the building's bin store and claims to have seen two people he recognized creeping out at around 2.00 a.m. He's named them as Grozdan Horvat and Marek Kováč. The police want to interview them and have issued warrants for their arrests. From what I see of their background, they're not very nice people. It'll be good for Cathy if she can charge them and close the case.'

Mick's expression softened at the mention of Cathy.

'Does she talk about it?' asked Tom curiously.

Mick shook his head. 'No, she said she's not the lead detective, but I can see she's excited to be working on it.'

'Has she asked you yet if you were out running that night? Whether you saw anything?'

'Yes, and I told her that unfortunately I hadn't; that it was my pill night.'

'Hmm. Those two ladies are going to be a complication. Be easier if we hadn't met them.'

'Why? I thought you liked Andrea.'

'I do, and that's the complication. Have you told them about our fishing trip to Scotland in a few weeks? We also have the offer of a job in Colombia. What do we tell our lovely ladies?'

'I see what you mean. Scotland might be OK. It's mid-week and they'll both be working. But Colombia?'

'We have to do Scotland, I've already accepted payment, but I think I'll turn down Colombia. The money's good, very good in fact, but it's too messy. We'd need to bring in more people, and that's never a good thing. But there'll be other jobs coming our way that'll be tough to explain. What do we do then? It's too soon to hang up our hats, and I'd like more in our accounts before we retire.' His fingers air-quoted the last word.

He turned serious eyes to Mick. 'We can't afford to get too involved with them, lad. We have to keep it casual, be prepared to break it off.'

Mick nodded, but he would not be happy about it. From Tom's expression, it seemed that neither would he.

# 16

# CATHY

**Friday 06 April**

'DI Collins!'

Cathy recognized Randolph Wilson's voice above the throng of journalists crowding the rear of the iconic Southampton City Police Headquarters. Even with extra-dark sunglasses on, the flash of a dozen cameras had her squinting as she stepped out of her car.

'Who do you have in custody? Why do you think they did it? Come on, give us something!'

*OK, how about a boot up your arse?* One day, she might even say it aloud.

Without bothering to offer a 'No comment,' Cathy hurried through the back entrance into the Solent Constabulary Headquarters and Southampton City Police Station housed within an unabashedly modern iconic limestone building with a glass-fronted facade. Unlike the classical architecture of its predecessor, the entire building looked more like an upmarket corporate office than a police station.

She took the stairs to basement level one that housed the two suspects. Despite the cutting-edge air-circulation system, the odour of sweat, stale breath, rancid food and bleach, combined with the indefinable scent of guilt, fear and malevolence, hit her smack in the face. At times like this, Cathy wished she didn't have such a keen sense of smell. To be fair, though, the custody suites here were among the best in the country, with a range of modern facilities, including shower blocks, testing facilities and an exercise yard. She'd been in some of the older stations where, despite their bright lights and attempts to tart up with powder and paint, the custody suites still felt dark, dingy, rank and filled with despair.

Because they did not want to alert the suspects and end up widening the search area, Cathy had asked Uniform to be discreet, so it had taken them almost a whole day to round up Grozdan Horvat and his mate Marek Kováč. According to Uniform, both men had looked shocked when told that they were being arrested on suspicion of murder and had loudly protested their innocence. They'd even tried to make a dash for it but had not got very far before the officers cuffed and bundled them into the patrol cars.

They were younger than Cathy expected. From the way Stanley had talked about them, she'd got the impression they were the epitome of hardened criminals. Yet here they were, two young men in their early twenties with their duty solicitors, their widened eyes belying their bravado.

Grozdan was big, just over 6 ft 2 in tall, with wide shoulders, deep chest and big hands. Already at 22, his flabby muscles, the rolls of fat around his middle and red spider veins on his nose betrayed an abuse of alcohol and possibly narcotics.

Marek, a small weedy looking 21-year-old, had wild curly brown hair, round brown eyes, a thin childish face and a permanent smile, which Cathy suspected was more to do with nervousness than his fondness for the police.

Both young men claimed to be Slovakian and even had passports to prove it. Their notes read they had first come with their parents and siblings to work as fruit-pickers in Kent, almost five years ago. The young men had stayed on, moved to London doing odd jobs, and were now Southampton's more recent acquisitions. Neither had a record, which did not necessarily mean that they were a law-abiding pair living clean, healthy lives. Just that they hadn't been caught yet.

Stanley's statement still worried Cathy. She was convinced he'd been going to say something else before blurting out Grozdan and Marek's names. She'd even questioned him about it at the interview, but apart from a sidelong glance out of his red-veined washed-out blue eyes, he stuck to his story, insisting he had seen these two leave the Naylands in the dead hours of Thursday, 22 March.

Stanley was lying. But why? Had he even seen anyone? Cathy could think of several reasons why he would want these thugs off the streets. Despite being aware of their reputation, there was little the police could do as no one had complained about the pair or provided evidence of intimidation.

This was the best lead the detectives had so far, and they needed to follow it up. Plus, do all the other usual things, like knocking on doors, checking CCTVs in the area, speaking to the victims' colleagues, friends, trying to pick up and follow their electronic footprints, going through their finances, tracking their movements via their credit cards, and so on.

Although it was only five days since discovering the bodies, those doctors had been killed almost a fortnight ago, which had given the killer, or killers, plenty of time to have disposed of the evidence and disappeared. Not that the media granted any dispensation. With none of them actually saying so, the implication was clear. The police were clueless even after two weeks. One blog even asked why they hadn't found the bodies sooner.

Cathy and her team now had to work out if the two suspects in custody were indeed the killers. And if they were, what were their three Ms: means, method and motive?

'Like I told you. In my flat, in bed, sleeping. All night. I not go to Naylands or anywhere. I sleep,' insisted Grozdan Horvat.

He reminded Cathy of a bear, an outraged one at that.

She and DC Larry Ives sat opposite Grozdan Horvat and his duty solicitor in the custom-built Interview Room Number 3. A basic but well-lit space equipped with high-quality audio and video equipment. The only furniture in the room was the sturdy brown table with black metal legs, and two chairs with wooden seats built on black metal frames, one each for the suspect and his solicitor. Cathy was glad that they were all screwed to the floor. A sensible precaution should the incensed bear decide to use the furniture as projectile weapons. The detectives had borrowed chairs from one of the meeting rooms.

'You ask my friends. They tell you I in flat all night,' insisted Grozdan.

Of course, they'd asked his flatmates, and all of them had corroborated his story. One of them — Marek Kováč — was being interviewed next door. They could all be lying, of course, providing the two suspects with false alibis, but apart from Stanley's claim, there was no other evidence of the pair's involvement.

'We have a witness who saw you leaving the Naylands at around 2.30 a.m. on Thursday, 22 March.' Cathy kept her voice calm, tone neutral.

'Who? Who say this lie? Big lie. Tell me name and I ask him to his face. Why—'

'Do you own a pair of Treaders Confidence boots?'

Grozdan swung his head to Larry, obviously thrown by the sudden change of subject and interrogator.

'Treaders? Like brand?' Grozdan shook his head in disgust. 'I look like I rich enough to buy expensive boots? Where I get money for Treaders boots? You tell me. Maybe Father Santa bring me present, eh?'

'I'm guessing that's a no, then,' muttered Larry. Cathy suppressed a smile.

A search of the suspects' two-bedroom flat, which they shared with two other men, had turned up nothing, certainly no Treaders boots. For a big man, Grozdan had relatively small feet. UK size nine. And Marek took a size eight. Therefore, the boot print was unlikely to belong to either of them. It was equally likely that the print in the flowerbed had nothing to do with the murder of the two doctors. But it was evidence the detectives couldn't ignore.

An hour into the interview and they had nothing. Grozdan brushed fine, straight, dirty-blond hair off his forehead yet again, a habit which was getting under Cathy's skin. His narrow brown eyes darted between her face and DC Larry Ives's, and unless he was an excellent actor, she'd say he was telling the truth.

They took a break, and Cathy went into the viewing room, where DI Paul Hayes and DC Salim Khan were monitoring both interviews.

'Anything from Marek?'

'Not a sodding thing.' Paul sighed in frustration. 'Their stories match, and their flatmates say they were in all night. They watched TV, had a meal, a few beers, and went to bed. If they crept out, I doubt if one of the others would have heard them leave the flat or noticed their absence. If they're telling the truth, that is.'

'We've got more eyes going through the CCTV footage collected from around where they live, from midnight to 4.00 a.m.,' said Salim. 'It looks like they might be telling the truth.'

'Did they look for cars going in and out of there in that timescale? They wouldn't walk from their flat to the Naylands.'

'Yes, they did. Sorry, Cath. No vehicles left their block of flats or neighbouring blocks after 1.00 a.m. One of their flatmates, the taxi driver chap, returned at quarter-past midnight, parked and didn't leave again until 8.00 a.m. the next morning. A shift worker from two buildings down returned home at 11.55 p.m., parked and stayed put until nearly midday on Thursday. There wasn't any other traffic about. Looks like it was a slow night all round.'

'Damn! We'll have to let them go. Their solicitors are already making noises.'

Their glum expressions mirrored Cathy's.

'Is it worth seeing if we can extend the 36 hours to grill them some more?'

'I doubt if the boss will agree, not without something solid to go on,' said Paul. 'He wasn't even happy about signing off to the 36 hours. In fact, he said he'd be having a word with you for arresting them in the first place simply on the say-so of a drunk.'

*Oh great! Something to look forward to then. I could wring Stanley's scrawny neck.* Her first big case was going nowhere, and their only lead was fizzling out, but at least she had the weekend to look forward to. Mick would be here tonight and even though she'd be working over the weekend, they'd still be able to spend some time together. Her heart lifted as her lips stretched involuntarily.

The two men turned to her in surprise. 'What the hell are you smiling about?' asked Paul.

'Just imagining the fright I'm going to give Stanley for lying to us.'

'Yeah. Let's get him back in and scare the shit out of him,' said Paul.

Cathy thought about it and reluctantly shook her head. 'Not sure that will work. He'll clam up. Plus, he'll have a brief who'll stop him from saying anything that could get him into trouble. I'll go speak to him. See if I can get him to tell the truth.'

'Do you think Stanley could've killed those guys?' asked Salim.

They thought about it seriously. Then Paul shook his head.

'No. I've known Stanley for a long time. He's just one of life's unfortunates, but essentially harmless.'

'Really? He was a soldier, wasn't he? They're trained to kill, and he must have taken lives before,' said Cathy.

'Sure. Maybe. Although I'm not sure Stanley ever did. Or perhaps he did, and that's what made him like he is. I could believe it if those two doctors had been shot, but I can't see Stanley planning the whole thing meticulously, restraining and torturing them, then strangling them like that, all without leaving a trace.'

'Hmm. Yes, you're right. Anyway, I'd better get back to Grozdan. I'll make him go over the whole thing again and then let him stew for the full 36 hours before releasing him under investigation.'

Paul and Salim grinned. 'Good one. I'll tell Esther and David to do the same with Marek.'

Cathy headed back to the interview room.

*Afterwards, I'll go find Stanley and have a chat with him. Hopefully, he'll be more forthcoming and tell me who he really saw that night, or rather, morning. If he truly saw anyone at all.*

In any case, she needed to warn him they were releasing Grozdan and Marek.

# 17

# CATHY

**Friday 06 April**

*D*amn it! Where the hell is Stanley?

Cathy had been trawling the underbelly of Southampton city for two hours, venturing into nooks and crannies where she wouldn't go after dark, at least not alone. She scoured the alleyways and neighbourhood around the estates, which were still relatively clean, a legacy from the daily early morning blitz by the council's street-cleansing team. But come nightfall, every imaginable vice, plus some beyond her scope of inventiveness, would sprout and spread its hooked and clawed tentacles across the city. Like vampires, they would vanish at daybreak, the debris left behind the only evidence of their presence, which the road sweepers would once again mop up each morning to present an impeccable façade to the world. A never-ending cycle.

Unseen eyes suspecting her intentions, assessing whether she was predator or prey, clocked her presence, but they left her alone, perhaps because they knew who she was, or maybe because she was not an unfamiliar sight.

Being new to Southampton, she had walked every street in the last 17 months. It was the only way to get to really know her patch. All of its glitz and glamour, its saints and sinners, as well as its warts and verrucae. Of course, the crackling of her open PR—her personal radio—also helped.

Uniformed officers were looking for Stanley too, but Cathy had given strict instructions that they were to be discreet and not approach or disclose her interest in him. They were simply to keep an eye on the veteran, and radio his location to her on the borrowed PR. She didn't want to spook the man, but more importantly, she didn't want to alert anyone else of the police's interest in him. These streets had a thousand eyes. The information could get back to Grozdan. They'd already made a mistake and probably endangered Stanley when they had picked him up. Someone would have seen him get into the patrol car. She just hoped it wasn't anyone wishing him harm.

Her radio crackled.

'Target sighted at 18.48 hours on Ripley Road, heading west.'

Cathy rolled her eyes. 'No need to go all military on me, Randeep. Any idea where he's headed?'

'He might be going to Palmerston Park. He usually goes there around this time.'

'Okay, I'm heading there. Follow him but do it discreetly and let me know if he changes direction. I know it's difficult, but try to blend in, will you?'

'Blending right in, Cathy. The next lamp post you pass could be me.'

She laughed. Fat chance. With his turban adding a good six inches to his 6 ft 2 in frame, PC Randeep Singh stuck out wherever he went.

Fifteen minutes later, armed with three tall polystyrene cups of coffee and six granola bars, she entered Palmerston Park. Cathy laughed when she spotted Randeep about 100 yards away, standing by a lamppost.

'Evening, ma'am. Blending in as instructed.' He grinned, his teeth flashing white in the gathering dusk. 'Stanley's on that bench there, eating his burger and chips. He also stopped at an off-licence.'

'Thanks, Randeep. He should be fine for the night. We've got him a room at Dickson House for a week while social services try to sort out a long-term solution for him. Here you go.' She handed him a coffee.

'Oh, thank you.'

'You're very welcome. Right, I'd better go have a chat with our friend. See you later.'

Taking a circuitous route to the bench, she approached stealthily from behind and sidled onto it.

'Hello, Stanley. No, don't go. Please stay. I'm not here to arrest you. I just want to have a chat. Here's a hot coffee for you.'

She placed the coffee and the cereal bars on the bench between them, then leaned back to sip her Americano. Ignoring the nervous glances darted at her, she admired the borders with their early flowering rhododendrons under-planted with daffodils and hyacinths. Cathy smiled into her cup when a stub-fingered, grubby hand reached out to pick up the coffee and pocket the granola bars.

'We arrested Grozdan Horvat and questioned him, but he has a strong alibi for that night. He was nowhere near the

Naylands. You lied to us, didn't you, Stanley? No, don't move. I meant what I said. I'm not here to arrest you right now, but you should know better than to lie to the police. You've wasted a lot of our time and caused a lot of problems.'

'I'm sorry,' came a whispered response.

Cathy turned to face him; saw the wreck of the man he had once been. One of life's casualties. Many had tried to help him, to reintroduce him into society, but he kept returning to the streets and showed no wish to be reformed. In the end, the community workers and uniformed officers like Randeep left him alone but looked out for him. On a good day, Stanley was a hoot, they said. He had tales as long as your arm and made your sides hurt with laughter. Not lately, though. Cathy had certainly never seen that side of his persona. After 28 years of service, he'd retired with a decent pension. However, over half went to an ex-wife and son he had not seen or heard from in 20 years. But he refused to do anything about it.

'Why, Stanley?'

No response. He just sat there with his hands wrapped around the polystyrene cup, chin on chest, staring at his feet.

'Were Grozdan and Marek bullying you? Did they hurt you?'

She caught the word 'thief' in his muttered reply.

'They steal from you? What exactly? Ah, your pension. Why didn't you come to us? We could've done something about it, put a stop to it.'

That earned her a sidelong glance. *Who am I fooling*? Stanley knew as well as she did that it would take more than a few instances of intimidation and theft to remove Grozdan from the streets, and a lot more determination to have him deported to Slovakia. The man sitting beside her certainly didn't have that kind of resolve.

Seated on that bench as twilight kissed the sky goodnight on that growingly chilly evening, Cathy wasn't to know that events, and Stanley, would prove her wrong.

She sighed. 'Drink your coffee before it gets cold. I also wanted to tell you that you have a room at Dickson House paid up for a week and we're working with Social Services to get you a permanent place. You should use it, Stanley, at least at night, even if you spend your days on the streets.'

His shoulders slumped at the kindness being forced on him.

'We have not, and will not, tell Grozdan that you named him, but someone might have seen you getting into the police car, and it won't take him long to find out. Then he'll come looking for you. You should go straight to Dickson House before it gets dark and stay there till late morning. Do you understand, Stanley?'

His eyes flashed in the lamplight as he raised the cup to his mouth with shaky hands. He nodded.

'Now, tell me, did you actually see anyone that night at the Naylands? Or did you just make that up?'

After a long pause, just when she was ready to give up, he whispered. 'I saw the ghost again.'

It was Cathy's turn to slump in despair. She wasn't surprised. He was probably more drunk than usual that night, and possibly on drugs, hallucinating.

'You saw a ghost? What was it doing? Tell me about this ghost then.'

But with another glance at her, he shook his head. Cathy squinted. *Was he smiling?*

'I'm sorry,' his voice was stronger as he straightened up. 'I must've been dreaming. I'm sorry I caused you all this trouble.'

She waited but got nothing more. Eventually, she rose.

'That's alright,' she sighed. 'Stanley, don't stay here for long. Go straight to Dickson House. You'll be safe there. OK?'

He nodded and lifted his coffee cup in salute. 'Thank you, beautiful lady.'

Cathy smiled as she walked away, heading home for a shower, to dress up for her dinner date with Mick, determined to try to live up to Stanley's name for her.

*Wait till I tell them at the station. Ghost indeed.*

It was not until 3.20 a.m. the next morning that it hit her. Cathy woke up cold and alone at the Bluebell Inn, the sound of the shower in full flow clueing her in to Mick's whereabouts. She still wasn't used to his midnight runs.

Not *a* ghost. *The* ghost. Stanley's words had been, 'I saw *the* ghost again', not 'I saw *a* ghost.'

# 18

## STANLEY

**Friday 06 April**

*Beautiful lady,* thought Stanley again, watching the tall, slim detective inspector walk away. He drained his cup. *Kind too.*

Somewhere a clock chimed 8.00 p.m. He really should get up and start walking. Go to Dickson House, as the beautiful lady said, but he was tired. And scared. He shouldn't have told her about the *ghost.* Nor Rafi.

*Think of the devil and ...*

'Hello, man. I bin looking everywhere for you, ha. Where you bin? I was worried.'

'Hey, Rafi. I'm fine. All good.'

'What did they want? The police. I saw them take you away. Sorry I ran, man.' Rafi shook his head, his long, grey stringy curls bouncing. 'Got scared. I waited outside the police station for hours, but you were still in there. Didn't come out.

Got dark. Then they made me go. Not hang around no mo',
they said.'

Stanley blinked. That he had not expected. He
swallowed the unfamiliar lump in his throat.

'They just asked some questions, then gave me dinner
and got me a room at Dickson House.' He laughed. 'I even had
a solicitor. She was kind. Took me straight there in her car. But
that was good of you, Rafi.'

'That's OK. You're my friend. I got worried. Asked
everyone if they'd seen you. Why the police took you? But you
OK now?'

Stanley stared at him as the implication of Rafi's
words sank in. The gossip mills amongst Southampton's
misfortunate, fuelled by the news of his and Grozdan's visits
to the police, would have been grinding overtime and would
soon reach his tormentors. His friend's concern had betrayed
him. Stanley's fate was now sealed.

'I'm OK, mate. It was nothing important.'

Rafi squinted at him, worry creasing his forehead. They
sat in companionable silence for a long while, then Rafi slowly
got to his feet. 'I got my money. That bugger didn't steal it last
night. I think I'll pay for a room tonight. You coming?'

'No thanks, man. You go on. I'll be fine.'

'Don't stay too long. I smell rain coming. Maybe a
storm too.'

'I won't. See ya.'

Stanley waved and watched Rafi trudge off into the
dark. He knew he should go, too. It would take nearly forty
minutes to get to his room. But he stayed. Sat on the bench
and waited.

Rafi sat up on the thin mattress and pulled the blankets tight around him. The tiny worry worm had grown and grown and was now a gargantuan Gippsland earthworm burrowing deep into his mind. He scratched his shaggy, grey head. He shouldn't have left Stanley alone. What kind of friend was he? He should have stayed and made sure Stanley was safe for the night.

He got out of bed. He had got in fully dressed, even down to his shoes, a habit now. When you lived on the streets, you kept everything on, always. Rafi crept out of the tiny room with its single bed, the mattress flattened by years of use and abuse, and its threadbare sheets and blankets. He slipped into the hallway with its single bare bulb and went into the toilet that desperately needed a clean.

When he finished, he waited outside in the shadows of the landing, listening hard. Heard nothing but creaks and groans and a few snores from behind closed doors. He peered over the banister, saw the night manager-cum-receptionist-cum-watchman fast asleep with his head cradled in his arms on the desk. The big wall clock told him it was only 11.50 p.m. even though it felt much later, well past midnight.

Noiselessly, he descended the stairs and slipped out of the boarding house. He didn't know where Stanley would be, but the park seemed a good place to start.

# I, SAID THE FLY

S tanley lost track of time sitting on the bench. The cramp in his arm and shoulder and a stiff neck testified he had dozed off, but he was far from rested. Beyond the range of the park's lamplights, it was pitch-black and still, the air thick and heavy, holding its breath. He shivered, drew his coat tighter around him, tucked his hands under his armpits, and settled down to wait some more.

An hour later, he was shivering in earnest. Maybe they wouldn't look for him tonight. This was a silly idea, waiting in the cold, especially with the impending rain. Rafi was usually right in his weather forecasts. He should leave. Use that warm room and bed in Dickson House those kind people had paid for. He could always come back here tomorrow.

But Stanley knew that if he left now, he would not find the courage to return tomorrow. Or ever. He would cower and hide. Be always looking over his shoulder every minute of every new day. So, he stayed and waited some more.

Another hour slipped away. Far off a ship or a trawler's horn sounded two short blasts. *Turning to the port side.* Stanley smiled as the memory resurfaced but he couldn't remember how he knew that. He was tired of waiting and didn't intend to freeze to death.

He got up, stretched his back, collected his belongings, turned and began walking. Through the East Park and out the West Park, then cutting across Devonshire and Morris Roads would be the quickest route to Dickson House. It was a 40-minute walk, but walking was one thing he could still do well.

They caught up with him on the edge of East Park.

Rafi tottered and stumbled towards Palmerston Park, wincing at the old pain in his leg. He stopped often to ease the stitch in his sides and pressed a hand to his thigh where Grozdan had kicked him two weeks ago, even after Rafi had handed over his money. There was a time when he could have easily taken Grozdan and his nasty friends, but that time was a distant memory.

He hoped Stanley hadn't planned to sleep on a bench in the park. The quiver of the hairs on his nape, sensitive to the electric charge of the looming storm, told him it wouldn't be a clever idea.

He entered Palmerston Park from the south and made his way to the bench where they'd sat earlier that evening, sharing the silence. A big grin lit up his thin face at the sight of the empty seat. Good! Stanley had heeded his advice, after all. He was warm and tucked up in a bed in Dickson House. And now he, Rafi, could also go back to use his bed in the hostel.

Rafi swivelled from the waist upwards to return to the route he had come from, but his feet had other intentions. He began walking towards the East Park, realising that he was going toward Dickson House. It wouldn't hurt to check on Stanley, make sure he'd got there OK. After all, he wouldn't sleep much even if he went back to bed.

Sounds of voices, rough staccato speech, thumps and muffled cries reached him. Rafi frowned. He recognized those noises. Someone was inflicting pain on someone else. He stepped off the hard paved path, moved on to the soft grass and, sliding behind the cover of shrubs, bushes and trees, approached the source of the sounds. From behind a massive oak, the thickness of its trunk easily concealing his scrawny frame, he watched two men kicking at something on the ground that grunted in pain.

'You miserable old man. Why you say lies about me? Huh?'

Rafi knew that voice, that big hulking figure with the brutish face. He also recognized the smaller man beside him. He started forward, but his head overruled the impulse and stayed his feet. Although Rafi could not see their victim clearly, curled up as he was to protect his head and face, Rafi knew without a doubt that it was Stanley. He also knew he couldn't help his friend.

So, he stayed behind the gigantic tree and watched the shadow dance. It wasn't a fight. You needed participation, however unequal, from both the attacker and the defender for a fight. This was wholly one-sided. Rafi covered his ears to block the grunts of pain from the target and those of pleasure from his attackers. It went on for a long time and then it stopped.

With one last strike, the two men glanced around, snatched Stanley's rucksack and his tote bag, and ran out of the park.

Rafi waited until he was sure they'd left, then crept out of his hiding place to approach the unmoving bundle on the ground. He knelt down painfully and turned the man over. Stanley. With blood on his face and arms flopped to his side, his friend lay still. Rafi tried to feel his heartbeat and pulse and found nothing.

He knelt there for a long time, unaware of the tears mingling with the steadily increasing drizzle. Eventually, he pushed himself up on his feet. He should go to the police, but while he had little doubt about their good intentions, he had no faith in their system.

Rafi made a decision as he turned away to return to his hostel. Tomorrow he'd buy or steal a knife and wait for them. He knew they would come looking for him before too long.

He was too easy a target for them to ignore.

# 19

## STANLEY

### Saturday 07 April

The pain was a shroud, enveloping him from head to toe, but the icy drizzle soothed and numbed some of it. Stanley rolled to his side, crying out in agony at the sharp pain inside him. He lay still, waiting for it to pass, waiting to wake up. As consciousness returned, so did his memory.

Ignoring the pain, he sat up, panting hard and fast to keep it at bay. He clenched his left fist and shoved it deep into his pocket to protect it. He hoped it would be enough, that it would get his attackers off the streets.

He wanted to lie back down and go to sleep on the hard ground under the open sky, but the image of an alcove intruded and, for reasons that not even he could understand, Stanley longed to return there. It felt like home.

Fifty slow and painful minutes later, he sidled along the hedges and limped to the back of the Naylands to the rubbish-bin store. To his hidey-hole, his haven, his home.

Relieved to find it unlocked, he stepped inside and found his usual spot. He couldn't remember what he'd done with his rucksack or his tote bag. Had his attackers taken them? He no longer had his fan-folded cardboard sheet to soften the concrete floor. Still, it was out of the rain, cosy and familiar.

The rumbles of thunder followed each other in quick succession. Stanley smiled. Once upon a long, long time ago, his mother used to say, 'It's the sky giant's tummy rumbling in hunger for naughty little boys. But you won't find any here, Mr Sky Giant. Our Stanley's been a very good boy.'

Lightning flashed across the sky, followed by a crash of cymbals. The storm was getting closer. Stanley lay down, his left hand still deep in his pocket.

*Meow, grruump.*

Stanley laughed as the big ginger tom crept up to him and nuzzled him. He couldn't remember when he'd last been this happy. He stoked the cat with his free hand, tried to get it to sit, but the animal couldn't seem to settle down. It patted his face with its paw, head-butted him and ran its rough tongue repeatedly across his face.

'I'm OK, Tommy. I just need to sleep a little.'

But the ginger tom knew better. It recognized the shadowy figure of death drawing ever closer to the man. It had seen that ghostly form many times before on the streets, often hovering over others, but at least seven times it had been close by, grimly crossing off yet another one of the cat's lives.

There wasn't much the stray could do for the man, so it lay down beside him, close and tight against Stanley's chest, sharing all the warmth of its little body. It purred its distress, huddled close and waited the last few hours as the heaving breaths grew farther apart. Stayed even when it felt the lurch of the man's heart and the slowing of his pulse, until finally, with a deep sigh, Stanley ceased his long-running struggle with life and relaxed.

But the cat stayed close, watching, waiting, hoping. Perhaps the man would return too, just like the cat did on more than one occasion. Eventually, as morning light crept into the threshold of the alcove, it rose to its feet. It crouched and washed Stanley's face, over and over again, dredging up saliva to do a thorough job of it. With a final pat and nudge, it leapt away and shot out of the bin store.

It returned half an hour later with a dead sparrow and laid it close to Stanley's cheek. Then, with one last glance, the cat disappeared into the undergrowth.

Now if the man wakes up hungry, he'd have something to eat.

# 20

# CATHY

**Saturday 07 April**

M rs Rosalind Harman, the indomitable owner and
resident of Flat 404, found Stanley at 11.00 a.m.
on Saturday morning when she went into the block's
communal bin store to dump her black sack of rubbish.

Getting no response to her angry and repeated
instruction to him to get up immediately and out of there,
she dialled 999. It gave a small insight into Mrs Harman's
character that she asked for an ambulance first before also
asking the emergency services to send for the police.

Cathy was at the station when Uniform notified
CID. At that stage, the attending police officer didn't know
the identity of the corpse, but her heart sank the moment
she heard the location.

Having already phoned the hostel earlier that morning,
she knew Stanley had not turned up last night. She'd been

getting ready to go out and find him, to ask him about the ghost when that call had come in.

*I should have guessed he'd go to the Naylands.*

'C'mon, Cath, let's go,' said DI Paul Hayes quietly by her shoulder. Unable to speak, she looked up. Paul's jaw was clenched tight, and he blinked rapidly.

She had a sense of déjà vu when they arrived at the Naylands. The same flashing blue lights parked along Harold Road and blue-and-white tape strung across the driveway. This time, they headed to the bin store at the back of the building. Paul had already asked Salim to call the path guys and forensics. The detectives heard them arrive.

Garbed in protective overshoes and gloves, they approached the bin store but kept their distance. Cathy was impressed when Paul pulled out a pair of small but powerful binoculars and surveyed the scene. With a sharply indrawn breath, he passed them to her.

There was no doubt it was Stanley. He lay huddled on his side, his right arm crooked at the elbow as if he was holding something. But it was empty.

'Hey, Cathy, we never got around to scheduling our evening out, did we? How about next week?' Dolly Qing, the assistant pathologist, grinned at her before pulling her mask up over her mouth and nose.

Her grin turned to a frown when she noticed their sombre expressions. 'Oh, you know the victim, eh?'

'Yeah, we did.' Cathy struggled to keep her eyes from filling up and her voice steady. Stanley's death was getting to her, yet she had barely known the man.

'So sorry. That's always hard. We'll look after him, I promise.'

Dolly put down stepping plates before kneeling beside Stanley. After what seemed like forever, she stood up and signalled her team.

'Rigor mortis is setting in, and I would like to get him to the morgue before it develops any further. I can't tell you anything at this stage. From what I've seen, it looks like he died of natural causes, of a cardiac arrest. But take nothing as read until I get him back and examine him more thoroughly. This place isn't exactly ideal. Apart from everything else, it is too cramped.'

A cardiac arrest. Cathy was glad it had been quick. That Stanley had not suffered.

Earlier in the morning, she had chided herself for not getting into work sooner.

Now it seemed that she could not have got in early enough.

Now she would never know what or who he meant by 'the ghost'.

# 21

## MICK

**Saturday 07 April**

'Mr O'Neal?'

Mick carefully lowered the bar weights into the slots before turning to the attractive young woman, one of the gym's trainers. He tried to remember her name. Lisa? Laura? That's the one, Laura.

'Yes, Laura?'

She smiled and flushed, thrilled that he remembered her name. 'There's a gentleman looking for you. A Major Cassidy? He says it's urgent.'

Mick shot upright on the bench press, making her jump back.

'Thank you, I'll be right out.'

He grabbed his towel and half-empty bottle of water and hastened out of the massive room lined with its array of professional equipment. He'd joined this gym a few weeks ago as it was an easy mile jog from the Bluebell Inn, had an impressive collection of equipment and best of all, was open 24/7, which meant he had other options besides pounding Southampton streets at night during his bouts of insomnia.

With Cathy being called in to work, his plans for the weekend were in tatters, especially with Tom spending most of his time with Andrea, so he'd sought refuge here again this morning.

'What's up?' Mick wiped the sweat from his brows and neck and frowned in concern at a grim-faced Tom Cassidy.

'Get your stuff. We need to go.'

He would have preferred to shower first, but years of gruelling training, combined with knowledge of the man and the logical assumption that he would not be here unless it was urgent, made Mick turn and head straight for the locker room, stopping only to change his shoes. Then, grabbing his gym bag and jacket out of the locker, he followed Tom outside to his car.

'Cathy's been trying to reach you. Andrea got a call from her with a message to say that she wouldn't be joining us for dinner.'

Mick frowned. His phone had been in the gym locker, but Cathy could easily have sent him a text message. This hardly warranted Tom coming to fetch him. He waited.

'Cathy was very upset. Andrea said she was calling from the ladies' toilet at the station and sounded like she'd been crying.'

Mick's jaws clenched.

'Why was Cathy crying?'

'Apparently, this morning they found the body of a homeless man in the rubbish-bin store of the same building as those two doctors. The initial conclusion was that he'd died of a cardiac arrest. But this afternoon about an hour ago, Cathy got a call from the pathologist to say that they'd run a series of X-rays on the body and found he had broken ribs and a cracked pelvis. The pathologist took a closer look at the body and now thinks that although the man might have died of a cardiac arrest, she suspects he'd been badly beaten before that.'

'Why was Cathy crying for him? She must have seen bodies before.'

'Andrea asked her exactly that. Cathy said that she'd known Stanley. Many in her team did. They all liked him and stopped to have a chat if they met him. Sort of looked out for him. She'd actually spoken to him the night before he died.'

'Stanley.'

'Yes, ex-Corporal James Stanley.'

Mick shut his eyes and drew in a deep breath. His eyes were cold grey pebbles when he turned to face Tom. 'I see.'

Tom nodded and turned on the ignition.

'I've been doing some research and making some calls to find other ex-forces people here. They keep in touch with each other. There are two other known homeless veterans in Southampton. Lance Corporal Mohammed Rafi and Sergeant Duncan McLeod. Rafi's our best bet right now, as McLeod's been in hospital since Wednesday with kidney problems. I'll park in town, then we can split up and look for him.'

Forty-five minutes later, Mick's phone buzzed.

'Found him. He's on Handel Road and seems to be heading towards the parks.'

'On my way.' Mick opened up a map app on his phone and looked for the quickest route from his location.

He arrived at Palmerston Park to find Tom leaning against a tree trunk.

'There he is.' Tom nodded towards a bench where a lone man sat hunched over a fast-food container.

Mick would not have recognized Rafi. The man he remembered had been tall, dignified, impeccably turned out and marked for promotion, not this dishevelled, grey-haired lost soul.

Tom started walking casually towards the bench and jerked his head at Mick, who looped around to the bushes behind the seated man.

'Hi, Rafi,' said Tom, standing in front of him.

Rafi's head jerked up. The food box flew out of his hands, scattering the chips to the ground as he leapt to his feet, mouth open in a big O of surprise, his right hand flying to his brow in a shaky salute.

'M ... m ... major! It really you?'

'Yes, Rafi. You remember me then?'

'Yeah, sure, I remember you, major.'

'Please sit, Rafi. Sorry, didn't mean to startle you.'

Mick saw Tom bend down, pick up the empty container, walk three paces to dump it into the litter bin. Returning to the bench, he lowered himself to the seat beside Rafi, who'd been watching his every single move.

'It's been a long time, Rafi. Many winters. How have you been?'

'I bin OK. I bin good.'

Hearing that voice again brought back memories of a much younger, lanky soldier with a slight stutter, a big smile and a beautiful tenor voice. Of that Christmas in an Iraqi desert camp nearly 12 years ago.

'Rafi, did you know Stanley?'

The shaggy grey curls nodded. 'Yes, he was my friend.'

'*Was*. I see. So, you already know he's dead?'

Another nod.

'Rafi, we'd like to ask you some questions.'

'Who's we?' Rafi's head swivelled on his scrawny neck.

Mick stepped out of the bushes and leaned over Rafi's shoulder.

'Boo.'

# 22

# GROZDAN

## Saturday 07 April

Grozdan's phone vibrated deep in his pocket. His arm jerked directing the spray of water from the pressure-washer's lance away from the tyres and on to Marek's trousers. The latter swore and jumped back. Laughing aloud, Grozdan released the trigger to shut off the water while Marek continued swearing and swiping at his trouser legs.

Although it was past 7.00 p.m., the two men were still at work at their car-wash stall in the car park of a large superstore just outside the city centre. Marek, the lazy sod, hadn't been enthusiastic with Grozdan's decision to stay open beyond their normal closing at 6 p.m., but his boss was certainly pleased. Business had been good today, with a steady flow of customers continuing late into the evening. Grozdan also refused their boss's offer of additional help, preferring to carry on alone, as it meant they wouldn't have to share their profits.

The phone buzzed a second time. *Must be important,* thought Grozdan , handing the pressure washer to Marek and digging into his pocket for his phone. Two text messages. He frowned, not recognising the sender's number on the screen. Had the message been in English, he would probably have deleted it without opening, but the first few words in Slovak intrigued him. He tapped on the icon.

*Grozdan, it's Anton. Have special deal, need your help. Meet me at 12.30am at Titanic Engineers' Memorial in East Park. Bring Marek. Secret deal, don't tell anyone.*

The second message read:

*Forgot to say, don't bring car. Come on foot. Don't want get caught on CCTV. Ciao, Anton.*

Excited, Grozdan called out, 'Marek, come here! Look!'

Grozdan handed over his phone and tapped his foot impatiently while his friend read the messages from one of their flatmates, Anton Gajdoš.

Several weeks ago, Anton, a private cab driver who also handled what he termed as 'special packages' for some of his customers. had included his flatmates in an invitation to one of his client's parties. An evening of what their host laughingly referred to as drugs, sex and rock n roll. It had been a memorable night for Grozdan, and especially for Marek. Particularly the sex part.

The two friends grinned at each other. This didn't sound like a party, but maybe it would lead to another one soon.

Both were oblivious of the man waiting by a car parked about fifteen yards away, fiddling with his phone while apparently waiting for someone. A man who surreptitiously noted their actions and movements, whether they were right or left-handed, and who left the site shortly after Grozdan received the second text message.

## Midnight, Saturday 07 April

Neither man would have agreed to the two-mile walk, especially at night and after drinking so much beer. But the anticipation of another special invite and the intrigue of a scheme, any scheme, to cheat their boss, buoyed their spirits and distorted their perception of the distance to their rendezvous.

Despite the clear, crisp night, Grozdan and Marek passed few people and fewer cars, but they stayed alert. They knew all about the predators that lurked in these street corners. Often enough, that had been them too.

The Titanic Engineers' Memorial in East Park – a poignant memorial to dedication to duty and sacrifice – glowed in the night. The floodlit bronze and granite monument with its towering statue of Nike, the Greek goddess of victory, her wings spread wide, appeared ready to take flight into the starlit night sky, while the marine engineers on the bronze bas-relief panels on either side continued to toil at their tasks.

The hundred-plus-year-old memorial was deserted. No one waited for the two men at their rendezvous point, but then, they were seven minutes early for their 12.30 a.m.

meeting. They strolled away from the lit-up monument, and Grozdan drew out his phone.

'I'll tell Anton we're here,' he said, his thumb hesitating between Anton's usual phone number and the new one from which the messages had been sent.

'Look,' said Marek, nudging him in the ribs, pointing to the shadows of the densely planted area.

The dark outline of the man in a hoodie standing in front of one of the park's densely planted borders would have been invisible but for the dim glow of a mobile phone in his hand. No light penetrated the wall of darkness in the space behind and beyond him. The figure beckoned to them urgently and stepped back into the shadows.

Shoving the phone hastily back into his pocket, Grozdan and Marek hurried towards him.

'Pod' sem.' *Come here,* whispered a voice from the undergrowth in Slovak.

Heads bent, forearms raised protectively in front of their faces, the two men thrust branches aside as they pushed their way into the little clearing behind the shrubs. They sounded like a herd of elephants trampling through the bushes.

'Ticho!' *Quietly!*

The faint glow of the phone torch clicked off. To their eyes, still influenced by the lights of the Titanic Engineers' Memorial, the blanket of darkness felt like someone had pulled a hood over their heads.

Grozdan swore. 'What the fuck, Anton!'

'Shut up,' ordered the voice, moving further into the blackness.

With sight now a worthless accessory, Grozdan and Marek followed the voice.

# 23

## CATHY

### Sunday 08 April

The warm hand on her bare shoulder and warmer kiss on her neck brought Cathy awake with a smile. She reluctantly opened her eyes to find Mick sitting on the edge of the bed, fully dressed.

*It must be much later than I thought.* Raising her head and shoulders she peered around expecting daylight, but the blinds and curtains were still drawn shut, Mick's bedside lamp the only light in the room.

'What time is it?'

'06:18.'

Her smile deepened. His precise answers still amused her, but she was getting used to it. That and his almost obsessive tidiness, his need to have everything just so.

*Why's he up and dressed so early*? She sat up, saw his packed case and backpack in the tiny hallway leading to the door. Her eyes widened as desolation flooded in.

'I'm sorry. I must go. We've a key client arriving unexpectedly this morning and I need to go pick him up.'

'Can't someone else do it?'

Mick shook his head. 'No, not this one. Can't afford to palm him off on someone else. He'll see it as an insult.'

She remembered Tom once saying that in their business they got just the one chance. If they turned down even one request from their egotistical celebrity clients or passed them on to a rival, even a friendly one, it could mean losing the client's business and possibly that of their family and friends, too. She slumped.

He leaned in, pressing her gently back against the pillows with a deep kiss. She inhaled the citrusy scent of shower gel on his skin.

'I didn't hear you come in after your run last night.'

'Tom was returning to Andrea's, so I used his shower. I didn't want to wake you.'

*Returning to Andrea's? What an odd turn of phrase.*

Although she knew Tom was staying overnight at her friend's, Cathy had still not dredged up the courage to ask Mick to hers. She hadn't dared to read more into their relationship.

'Go back to sleep. Check-out's not until ten, so you have plenty of time.'

He got up, limped a few paces to pick up his black leather jacket. She shot up in bed.

'What happened? Why're you limping?'

'It's nothing serious, just a sprain. I twisted my ankle last night while running in the park and got Tom out to bring me back in his car.'

135

'You could have called me. I'd have come out.' For a moment, she was well and truly jealous of his relationship with Tom.

'I know.' He turned to her with a devastating smile, turning her insides to mush and squeezing her heart. 'But I knew you were working today, whereas that lazy sod wasn't.'

*Aww.*

'Does it hurt? Is it bad?'

He shot her a glance, amusement crinkling the corners of his dark-lashed grey eyes.

'No. I only taped it, so I don't damage it further. Andrea's also armed me with a crutch,' he pointed to one leaning against the bottom of the bed.

His phone buzzed. He glanced at it, shoved it back into his jacket pocket.

'I've got to go.'

Her heart sank. He'd said nothing about seeing her again. She bit her lip as he came back for a last goodbye kiss.

'Can I see you next weekend?'

*Was there a concert playing in the room?* Her grin threatened to take the top of her head off.

She tightened her arms around his neck and nodded. *In for a penny...*

'Would ... would you like to come to my place?' She stopped breathing as he pulled back, the smile disappearing as he stared at her, narrowed eyes probing deep into hers.

Slowly, the dimples on his cheeks reappeared as his eyes glowed. 'I thought you'd never ask.'

# 24

# MICK

## Sunday 08 April

A knock on a door can speak volumes. It can be a tentative tap, almost afraid of being heard. Like a whisper asking, *Are you there?* Or it can be a firmer *rap, rap, rap.* Usually three times, with the middle joint of the index finger. Posed in a normal tone of voice, it's an inquiry. *Are you there?* An action usually follows it: turning the doorknob or if the door is locked, the caller leans in to repeat those *raps.* Only, they are a lot louder and faster this time. Or the knocks notch up a stage: the caller stands really close, banging a fist on the door. Starting slowly with a well-paced *thump, thump, thump,* it spins into a series of harder, faster, staccato *thumps.* Imperative. Hard to ignore.

No one could knock on a door quite like Tom Cassidy. He used his knuckles. Three sharp raps, a microsecond's pause followed by a firmer *rap.* There was nothing tentative about it. It didn't ask permission. It was both an announcement and an order, always delivered just the once. An unequivocal statement: *Come out or I'm coming in.*

At the sound of Tom's unmistakable knock on the door, Mick grabbed a deep kiss, untwined Cathy's arms from around his neck and straightened up, all in one smooth motion. A last look around the room, his glance lingered on her tousled silky black hair, honey-brown eyes, soft parted lips, bedsheet clutched between clenched fists at the hollow of her neck.

Mick turned away before she could see the regret in his eyes. He slung his backpack over his right shoulder, picked up the crutch, hobbled to the door, and stepped aside while Tom reached in to pick up his overnight case. Without a backward glance, he pulled the door firmly shut behind him and followed the older man, the rubber tip of the crutch and carpeted floor muffling the sound of their departure.

Neither said a word until they were outside the main doors of the Bluebell Inn.

'Alright?' Tom scanned Mick's face before raising his eyes upwards to a second-floor window where the distinctive silhouette of a torso stood beside the partially opened curtains framed in the soft glow of the table lamp light.

'Yep,' said Mick, hefting his backpack further up his shoulder to raise a hand in a wave.

Despite the empty car-parking spaces in front of the Inn's main entrance, Tom had parked his Land Rover around the side of the building. The men halted and scanned the area before approaching it.

They both grinned as the puppy in the back seat tried to reach the window. Even with the doors closed, they could hear Calamity Jane – CJ as they now called her – yapping and whining to get to them.

They opened the rear passenger doors, loaded Mick's case and backpack along with the crutch beside Tom's luggage, and made a fuss of the overexcited little animal. Then, while Mick got in and fastened his passenger seat belt, Tom went around to check that the car boot was securely locked.

As Tom drove out of the Bluebell Inn's car park, Mick bent down to undo the strapping around his foot.

'Stop, don't. You need to leave that on for at least three days.'

With a groan, Mick settled for loosening the straps.

'And as you're now an invalid, you'd better stay with me for the next few days.'

Mick's groan was louder this time.

'Do I have to?' he asked, knowing he sounded like a 5-year-old.

'I hate not being able to go for a run,' he added lamely in the face of Tom's glower.

'That's definitely out of the question,' scoffed Tom. 'Besides, we have some serious work to do tonight.'

'Yeah, I know.' With a sigh, he settled back to stare at the brightening day and the steady build-up of traffic. In the back seat, CJ lay curled up, fast asleep, lulled by the motion of the car.

'Ricardo will drive the main limo today. You take the second.'

Mick turned to him in surprise.

'Your foot. Rick knows to help with the luggage, so don't lift anything heavy. I'll be the outrider today and arrange for help with the bags at the airport and at the hotel.'

Mick's mouth twisted in a wry smile. 'Okay.'

This was an act they'd perfected over their years in the business. Once they met the client and his entourage, Tom or one of the other veterans they employed would act as the outrider, making a show of checking the airport and reporting back to Mick and the other chauffeurs on duty. The airport security staff were familiar with their act and showmanship, so their actions weren't reported as suspicious.

After picking up the client, the motorbike-mounted outrider would ride close to the main limousine, sometimes in front and sometimes at the back, but visibly present, making a show of checking the route in both directions.

The smartly dressed, black-suited chauffeurs with their dark wrap-around sunglasses, who looked like the cast of *Men in Black,* hovered protectively over the client and his or her entourage as they herded them into the cars, adding to their celebrity status and aura of self-importance. It certainly seemed to impress the clients who paid well above the odds for the show. Tom was an astute businessman, and their appointment books were full. He was also an excellent judge of character and only employed
veterans he knew and trusted.

'Is Cathy better now? She seemed to take Stanley's death quite hard,' Tom asked after a while.

'She'll be fine.' Mick's eyes clouded at the memory of Cathy crying herself to sleep in his arms, her body wracked with sobs for a man she barely knew.

'Will Stanley's family have a funeral for him, d'you think?'

'I don't know if that cow, his wife Doreen, will even claim his body. She's quite happy taking his pension though,' said Tom. 'But probably the British Legion, the council or one of the volunteer organisations will arrange something. Won't be much of a send-off for him, poor soul.'

'That's a shame. He deserves better.'

'True.'

They made the journey to Tom's home-cum-business premises in two hours. Not bad considering the peak-hour traffic build-up the nearer they got to London. But luckily, their route from Southampton to Kingston upon Thames was straightforward, and they didn't have to use the M25, which, at this time of the morning, would have the London traffic entangled in its vicious grip.

Tom drove past the tall security gates to the back of a two-storeyed building that was his office and home. Set on a large plot of land, it had an industrial type building in the back yard providing secure garages to house the limousines. A smaller brick-built garage attached to the side of the office block accommodated his Land Rover.

Once behind the locked doors of the garage, they picked their luggage up from the passenger seat of the car and followed CJ as she skipped up the utilitarian metal stairs to Tom's three-bedroomed apartment above their offices.

Both men deliberately ignored the elephant in the room, or rather in the car's boot.

Mick headed into what they now regarded as his bedroom with its own ensuite to unpack and place his belongings in their precisely allocated locations. This was a space he had used often enough over the years, especially when they worked on their *special* assignments. It reflected his own personality. Austere with no frills and nothing that he couldn't walk away from. Apart from having it vacuumed and dusted each week, Tom left the room undisturbed.

Tom simply dumped his cases in the master bedroom before going into the kitchen to feed CJ, set coffee brewing, and check his messages.

'Oh. We have a booking request from Missy's office for next week. And guess what? They've asked for you.'

Mick's face was a picture of dismay. He remembered her vulnerability the last time he'd been with her. Missy's sleepy voice murmuring, 'Stay, please,' as he got up to leave. It was the first time she'd ever asked him to stay. He'd been tempted, but Tom's warning about a chauffeur in every airport clanged in his brain. So, after gently lifting her hair away from a damp forehead, whispering 'Shhh, go to sleep' and kissing her lightly on the temple, he'd left.

But that was eight weeks ago. A lot had happened since then. Meeting Cathy for one. A lot had changed

His eyes slid away from Tom's penetrating scrutiny and focussed on his hands wrapped around his coffee mug. He shook his head. 'I can't.'

'Is it because of Cathy?'

'I think so.'

Tom stared at him for an uncomfortably long moment before sighing. 'OK, lad. Don't worry about it. I'll make your excuses and find her an irresistible replacement.' His short bark of laughter was humourless.

Something in his tone alerted Mick. He scanned Tom's face, which had settled into its normal cheerful craggy lines, but not before Mick caught the sadness in his eyes and dejection in the downturn of his mouth.

'What is it?'

But Tom just shook his head. 'It's nothing. Just a complication I wasn't expecting.'

Mick was conscious of his weak radar for other people's sensitivity and emotions. Usually, it was because he simply didn't care enough.

'Is it Andrea?'

142

Tom froze before turning back to Mick.

'Yes, I'm afraid so. Her and now your Cathy. I'll have to think what we're going to do about them.'

Mick's shocked grey gaze landed on Tom's tired and clouded blues. He didn't like where this was going. Not one bit.

# 25

# CATHY

## Sunday 08 April

The discovery of Marek's body turned out to be a spectator sport.

It started with Chloe Mullen. The young mum with her 8-month-old daughter in a pram and her 4-year-old son skipping alongside were heading to the park's play area, as they did most Sunday mornings. She stopped a little way past the Titanic Engineers' Memorial to dig out her phone from her handbag. Bored, or because he glimpsed something behind the bushes, young Oliver wandered off a few yards to investigate. His mum immediately called him back, grabbed his hand and reprimanded him.

'But you could see me,' argued her son.

Cathy would come to learn that little Ollie had a lot of opinions and did not hesitate to share them.

'I couldn't see you in those bushes. You never know what could be hiding in there, waiting to catch little boys. There could even be a Gruffalo.'

'There's no Gruffalo there! Only a man sleeping on the ground.'

'A man?' The mum snapped into *stranger-danger* alert mode. Holding on tightly to Oliver's hand, she began trotting, pushing her baby's carriage before her, stopping only when her son's plaintive cries of 'You're hurting me, Mummy' reached her. A quick check of her surroundings reassured her. There were more people around here. A couple of dog-walkers, four joggers, two determined speed-walkers and three people just out for a stroll.

She examined the little boy's hand, red where she had gripped it. 'I'm sorry, Ollie. There, kiss better. I didn't want to wake the man up.'

'He was naughty. He spilled ketchup all over his jacket and didn't take it off.'

It took almost a minute before the import of her son's comment clicked. Chloe Mullen stopped, turned and hesitated. On the one hand, the man in the bushes could be hurt and in need of help. On the other, she was pragmatic enough to realize that she could not provide it. Not with two children beside her. She brought her phone up, preparing to dial 999, but hesitated. *What if Ollie was making it up, had imagined it? Maybe the ketchup was just that.* She should check it out before calling emergency services, but she certainly wasn't going back alone.

Chloe waved down the two approaching joggers, told them what her son said he'd seen, and explained her concern that the person might be hurt. The dog-walkers stopped to listen, as did two strollers. They would all go check it out.

There had recently been reports about assaults and rape in the park and they'd soon take care of any pervert lurking in the bushes.

In the Solent Constabulary HQ, Cathy was at her desk reviewing the scores of reports and transcripts of interviews the team had gathered about the murder of the Dwyer twins, looking for a nugget of anything that would help move the investigation forward. But mainly she was thinking about Stanley.

'His bruises developed after a few hours in the mortuary. He'd been badly beaten up,' Dolly told her.

Cathy had a good idea who was responsible. *I'm sure it's those two thugs. Grozdan and Marek.*

But she had to wait for the pathologist's report. Dolly had promised she would try to jump his PM to the front of the queue. *Did that battering lead to Stanley's death? If so, we could be looking at manslaughter. Could we push for murder charges?*

It was almost 10.00 a.m. when the call about the body in the park came to CID. Since Cathy was already at work, the DCI asked her to attend the crime scene with DC David Plummer. Thinking about the twins' murder was making her head ache and thinking about Stanley made her heart ache, so she grabbed a fresh new notebook and headed out. Maybe some fresh air, even if it was to the scene of a new crime, would give her a different perspective.

The two detectives shook their heads at the crowd gathered around the blue and white police cordon manned by uniformed officers. The FAO – the first attending officer – called for more help when it became apparent that many of the local residents decided it would be an interesting way to spend a Sunday morning. Although the corpse was behind tall bushy shrubs, most of them had their mobile phones held high to video or photograph the scene.

The FAO had also isolated the group of people who had discovered the body. Two officers were talking to them, jotting down their details and taking their statements.

Cathy and David showed their warrant cards and ducked under the tape.

Marek Kováč lay curled up on his side, hands clutching his stomach, his torso covered in blood. He was very dead indeed. And just four yards away lay what could be the murder weapon.

The crime scene was a total mess. The CSIs tutted and shook their heads in disgust. Seven people and two dogs had trampled and mucked up the ground before paramedics and Uniform arrived to set up a cordon. Luckily for the police, the knife had been sufficiently far from the body to have escaped the stampede.

The attending pathologist – not Dolly this time – put the estimated time of death at between 11.00 p.m. and 2.00 a.m. The victim appeared to have been stabbed. He refused to tell Cathy and David anything more until he took a proper look.

It did not take the lab long to confirm that the blood on the switchblade was Marek's. Forensics also identified the only set of fingerprints found on the knife.

The injuries on Marek showed he had taken a fist to his face, which had split his lip and loosened a tooth. His assailant had scraped his knuckle against Marek's teeth and left a fragment of skin. It did not surprise them to learn that it belonged to Grozdan Horvat.

The detectives were aware of Grozdan's temper, but what had his childhood friend done to incense him so much that he not only punched Marek's face, but also put a knife through his heart and stomach?

*What on earth happened between those two? Did they have a falling-out? Was it to do with Stanley? We have evidence that the two men attacked him. Where the devil's Grozdan?*

Paul's theory was that beating up Stanley had given Grozdan a taste for hurting people, and with Marek, he had most likely got carried away. Cathy was willing to accept that Grozdan might well be a psychopath and sadist. What she found difficult to digest was that Marek would do anything to infuriate or push his friend so far out of control. Her view was that Marek's role in life was to massage Grozdan's ego, to bloat his self-esteem and blindly follow his big, burly friend.

But all the evidence pointed to a fatal disagreement between friends. *Or maybe Marek was like Shakespeare's Iago. Not a true friend at all.*

The manhunt for Grozdan began. CSIs found his phone to the south of the park in the verges of the roads leading towards the port. It was well and truly smashed up. Of the man himself, there was no sign.

Cathy shook her head. The bodies were piling up, and now they had a missing person, too.

As with every case, the jobs got divvied up. Her task was to talk to Grozdan and Marek's employer.

When she turned up at the car-wash stall, she found the owner raging that neither Grozdan nor Marek had showed up for work. He stabbed at his phone, trying to find someone to cover in their stead.

Although he paled in shock upon learning the reason for the two men's absence, he didn't seem too devastated by the news.

'They good workers,' he told Cathy, 'Fast and efficient. Grozdan have good head for numbers. He makes me good money.'

The man looked like a much older version of Grozdan, and she learnt he was the young man's mother's second or maybe third cousin. He seemed keen to emphasize the distance of the relationship and almost convinced her he was a closer kin to *Lucy*, the 3.2 million-year old skeleton fossils of one of the oldest known human, than he was to Grozdan. Cathy also got the impression that despite his *very distant* cousin's money-making skills, he was not too keen on the young man.

And of course, he insisted on telling her all about himself. How he'd arrive in England 12 years ago with nothing but the clothes he stood in, a bucket, sponge and a few washcloths. He went around cleaning cars and now owned three car washes.

When he began grumbling all over again about their lack of consideration for the inconvenience they were causing him by getting killed and going missing, Cathy left him to it.

Back at the station, the team's IT whiz kid, DC Ian Shepherd, had moved things along and got a warrant for Grozdan's phone records. Cell site showed his phone had still been on at 12.45 a.m. around Houndwell Park, to the south of the city. The previous evening, he had received two texts from one of his flatmates, Anton Gajdoš, via an unregistered phone.

Cathy recalled interviewing Anton Gajdoš a few days ago when they had arrested Grozdan and Marek based on Stanley's accusation. Anton was a taxi driver, and their other flatmate was a waiter in a local nightclub. She put a call out to Uniform to pick up both men and bring them in for questioning.

This was more complex than it first appeared, made even more complicated because she remembered Mick had been out running at approximately the same time that Marek met his maker.

Mick and Tom would have to be interviewed, which meant that she would have to disclose their relationship.

She was not looking forward to that at all.

# 26

# CATHY

## Monday 09 April

'You're dating a robot.'

'I'm what?' Cathy swivelled her chair around to face DI Paul Hayes, who was staring at his computer screen.

'You – are – dating – a – robot,' he enunciated, which wasn't helpful as she'd heard him clearly the first time. 'Your boyfriend is a robot. All he does is his job, eat, sleep and work out. No social-media presence, doesn't seem to go out much, has no friends to speak of. His only regular contacts seem to be his boss and, recently, you. Not been married and no sign of any previous girlfriend. Cannot find any living family. His bank balance makes me want to weep, and...'

'Why are you doing such a deep search on him? All we need to do is ask him whether he saw or heard anything while he was out running last night.'

'What do you know about him, Cathy? Did you check him out before you, er, started a relationship with him? You've only just met the man, and I wanted to check that he is who he claims to be.'

'Paul, shut that down right now.'

The detectives jumped and turned at DCI Holt's voice behind them. Stone-faced, eyes narrowed, he said, 'in my office. Now. You too, Cathy.'

He spun on his heels and strode off with the pair following like schoolchildren heading to the principal's office.

'I've just had a call from MOD. They received an alert of a search being run on two of their personnel. Michael O'Neal and Tom Cassidy. And they want you to cease and desist immediately. Their words. Why're you running a search on them?'

Cathy met Paul's desperate glance and felt the heat rising to her face.

'Sir, Mick, I mean Michael O'Neal, might be a material witness. He was out running the night Marek was killed,' said Paul.

'I see. How did you come by this information?'

Her cheeks on fire, Cathy felt even her neck burn. When the DCI's slate-grey eyes narrowed, she took the plunge.

'I'm, er, I'm in a relationship with him, sir.' Her voice was barely above a whisper.

'So, you were running this search for personal reasons?'

Cathy gasped aloud and realized the echo she heard came from Paul. Their boss hadn't raised his voice nor moved a muscle, yet his tone sent a sliver of ice down her spine.

'No, sir.'

'It was my fault. I ran the search to check him out. Since he isn't from Southampton, I wanted to make sure he is who he says he is, and that Cathy's safe with him.'

She breathed a sigh of relief. She had been terrified that he wouldn't own up and knowing she couldn't snitch on him meant the crap would land on her. DI Paul Hayes went up a few notches in her estimation. It was also nice of him to care for her safety. But while some of his concern might have been genuine, she suspected it was so he would have something juicy to recount to the others at the pub.

'I see. Why didn't you run the search yourself, DI Collins?'

*Oops. My title and surname. He isn't happy.* Cathy went for honesty.

'I wanted to, sir, but I didn't have any work reason to run a search and I was afraid of getting caught.'

*Was that a twitch to his mouth?* DCI Holt turned to Paul. It was the first time she had heard the cocky DI stutter.

'I'm— I'm sorry, sir. I got a little carried away, especially as there was so little about the man in the public domain. The more I looked, the less there was to find. It triggered my curiosity and suspicions. Sorry, sir. I should have cleared it with you first.'

'Yes, you should, and you should have known better. You're supposed to be showing DI Collins the ropes. This isn't one of them.'

'The records say that he was invalided out in 2012. Why is the MOD still keeping tabs on him? Is he still in active service?'

'Which word did you not understand: cease or desist?'

They deflated like pricked balloons. Suddenly, the boss smiled and leaned back.

'Look, the instructions come from the very top, and your searches seemed to have touched a nerve. For national security reasons, his military records would be sealed, and we wouldn't have access to it for any reason. But that should have no bearing or relevance on our case. As you said, he's retired, but there must be a reason for MOD's ongoing interest in him, which they're very unlikely to reveal.' He paused in thought. 'If, however, you suspect these two men of any involvement in any crime, that changes everything. Do you? Suspect them, I mean.'

'No, sir,' said Cathy.

'Yes, sir,' said Paul. He grinned sheepishly when both Cathy and the DCI glared at him.

'Not really, sir. He's a man of mystery, but it seems a too much of a coincidence that he was out running on the night that Marek Kováč was killed.'

'He goes out running most nights!' she protested. 'Running or to the gym. He suffers from insomnia.' Cathy could see the thought spring into Paul's mind, probably the DCI's too, that she was not tiring Mick out enough in bed. But neither men cracked a joke. 'He has nightmares,' she added sadly, more to herself than to them.

DCI Holt nodded. 'I got a précis of ex-Captain O'Neal's background. His father was Irish, died in Belfast when the boy was ten. Details classified. His mother was English, brought him up on her own. She died of leukaemia in 2000. O'Neal joined the regular army when he was eighteen and then the SAS three years later. In 2010, on his tour in Afghanistan, he was captured and tortured before he somehow got away and his squad rescued him. He'd been shot, almost died and was hospitalized for several months. I imagine it must have been a traumatic experience.'

*That explains a lot. My poor Mick!*

'What about Major Cassidy, sir?'

'He retired after 22 years of service, won several medals and citations, though they wouldn't say what for. But it certainly wasn't for neat handwriting. His superiors and his team thought well of him. He now runs a limo-chauffeuring service for celebrities and is doing very well. He's been looking to expand their services to cruises, I understand.'

Cathy nodded. This tied in with what they'd told her and Andrea. It was good to have confirmation that they were really who they said they were, and she was glad for her friend that Tom checked out OK. Andrea seemed to be taking Major (Ret'd) Tom Cassidy very seriously.

'Yes, sir. He said they'd been thinking about it for several months and exploring potential partnerships since mid-January.'

'What time did he leave on Sunday?'

'Really early. Just after 6.00 a.m. They had clients to pick up from Heathrow.'

'That's true, sir. I ran ANPRs and got confirmation from Heathrow Security as well. Both Tom Cassidy and Mick O'Neal, plus another veteran, ex-Sergeant Ricardo Perez, were at the airport. They picked up a Sheikh Abdullah and his family members – seven in total – in two limos and took them to the Corinthia in London.'

Cathy could not believe her ears. *He's actually run a check on Mick and Tom. He's treating them as suspects!* Her fists clenched, but she swallowed a retort when the DCI nodded his approval.

'Hmm. So, no reason apart from personal curiosity for you to dig any deeper. Unless you have actual evidence of their involvement in a crime, stick to the rules. Interview them by all means. If they've committed a crime, then all bets are off, and we treat them like we would any other criminals. But until then, kid gloves. Right?'

'Yes, sir.'

'And DI Hayes, don't blot your copy book again.'

*Seriously? Who says that anymore? These days it was more like 'Don't get crumbs on your keyboard or peanut butter on your screen'.* The DCI's speech pattern was very neutral, more London than anything, but occasional slips like that betrayed his public-school background.

'Now get out of here and take your daughter with you.'

*Ha, ha. Hilarious.*

# 27

# CATHY

## Monday 09 April

Anton Gajdoš protested his innocence. Loudly. He had a passenger in the back when the police arrived with their sirens blaring and blocked his taxi. His terrified passenger scooted out of the car, but not before the officers collected his name, address, and contact number. Startled as he appeared by the turn of events, the passenger still tried to get a photo or two of the police escorting Anton away in their patrol car. He might have managed a couple more shots, but an officer told him, politely but sternly, to 'Please put that away, sir'.

After processing him through the custody suite, Anton was brought to Interview Room Number 3, where Cathy and DI Larry Ives waited.

Cathy surveyed the room glumly. *I'm spending so much time here that pretty soon I can claim it as my office. Maybe even hang a nameplate on the door.*

Anton looked shocked at the news of Marek's death. He asked several times if they were sure, and how he'd died. He even asked where Grozdan was.

'Do you recognize this phone number, Anton?' asked Cathy, showing him the burner phone number from which the two messages to Grozdan had originated.

He frowned at the number on the screen, his mouth moving as he read out each digit to himself.

Crime scene officers had already searched his flat and taxi but discovered no unregistered phones or anything else incriminating. Whatever Anton and his flatmates were into, they were careful to leave no trace of it in their home.

'No, that's not my phone number. My number is...' He rattled off his normal registered number.

'So, whose number is this then, Anton?'

'How should I know?' His answers, in good English, were delivered in a strong East-European accent.

'Well then, it's strange that you sent a text message to Grozdan from a phone you say you don't recognize.'

'Sorry, I don't understand.' The puzzlement on his face looked almost genuine and would have been believable if it weren't for the wariness in his eyes.

The detectives directed his attention to the two text messages up on the screen, in their original form in Slovak. Again, Anton's lips moved as he read the messages, then raised wide watery blue eyes to his interrogators.

'I didn't send those messages. It's not my number and I know nothing about it.'

'We find that hard to believe, Anton. What is this deal you mention?'

Something shifted in his stance and his eyes lowered, darted around the room like mice scurrying to the corners. He tensed.

'I don't know anything about any deal. I didn't send those messages to Grozdan. I was working. Why would I want to meet him?'

'You tell us. Why did you need Grozdan and Marek's help? Why did you ask them to meet you at the Titanic Memorial at that time of the night?'

'I didn't.' His voice grew louder and higher pitched. 'I'm telling you I didn't. I was home asleep. You can check.'

'How? Were you with someone between midnight and 2.00 a.m.?'

'No, I was in my flat alone. Asleep.'

'Well, then you have no one to corroborate your statement, do you? Grozdan and Marek were definitely not there, and your other flatmate was working at the nightclub. So, we only have your word that you were in your flat.'

And so it went on, with him denying ownership of the phone and disclaiming all knowledge of the text messages. Cathy knew they had no way of proving otherwise. The phone from which the text messages originated had no GPS. Cell-tower triangulation put its location within a half-mile radius of the busiest part of Southampton city. Not helpful, especially as the phone had gone dead after those two messages.

In his statement, Anton persisted he hadn't left the flat after returning there at 11.55 p.m.

'I was tired and went straight to my room and to bed. I didn't go into Grozdan and Marek's room. It was late, and I assumed they were asleep. And no, I didn't go out again. I go to sleep.'

The detectives had no evidence to show that he had gone to meet his flatmates at the park. There was no CCTV footage of his presence in the streets of Southampton and no log on the ANPR database of his car after midnight, either.

Although they pushed hard, neither Cathy nor Larry could budge him. Their persistence ended with his solicitor protesting that they were harassing his client.

With no choice but to let him go, they released him under investigation, warning him not to leave the city.

'I'm certain he's hiding something,' said Cathy, watching Anton depart hastily before anyone changed their mind.

'So am I. I think it's related to Marek's death and to Grozdan taking off, probably with enough cash to buy his way out.' But when asked to elaborate, DI Paul Hayes could not offer any details for his assumption.

'I'm not so sure it's linked to Marek's death or Grozdan's disappearance,' said Cathy. But when challenged, she had no answers either. Just plenty of doubts and even more questions.

# 28

# CATHY

## Wednesday 11 April

Much to her disgust, Cathy was not allowed to interview Mick or Tom, but had to be content with watching the recordings afterwards. She also had to endure the knowing looks, teasing and calls for her to bring him to the pub and introduce him to the team.

*Yeah, Mick would love that! I don't think so.*

The two men were busy with clients and couldn't come to Southampton until Wednesday, so DI Paul Hayes and DC David Plummer interviewed them remotely by video.

Her heart tightened at the sight of Mick's handsome face on the computer screen, but she also felt sorry for him. He was so stiff and uncomfortable before the camera, whereas Tom was a natural and totally at ease.

'What time did you go for your run?' Paul asked.

Mick sat upright in an executive chair in a small, unpretentious office, which Cathy learnt was Tom's. She smiled at the pictures on the wall behind. Dotted between the posters of three gorgeous limousines were a hoard of pictures of Tom's puppy, Calamity Jane.

'At 23:03 hours.'

Paul and David looked surprised, both by Mick's use of the more formal 24-hour clock and knowing the time so precisely, to the exact minute. Cathy grinned. *Welcome to my world.*

But Mick's response also surprised her. That was very early for Mick. He usually went out around 3.00 a.m.

*Why hadn't I heard him go?* But that didn't surprise her. It had been a harrowing Saturday, especially after her emotional reaction to the news about Stanley. She had also downed several glasses of wine at dinner, then gone upstairs with Mick. Afterwards, Cathy had fallen into a deep sleep. By 10.30 p.m. she'd been dead to the world.

'Can you describe the route you took, and what you saw or heard?'

Mick frowned as his eyes lowered and shifted left, trying to recollect.

'I didn't plan on any particular route, just kept to the main streets on the A3057 and headed south towards the quayside. On my way back, I ran through the south park — Houndwell, I think it's called.'

'Did you see or hear anything along the way?'

'Nothing unusual. Few cars, a couple of vans, and few people including dog-walkers and two or three groups of young people. I had my earphones in, so couldn't hear much.'

'Go on.'

'From Houndwell, I ran across the road into the next park. Palmerston Park. That's where I twisted my ankle. I found a bench and called Tom, that's Major Tom Cassidy, asked him to come and get me.'

'What time was that?'

Mick got his phone out, flicked through the screen.

'At 23:43 hours and then again at 23:48.'

'And then?'

'I sat and waited for him.'

'You just sat and waited inside the park? Didn't go nearer a road so he could pick you up more easily?'

Mick looked puzzled. 'No, I sat and waited for him to come.'

'You said you crossed the road from Houndwell Park into the next one. How far in did you go?'

'Not far, about 150 yards.'

'Did you go as far as the Titanic Engineers' Memorial?'

'That's at the other end, isn't it? The north end? No, I stopped in Palmerston Park and waited.'

'What time did Tom Cassidy get to you?'

'At 00:22 hours.'

There was a pause while Paul translated the time in his head.

'Did you see anyone in the park?'

'No, it seemed pretty deserted. I didn't see—' He paused; his eyes widened. 'I saw someone. Just the back of a person, walking south through the bushes.'

'What time was this? How far away? Can you describe the person?'

'Hmm. I didn't check my watch. Maybe 00:35 hours? Tom was with me then, strapping my foot. He might have seen something, too. The person was about fifty yards away. Near the road. Let me see.'

He glanced down at his phone again. Cathy made out the image of a map.

'Near Pound Tree Road. And I just caught a glimpse of his back in the shadows. Looked like a man. Big, kind of bulky figure. Hunched over, sort of staggering. A drunk, I thought.'

*Bingo! That must have been Grozdan, heading out of the park. Such a shame Mick had not gone in deeper and through to the adjoining East Park. He might even have prevented Marek's death.*

'Did you see the person again?'

'No, sorry. He was heading south when I saw him. We walked to Tom's car, and he drove me straight back, north on the A33, to Bluebell Inn.'

*So, someone who looked like Grozdan was last seen heading towards the docks.* Cathy glanced at the clock. *He's had 36 hours to find a boat or a trawler to take him either as a passenger or a stowaway.*

The interview with Tom Cassidy was just as unproductive, although the tone of the interview could not have been more different. Tom was a real charmer, open and friendly, and he was soon chatting away to Paul and David like old friends.

His story tied in with his associate's. He'd been at Andrea's when he got Mick's calls. Tom said they were both awake and Andrea gave him strapping tape and a pair of adjustable crutches to take to the injured man. *Trust Andrea to have those things to hand.* Tom said she also gave him a special protective walker boot, but as Cathy hadn't seen him wearing it, she thought Mick must have decided he didn't need it. But she clearly recalled the strapping on his ankle and the crutch.

Tom hadn't seen the man in the park. 'I probably had my head down strapping that clumsy bugger's foot at the time.'

Net result at the end of the day — they'd made no discernible progress towards solving any of the deaths or finding the missing Grozdan.

The team still had nothing new on the Dwyer twins' murder and it looked like Stanley's death was due to a cardiac arrest, with no evidence that the assault caused his death. But it certainly caused his serious injuries and Dolly said that if Stanley had been found soon after the GBH, he might have survived.

And now, they had a fourth body. Marek's. Killed by his best friend for reasons as yet unknown.

Cathy had no doubt that Grozdan and Marek were responsible for the brutal attack on Stanley. Much as she ached to have Grozdan incarcerated for killing the homeless veteran, she might have to settle for putting him away for GBH.

*But at least he'll still be going down for Marek's murder. All we have to do is to find him.*

And she'd learnt a little more about Mick. Or 'the Robot', as DI Paul Hayes now called him.

Hard to believe it was less than three weeks since she first met Mick. Sometimes it felt as though it had happened to someone else a lifetime ago and at other times, as if it were yesterday. The memory of their meeting was so sharp and clear, every touch, every sensation still vivid.

# 29

# CATHY

## Wednesday 11 April

'Why're you asking me about that? It has nothing to do with those brothers' deaths. I wasn't even here last week.' Parnell Walker of Flat 306, who'd been away when the detectives interviewed the other residents of the Naylands, sounded more bewildered than belligerent.

'Their bodies were found last week, but that's not when they were killed. And we'll decide what's relevant to the case, Mr Walker.'

It had been a long day tagged on to a sleepless night, added to which Cathy was hungry and cranky. From the scowl on DC Larry Ives's face, he was not in a mood to be messed around with either.

'Oh, OK then. Should I have a solicitor present?'

*Give me strength!* Cathy drew in a deep breath, stretched her mouth in what she hoped was a convincing smile.

'That's certainly your right, Mr Walker. Look, we've spoken to every resident in this building and taken their statements. You've been away, so you're the only one left. It's routine in any investigation. But we can always move this interview to the police station if you prefer.'

'No, no, that's OK.' Parnell Walker held up his hands in surrender and sagged into his armchair. The man's eyes were red-rimmed, and he looked tired. They could still smell booze on his breath and guessed his days away at a conference had included a lot of heavy drinking.

His two-bedroomed apartment was a typical bachelor pad with big fake leather recliner armchairs and modular furniture, chosen for comfort rather than looks. But dotted around were a few feminine touches. Bright flowery cushions, cheerful prints on the walls and a few knick-knacks on the pale wooden sideboard. Cathy had also noticed a pair of fluffy pink mules in the hallway.

'Where were you between 10.00 p.m. on Wednesday, 21$^{st}$ and 8.00 a.m. on Thursday, 22 March?'

'Here! I went out for a drink after work with Janine, my, er, lady friend, and then we came back here. Is that when it happened? When were they killed?'

Cathy ignored his question.

'Did your lady friend stay here all night? Did either of you hear or see anything?'

'Yes, she did. Stayed overnight, I mean.' He closed his eyes for so long that the detectives thought he'd fallen asleep. When he reopened them, the red-veined whites glistened around his widened black irises.

'Janine didn't wake as far as I know, but I woke up in the middle of the night. I heard nothing unusual, but I saw the outside security light come on. But when I looked outside,

I saw nothing and thought it must be a fox or a cat. I went back to bed.'

'What time was that, Mr Walker?'

'Oh, I don't know. After midnight, but I didn't check the time.'

'We'll need to speak to Janine too. Could you give us her contact details?'

He flicked through his mobile phone and held it out as Larry jotted down the details.

'Did you see anything at all outside? Any shadows? Any car passing?'

'No nothing, just that the light was on and then it turned itself off after a while.'

'What was your argument with the Dwyer twins about?'

The abrupt change of subject threw Walker. His face flushed. 'What? Who told you about that? It must've been that Harman woman, the nosy cow.'

Expressionless, the detectives waited.

Walker sat up, seemed to reach a decision.

'Those two! Everyone thinks they're so good and kind and perfect. Like hell they are. They're perverts if you ask me. Oh, I mean, they *were*.'

'Now, why would you say that, Mr Walker?'

'Please, it could be important,' Cathy added when he hesitated.

'They took my daughter out for drinks and invited her up to their flat. God knows what would have happened if I hadn't seen the message.'

*Bingo!*

'Tell us about it from the beginning, please, Mr Walker.' She wondered if the man realized he was talking himself into suspect territory.

'After my divorce, my daughter, Phoebe, used to come and spend every other weekend with me, but as she got older, it became once a month. Anyway, about five or six months ago when she came to stay, we were downstairs bringing her bags up and I was having a go at her for wearing make-up and dressing inappropriately, when the twins showed up. Naturally, I introduced my girl, but I didn't like the way they looked at her.'

*What parent does?* Cathy thought of her own daughter and the constant battles she seemed to have with her recently about practically everything.

'My daughter asked to come and visit more often after that. I was just happy and thought nothing of it. Then a couple of months later, she left her phone on the armchair and went to the bathroom. It pinged a text message and when I saw it was still on, I read it. It was from those two perverts upstairs inviting her to their flat that evening. They were having a small party. Bring a friend if you like, it said. Can you believe that?'

'Go on.'

'I saw other messages between them. They'd even met her in town one evening and bought her drinks. I was so angry I could've killed them.'

*Yep. He's definitely a suspect now.*

'I marched straight upstairs and almost punched them. But I didn't hit them. I promise. I only threatened to report them to the police if they came anywhere near my daughter again.'

He paused, his anger and fear emanating from him in waves.

Cathy and Larry leaned forward and nodded encouragingly.

He slumped in his seat. 'They looked shocked and puzzled. One of them, I don't know which one, said that they had done nothing wrong. Just invited her to a party. I started shouting at them again, called them paedophiles and accused them of grooming my daughter. Finally, I ran out of breath and saw their expressions. They looked stunned. I started to leave, determined to report them, when one of them said, "What do you mean, paedophiles? Your daughter's 18, isn't she?" "No, you pervert," I said. "She's only 15!"'

He took a deep breath. 'Even I could see how shocked they were. "She told us she was 18," they said. One of them brought out his phone and showed me a message from Phoebe, thanking them for treating her to a late eighteenth-birthday drink. They also showed me a note she'd slipped under their door when she first met them, giving them her phone number and asking if they would like to buy her a drink to celebrate her eighteenth birthday.'

Parnell turned to the detectives, his expression revealing his incomprehension. 'I was stumped. That stupid, stupid girl. Even after everything you hear on the news, after her mother and I telling her a million times.'

He shook his head in despair.

'What happened then?'

'They showed me photos she'd sent them. Definitely not something a father wants to see. One of them was of her all dressed up, holding a wine bottle. I'm ashamed to say she looked like a tart. The message said, *Celebrating my eighteenth birthday. Wish you guys were here.* She looked much older than 15, so maybe it wasn't all their fault. But they are doctors and

I think they should be able to tell how old a person is. I believe they knew, but continued to groom my child.'

'So, did you report it to the police?' They would, of course, check the records, but it was worth asking first.

'No, I didn't. They messaged Phoebe right in front of me. Called her a liar and said that they didn't want to hear from her again. They also told her that if she contacted them, they would report her as a stalker to the police. They told me they were keeping all her messages and photos as proof that she'd tried to entrap them.'

Cathy and Larry exchanged glances. Here was Walker, giving them a damn good reason for the missing phones and laptop.

'Did you talk to your daughter about it?'

'Talk! I shouted at her. Confiscated her phone right then and there, phoned her mother and we both grounded her. Phoebe blames me and refuses to see me now. Both her mum and I tried explaining that we were protecting her, but she won't listen. I only hope she understands someday.'

*And there he goes, giving us his motive for killing those two men.* He could have easily gone upstairs and killed them while his girlfriend was asleep, possibly with chemical assistance. Looking at the roll of fat around his waist, the beginnings of a double chin and flabby muscles, Cathy doubted he could deal with two of them, but rage could drive a man to commit desperate acts and give him the strength to carry them out.

*If he were guilty, though, would he have told us about his daughter? He could have made up a trivial but annoying excuse, like the twins parked in his space or left trash out. Or was he being clever by telling us the truth? Was his innocence an act? We need to interview him under caution.*

Cathy and Larry rose to their feet, their expressions sombre.

'Mr Parnell Walker, we'd like you to accompany us to the Station...'

# 30

## CATHY

### Friday 13 April

Two weeks into the twins' murders, yet Cathy and her team had hardly made any progress. And this despite tripling the number of detectives and support staff working on Operation Silhouette. Even the normally cool, calm and collected DCI was looking anything but. As for their superintendent, his explosive rants had everyone cringing in their seats if they were dumb enough not to have made a quick getaway. Cathy couldn't blame her bosses. The senior officers were getting a lot of flak from the media, as well as the public, and pressure from the very top.

After holding him for a full 36 hours, they had released Parnell Walker under investigation. Opinion on Mr Walker was divided. One camp thought him an innocent who'd had an unlucky fallout with the victims. The other believed him to be a clever psychopath who'd cunningly hidden the evidence.

Cathy vacillated between the two. So, although they released him under investigation, they also kept an eye on him.

The team assembled in the incident management room for their daily evening briefing. Having exhausted potential suspects, they were back to re-examining one of their pet theories about the motive for the crime — that one or both twins might have overheard or seen something they shouldn't have. Something potentially damaging or dangerous to someone, maybe to one or more of the staff, but it was much more likely to be a patient.

'Has to be a patient in one of the private rooms,' said Cathy. 'It'd be far too risky discussing anything sensitive in one of the general wards. The smaller ones have four beds and some of the larger ones have ten to twelve. There are always people walking about and even with the curtains pulled all the way around the bed, you could never be sure you wouldn't be heard.'

'That's true,' said DI Paul Hayes. 'We need to get a full list of all patients admitted to St John's.'

'I can't see the hospital simply giving it to us. It's too broad a scope,' said DC David Plummer in his quiet voice. 'We'll have to narrow it down.'

'I agree, in theory,' said Paul. 'But how? We've no idea of the gender of the suspect. Did they overhear anything? A phone call or a discussion between a patient, visitor, or staff member? Or was it something they saw? What? What could they've seen that got them killed so viciously?'

'Not something. Someone,' said DC Salim Khan, practically bouncing in his seat with excitement. 'They saw someone they recognized. Someone who wasn't who he or she said they were, or someone who shouldn't have been there, or—'

That reminded Cathy of Stanley's ghost.

'What if it was a visitor and not a patient?' asked David.

The team's horrified expressions were mirrored on each other's faces. The hospital had no log or register of visitors. People just came and went during visiting hours. It would mean trawling through hours and hours of CCTV footage, searching for a needle without knowing what it even looked like.

'Please stop,' groaned Paul. 'Let's not get into wild speculations. Let's focus on what we can actually find out and substantiate. If we can't narrow it down, we'll need a list of all patients.'

'We could narrow it down to the days or nights when the doctors were on duty and to the wards they worked,' said Larry.

'Good point,' said Paul, scribbling in his notebook. 'I'm thinking we'll need to get a court order. I'll run it by the boss, but it's the safest bet given how wide the request still is.'

'Considering how they died, it's not unreasonable for us to want to ask the patients if they saw or heard anything while they were at St John's. Whether they noticed or heard anything odd, even if it was something innocuous,' said Cathy.

Paul smiled, and several heads nodded.

'What time period are we looking at, sir?' asked an admin staff who would help with getting the court order written up and processed.

'I'm going on the hypothesis that whatever the conspiracy, it couldn't have occurred too long before their deaths. If the twins intended blackmail, they would've only waited for a couple of weeks, a month at most. If the conspirators thought they'd been seen or overheard, I doubt they'd wait half as long to deal with the two doctors,' said Paul.

'What if the doctors failed to recognize the significance of what they witnessed until later? Maybe as long as a month after. Then they took, let's say, another week or two to work out what to do with the information.' Cathy had her diary open and worked backwards from the doctors' deaths. 'They'd have had to approach the person, rattle his or her cage, make their demands and wait for a response. That puts us in the latter part of January. Shall we say from 1 January? That should cover a safe period.'

Paul nodded. 'With our luck, the Court will insist we really narrow it down. We'll be lucky to get it for two weeks before their deaths, let alone three months. It could even be something they saw or heard last year,' Paul muttered glumly, heading off to see the DCI.

Despite his pessimism, the gods must have been smiling on the team or the magistrate must have had a really good day on the golf course or else he'd been very drunk. They got the court order for the entire period of their request, starting from 1 January.

The following morning, Cathy nabbed Ian as her tactical weapon should the manager try to bamboozle her with the complexity of their database and the difficulty of extracting information from it. Clutching the precious court order, the detectives headed off to St John's Hospital.

'I see you haven't asked for their medical records,' said Shari Thundé, the manager scrutinising the order. 'Don't you need to know what they were in for?'

'Probably, but we're more interested in whether they saw or heard anything, regardless of how insignificant it seems. Besides, we can always ask them what they were in for. People love to talk about their ailments and hospital experience, especially if we ask them sympathetically.'

# I, SAID THE FLY

Ian turned to Cathy, blinking in disbelief.

'What? I can do sympathetic ... when I need to.'

# 31

# CATHY

## Saturday 14 April

Semi-awake, huddled in the warmth of her duvet, Cathy rolled over to answer her phone. Her heartbeats quickened when Mick's face filled the screen, but disappointment soon replaced anticipation when he apologized and cancelled their weekend together.

'Our clients have stayed on in London and both Tom and I'll be busy chauffeuring them to wherever their whims dictate,' he said. 'I'm really sorry, Cathy. I was looking forward to our weekend.'

'Me too. But I understand. How's your foot?' she asked, hiding her dejection as best as she could.

'It's absolutely fine. Back to normal.' His eyes crinkled in amusement at her mothering. 'I tried to use it as an excuse to duck out of the job,' he laughed. 'But the old man wouldn't buy it. "The sprain's on your left foot and the limos are automatic," he said, so I'm stuck here this weekend. But I have only one morning booking on Monday, so I can come right after.'

'Yes, please. I'd love that. But I'll be working late.'

'I know, but I'd still like to see you before Tom and I leave for Scotland next week.'

Apparently, the men had booked and paid for the fishing trip ages ago. Cathy and Andrea had laughed when Mick said they were exploring hobbies for Tom for when he retired.

Two minutes later, she hung up, surprised at the wave of loneliness flooding her.

Sat at her desk at the Station, Cathy stared sadly at the pathologist's report. The rest of her Saturday was turning out to be as bleak as the document on her screen.

Stripped of jargon, the report stated the cause of Stanley's death was a fatal cardiac arrest. The scars on his heart showed that he had previously had a series of minor heart attacks, which he'd ignored and certainly not gone to any physician for treatment. Stanley's heart had simply been marking time, waiting for the big one to strike.

Besides the cuts and bruises on his face and upper body, his X-rays showed a fractured rib, which had not penetrated his heart or lung. Blunt-force trauma to the left kidney had caused internal bleeding, and he had a cracked pelvis. The latter had been aggravated by his walking – or rather, limping – from the location of his attack to his hidey-hole in the Naylands. *He must have been in agony*!

The most interesting element in the report was the contents of his tightly clenched left fist. Stanley had been found lying on his left side, and no one noticed that his left hand was tucked into his pocket.

He hadn't put up a fight or defended himself during the attack except to grab at his assailant's head. After that, he'd taken the gruelling punishment and concentrated on protecting the evidence in his fist.

During the autopsy, Dolly had uncurled Stanley's fist to discover a few strands of hair, several with the roots intact. The DNA confirmed a match for Grozdan Horvat.

*I so badly wish I could charge Grozdan for Stanley's murder, too.* However, with the cause of death stated as cardiac arrest, Cathy knew the best they could get him for would be manslaughter. But they had to find him first.

The pathologist had found feline saliva on Stanley's face and ginger cat fur on his skin and clothes, especially around his neck and shoulder. There was also cat fur, both old and freshly shed, all around Stanley's den, and a dead sparrow. She recognized the signs: they were so familiar to her, a part of her life she could not imagine living without. Her own cat, Sooty.

*At least in his last moments, Stanley hadn't been alone. He'd been with a sentient creature who'd offered him what comfort it could.*

# 32

# MICK

## Wednesday 18 April

While driving to Scotland may not be the quickest option, Mick and Tom decided it would be the safest as they'd be able to take everything they needed without worrying about luggage weight or airport security.

Stashed in the boot of Tom's Land Rover was a full set of brand-new fishing gear, along with their night-surveillance kit, closed-circuit two-way radios, and night-camouflage outfits. After all, this was a fishing trip in more ways than one.

With pit stops for CJ, the journey had taken far longer than the sat-nav's estimate. Now eight and a half hours later, Tom was at the wheel for the 180-mile drive from Tebay to Perth. He smiled at the puppy asleep in the back seat and glanced at the man beside him.

Mick had the passenger seat tilted back and appeared relaxed with his legs stretched out, but his eyes were still alert. As he often did, Tom wondered what was going through his friend's head, if anything at all. While Mick was at the wheel, Tom had used the time to catch up on emails, schedule and assign chauffeuring jobs, and when that was done, had even played a few games and dozed off for a while. But not Mick. He didn't keep checking his phone, play games, watch movies or even read. Yet he absorbed information like a sponge and had a retentive, near-photographic memory. Tom had often seen him flick through newspapers, magazines or any non-fiction books in sight, yet every word was not only etched in his memory forever but also sorted, referenced, linked and filed, available to him at an instant's notice. And when there was nothing to do, that's what Mick did. Nothing. Tom knew no one who could stay as still or as unoccupied for as long as Mick, nor be as focused when he needed to be. Maybe that's why he was so good at his job, or rather, jobs. That combined with his good looks.

Tom sighed. The trouble with Mick was that he couldn't let go, didn't know how to forget. Everything stayed locked up in that head of his, trapped, unable to escape. Out of the corner of his eye, he saw Mick's head turn towards him, mouth twitch in a smile.

'Stop worrying. I'm fine.'

'What are you now? A psychic?'

With Mick once again at the wheel for the last leg of their journey, they reached their holiday cottage just before 7.30 p.m.

Located 20 miles from the village of Beauly and about an hour's drive south-west of Inverness, the small two-bedroomed stone cottage was cosy, clean, well-furnished and well-stocked with items from a list which Tom had sent the owners. Best of all, it was isolated and perfectly suited to their needs.

After unloading their car and having a quick wash, they walked the mile with CJ on a leash to the nearest family-owned restaurant recommended by the cottage owners.

The cosy bar at the Fairlea with its roaring fire was welcoming after the chilly, drizzly walk, especially for CJ, who made a beeline for the hearth to make friends with an elderly retriever. Although it was still early in the season, three couples sat at tables in the restaurant area while five men drooped over the bar.

Tom bought everyone a round of drinks, admitting that this was their first attempt ever at fishing and that he had lessons booked for early the next morning with the cottage owner.

One elderly local rooted around his jacket and brought out a small flat tin with a realistic-looking fly nestling inside, which he insisted was the best in business. This started a lively discussion at the bar, with a couple of guests bringing out their own special flies, which they swore by. To their gratification, Tom took photos of each one and even made notes of their advice, but his focus was on the local man, whose name also was Tom. Tom MacLeay.

'Tom, would you care to join us for dinner? Mick here is not into fishing, but he's a hiker and a history buff. We'd love to hear about the area from someone who lives here rather than just what we've read.'

'Thank ye, that's verra kind. And no, you don't wan' ta believe everything ye read,' said Old Tom in a gruff voice and a strong accent, nodding sagely all the while.

The two men had to concentrate to decipher Old Tom's lilting Highland burr.

'We got lost on our way, took a wrong turn and passed what looks like a manor house about 5 miles west of here. It looked pretty big, but we couldn't see it mentioned as a tourist attraction.'

'Ah, that be the Brannick House. A big estate, it is too. Nigh on 600 acres. No, laddie, you wouldn't see it on any tourist map. That's because the owner, Simon Brannick, won't let anyone near it. He keeps to himself. He's getting on now. Bit older than me he is. I'm 75, would ye believe?'

To the old man's delight, Tom looked appropriately and admiringly surprised. Truth be told, he'd thought their dinner guest to be much older, in his mid-eighties at least.

'Me, I come here for a drink an' company. But not Si Brannick. Since my Maggie died seven years ago, it's just old Bess and me now.' He pointed to the old dog curled around CJ, the pair of them fast asleep by the fireside.

It required some mental gymnastics, but they found it got easier to follow the old man's speech. 'Simon Brannick,' mused Tom aloud. 'Why does the name sound familiar?' His speech had picked up the cadence of Old Tom's accent and he already looked like he belonged, no longer a tourist.

'Ah, it's that scandal ye might've heard about. Back when Simon Brannick lived in England. It's a few years ago, mind. I'm not one for gossip, but since you've already heard about it...' The old man relished telling them the sorry tale.

Years ago, when Simon Brannick was arrested for fraud and his wife had also gone missing, everyone thought he'd done her in. But it turned out he was just a patsy. His partners had cleared off with all his money, and his wife had run off with one of them. It had broken poor, naïve Simon, but he still had the Brannick Estate, so he came here and never left. Eventually, he'd married a local woman, Doreen, and rebuilt his life in the area.

'Right angel was our Doreen. Third cousin to my Maggie, she was. Sad day when she died four years ago, an' poor Si's been a virtual recluse since.'

'It looks like a big place, from the outside anyway. Does Simon's family live with him?'

'Nae, he's got nobody. Just auld Ross McKay, his butler-cum handyman. And two auld dogs. Ross is gettin' on a bit, too. Near 70 he is. Likes his drink and is often in here.'

But old Simon Brannick was not a fool, Old Tom assured them. He'd had the house fitted with a new security system about ten years ago. One of them new-fangled electronic ones. Which, according to Old Tom, would be good if the old codger remembered to set the alarms. Not that there was much left in the house worth stealing, for Simon had sold off much of it to clear his debts and pay for repairs.

Promising to return tomorrow and buy Old Tom and his mate Ross, the butler, a drink if he showed up, Tom and Mick made their way back to the cottage.

'That sounds easy enough,' said Tom.

'Famous last words.'

'Well, you heard. A ten-year-old security system that may, or may not be turned on, a butler who likes a drink and two old dogs. How hard can it be? Shame that Simon's a recluse. It means it has to be an inside job. Anything else will raise questions. You OK with that?'

'Should be fine if you can get me in. I'd like to have a quick look tonight at the layout outside, see how close we can get without alerting the dogs or setting off any alarms.'

'I'll come with you. I'd like to see if I can tap into the alarm system. Let's drop CJ off at the cottage first, then we can take the car.'

Half an hour later, the two men, dressed in night-camouflage clothing with a paraphernalia of gadgets stashed about their person, crouched just short of 100 yards from Brannick House. The U-shaped building towered before them like a black, turreted, hulking monster waiting to pounce. A glow of light behind dark curtains in an upstairs room showed that one or more of the residents were still up at 11.45 p.m. Or, as they would put it, at 23:45 hours.

Mick and Tom wove their way to the back, keeping well away from the house. Clearly visible under a bright exterior security lamp were two dogs rooting around within a fenced-off area. Beyond them, yet another light shone through an open doorway. A few minutes later, the faint sound of a whistle reached them.

They watched the dogs trot back indoors, and the door shut behind them. Old Simon and his butler's idea of letting the dogs out last thing at night was simply to open the back door and whistle for them when it was bedtime.

Creeping closer, Mick trained his binoculars on the upstairs window. 'I don't believe it. That window's wedged open, right next to a cast-iron drainpipe too.'

Tom tutted as he edged closer to the front door of the house. Scooting past the range of the bright security light, he stood with his back pressed against the wall to one side of the doorway. He pulled out a professional-grade frequency jammer from one of his many pockets. Ten minutes later, he looked up with a grin and gave Mick a thumbs-up signal.

'Right, that just leaves the dogs to take care of,' said Tom as they headed back to their cottage. 'I've got my fishing lesson at 07:00 and will be at it all day. Are you going to try your hand at it too?'

'No way. I'll go for a walk. See how far I get.'

'On your way back, stop by a butcher's and buy half a kilo of minced steak.'

# 33

## CATHY

### Wednesday 18 April

The admin staff at St John's hospital had finally collated the information from their database matching the parameters of the court order.

'Why didn't you just ask for the records for all the patients?' the manager had grumbled. 'It'd have been so much easier.'

Cathy and Ian nodded. They could see what she meant. Even though they tried, their managers could only roster the Dwyer twins on the same shifts for around 40 per cent of the time. But even then, they worked in different wards. For the remaining 60 per cent, their schedules were all over the place. In the end, the rostering team did a data dump into an Excel spreadsheet and Ian worked his magic with macros and formulae to extract the information the detectives needed.

It was still a long list, but Ian soon reorganized it, separating those in private rooms from the general wards and highlighting patients who'd stayed for over two nights.

'Paul, come here. Look at this.' Cathy pointed to a name on her screen. 'Isn't that—?'

Paul Hayes scooted his chair closer, peered at her monitor. 'I think it is.' His voice quivered with excitement. 'Wait. Let me check something.'

With a whoosh, his chair rolled back to his desk, and he furiously worked his keyboard and mouse. Eventually, he sat back with a satisfied grin.

'Ta da!'

'Are you sure it's him?' asked DCI Holt.

Cathy and Paul were in their boss's office, brimming with pride at the gigantic gold nugget in their pan. On reflection, maybe it wasn't a precious metal they had sifted and panned, but an unexploded bomb.

'Yes, sir. That's definitely his address and the phone number alongside his name is registered to him,' replied Cathy.

'You haven't already contacted him, have you?'

'No, sir.' The two DIs held their hands up in surrender. 'We came straight to you. But we need to question him.'

'What did you have in mind? To ask him if he killed those two young men?'

'Of course not, sir. Our line of questioning, for him and others on the list, is to ask whether they saw or spoke to either of the doctors or if they saw or heard anything, particularly when either of them was around,' said Cathy.

The DCI nodded thoughtfully, then sat drumming his fingers on the desktop, darting the occasional glances at them.

'We need to question him, sir,' prompted Paul, unable to stand the silence.

'OK, I'll allow it and I'll warn the super what's going on.' He glared at the two detectives.

*It's not our fault that man was in hospital within our time frame,* thought Cathy, but stayed schtum. She sympathized with him. Once the DCI told the superintendent, it would trigger a chain reaction of worry about the fallout all the way up the chain. What flowed back would not be pleasant for the detectives.

'Right. Cathy, I want you and David to set up a meeting with him.'

Paul's mouth opened to protest but the DCI simply held up a finger in warning and he backed down. Cathy's jaw ached from trying not to grin, or at least not look too smug.

'Cathy and DC David Plummer are to do this one. Reassure him it's a standard line of inquiry and that you are contacting all patients who stayed overnight,' said DCI Holt.

'Yes, sir.' *It's actually a good strategy.* Cathy was senior enough in rank to satisfy that patient's ego, but not senior enough to make the interview appear too formal. Plus, being a woman, her presence would be deemed non-threatening, by most people anyway, and DC David Plummer was brilliant with people.

'And for god's sake, don't make me regret this. Be careful and be subtle. You do know how to be subtle, don't you, DI Collins?'

'Oh, yes, sir. I can do subtle. When I need to.'

# 34

## MICK

**Thursday 19 April**

Backpack laden with water, binoculars, spare socks, maps, compass and sandwiches in an insulated lunchbox, Mick left on his walk early the next morning. He planned to get a good look at Brannick House and its surroundings in daylight before trekking around Loch Affric while Tom and CJ drove off for a day's fishing lesson. They'd then meet back at the cottage at 6.00 p.m. before returning to the Fairlea.

Mick's reconnaissance of the Brannick House and Estate that morning as part of his hike turned out to have been a totally unnecessary exercise. For here they were again, at almost midnight, sitting in the Land Rover, watching Ross the butler stagger into the house, having refused his invitation to go inside for a 'wee un' for the road.

The evening had gone like clockwork. They'd hosted Old Tom and his mate Ross for dinner. When the old man protested, Tom had whispered that it was all going to be charged as a business expense, after which neither of their guests felt guilty about the quality or quantity of their drink or food orders.

The butler's last drink had included a mild sedative, which would ensure he got a restful night's sleep with no ill effects.

As Tom reversed the car and drove away to park it out of sight of the house, Mick slipped off round to the back with the insulated lunch box containing the doctored minced meat and dropped it in two separate piles inside the dogs' fenced-off area. Sure enough, five minutes later, no sooner had the animals been let out, they found and scoffed down their unexpected treat.

The two men, clothed in dark camouflage, balaclavas and night-vision glasses, waited a full thirty minutes before creeping around to the front of the property. Tom disarmed the burglar alarm.

Mick eyed the cast-iron drainpipe longingly.

'Don't be a fool. Those restraining clips are rusted and the whole thing could come off the wall. Use the front door like any respectable burglar, will ya?' said Tom.

Mick sighed, trudged to the front door, picked the lock and slipped inside while Tom kept watch.

Earlier, they'd discussed their options and the best way to fulfil the contract.

'Drugs are not an option,' Tom had said. 'They might conduct a post-mortem.'

'Maybe he slips in the bathroom and cracks his head on the edge of the bath or toilet?'

'Possible, although he might survive that.'

Mick's derisive glance spoke volumes. Mostly it said, 'Don't be silly'.

'How about he breaks his neck falling down the stairs?' he had suggested.

'Yes, that sounds better and a lot less messy. Let's go with that. So, this mission is to recon the layout, check the stairs, make sure that there is enough of a sloping run to justify someone breaking their neck in a fall. That it isn't one of those silly ones you see in big houses with two or three landings. Take a peek at the old man too, if you can. We can come back in a couple of weeks to finish the job.'

A light at the end of the passage illuminated the generous hallway with its dark wood panelling and an elaborate but unlit chandelier. Upstairs, another bulb on the first-floor landing provided adequate light to the curved sweep of the wide staircase, with its threadbare runner down the middle, held in place by brass rods that begged for some polish and elbow grease. Mick nodded in satisfaction. A nice fall all the way down.

Although they'd given enough time for the sedatives to take full effect on the butler and the dogs, Mick stood still, alert for any sounds or movements. All was quiet except for a faint snore from behind one of the closed doors upstairs and so far, neither of the dogs had barked.

An elaborate, dusty, crystal chandelier, twin to the one below, hung from the high ceiling. Only one of its many candle-shaped bulbs worked. He flicked off a switch on the small stretch of wall, plunging the area into darkness and lowered his night-vision glasses into position.

The snores grew louder as Mick mounted the stairs. He reached out a gloved hand, turned the doorknob carefully, and peered in. As he suspected, it belonged to Ross, the butler, who lay sprawled on the bed with his mouth open.

Mick grinned, left him to it and moved on to the next room. The door was ajar. He nudged it open wider. The gleam of white porcelain and odour identified it easily enough. The discarded clothes on the floor revealed that the snoring butler had been the last to use the bathroom. He memorized the layout before moving on to the next room.

A floorboard creaked as he stepped stepped up to the closed door. Mick froze, counted off the seconds to two whole minutes. People hearing odd noises in their home usually listened for 15 to 30 seconds for a repeat of the sounds before deciding it was nothing or got up to investigate.

This is where he had to be extra careful. More intel would have come in handy. Was Simon Brannick a light sleeper, who needed less sleep the older he got? Did he get up and wander about the house at night? Or did he slumber on blissfully, regardless?

Satisfied that his literal *faux pas* had not disturbed anyone, Mick gripped the doorknob, and in one smooth movement, twisted it to swing the door open just wide enough for him to slip in and drop into a crouch in the corner of the dark bedroom.

He rose cautiously to his feet and heard a sharp intake of breath from the room's occupant.

# 35

# CATHY

## Thursday 19 April

C athy and David waited until the peak hour traffic had subsided before setting out on their hour-and-half drive to Bertling near Reading to meet the Right Honourable Sir Nicholas John Hubbard. The 46-year-old was a VIP in politics. He was not only a Member of Parliament but also a senior cabinet minister – the Secretary of State for Defence. Or rather, now an ex-cabinet minister and ex-Secretary of State for Defence.

As the late Labour Prime Minister, Harold Wilson, had famously said, 'A week is a long time in politics.' These days, however, even 24 hours was a long time in politics. A week was a lifetime, and 3 months an aeon.

Much had happened to the Rt. Hon. Sir Nicholas Hubbard since January.

He appeared on the list of inpatients from Tuesday to Friday, 16 to 18 January, when he'd spent three nights and four days at the hospital. Apart from his surgery on the first day, when he had a stent put in to treat a heart attack, he had been kept in to monitor his recovery and progress, which meant that he was fully conscious and able to make decisions. Totally *compos mentis*. Capable of setting an assassination in motion. If he was guilty, that is. And he was astute enough to detect any discrepancies even if he was innocent. But Cathy wondered whether people like him observed or actually took any interest in anything that was not directly connected to them. They would know soon enough.

When she'd spotted his name among the patients in private rooms, Paul had dug up the media reports about him. On the day of his admission, Hubbard had been visiting the Greengage Barracks on Ecclestone Road, where he collapsed during a dinner hosted for him. Diagnosed as a heart attack, he was rushed to St John's Hospital and had a coronary angioplasty with a stent insertion that same evening. The surgery was a success, and three days later, he was discharged.

There had been photos of his wife, Lady Elizabeth, daughter of the 10th Earl of Seddingfold, and their two daughters arriving to visit him. However, despite the description, the photos merely showed a big car and the backs of a woman and two children in coats and hats. They hadn't stayed long and apparently, reassured by his recovery, had not returned for a second visit.

When Cathy phoned to arrange the meeting, she'd rather hoped that it would be at the politician's family home on the southern edge of Oxfordshire. The country home, set in 49 acres of landscaped grounds, looked stunning in the pictures, and she'd been looking forward to getting a glimpse of how the other half – or rather, one per cent – lived. Even better would have been the chance to visit Lady Elizabeth's childhood home, the stately home of Seddingfold in the centre of Oxfordshire, which was not open to the public. Instead, they were heading to Bertling, a mile or so north of Reading, to Nicholas Hubbard's modern, five-bedroomed, river-front property.

Cathy rolled the car closer to the black box mounted on a pillar at the entrance and announced themselves. One of the tall wrought-iron electric sliding gates rolled laboriously aside to let them in. As instructed, she parked on the drive beside a double garage and walked up to the porch. Though far less sumptuous and imposing than their other homes, this was still a very nice designer property. Painted white with grey tiles and trimmings, it had clean lines and a modern, minimalistic appearance.

The man himself greeted them at the door. Cathy had, of course, seen his photos and he had featured often enough on news broadcasts, but she thought he was better looking in person. About 5 ft 9 in tall, he was of average build, and square-jawed, with thick, greying, wavy hair parted on the side over a broad forehead, a biggish nose. Unlike many of his more bluff, garrulous colleagues, Hubbard was quiet, sombre, and dignified. His clipped accent reflected his background and education: Eton followed by a business and politics degree from King's College, Cambridge, where he had met his wife. They married when they were in their late twenties and had two daughters, now aged 15 and 13.

Cathy kept a lookout for them as Hubbard led her and David through a nicely appointed living room and then through to a sleek, modern kitchen. But the house was devoid of any sign of his wife or children. In fact, there were no signs of them living with Hubbard, but he clearly had been living here for some time.

A woman in her mid-forties and a man in his early thirties, both smartly dressed, were busy at a dazzling white central island assembling trays of sandwiches and coffees. Hubbard introduced them as Miranda Preston, his PA, and Richard Pearson, his PR manager. It was obvious that Hubbard's staff knew who the visitors were and why they were here.

'I hope you won't mind if Miranda joins us?' he asked, and when Cathy hesitated, he added, 'I have no secrets from her, and she is most discreet.'

'That'll be fine.'

They followed him through to the back of the house to an enclosed terrace that encompassed the width of the kitchen and extended to cover half of the living room. The terrace faced a well-maintained garden and led directly to the river Thames. It was breath-taking. The water glinted and sparkled under a soft blue sky. Despite the bright April sunshine, it was sadly still too cold to sit outside, but, as they lowered themselves into the cushioned, low-backed rattan armchairs around a large oval, glass-topped coffee table, Cathy thought this would do nicely instead. It was easy to see why Hubbard wouldn't be too unhappy settling for this.

'Won't Mr Pearson be joining us?' David asked when Miranda appeared rolling a two-tiered trolley laden with a tray of sandwiches, pots of tea, coffee and condiments. The lower shelf held crockery, cutlery, and cloth napkins.

'No, he's busy working on my PR material.' He smiled grimly. 'As you've no doubt read in the press and various social-media sites, my image sorely needs some serious PR work.'

Cathy took that as her cue. 'We're so sorry about your friend. It's very sad losing someone you love and trust.'

Both Hubbard and Miranda froze in the act of handing out plates and napkins. Eyes narrowed, Hubbard turned sharply around to face her. But Cathy was being sincere. At that moment, she was thinking how devastated she would be if she lost Andrea. Some of that must have shown in her eyes, for his softened. He nodded and returned to his task.

Cathy glanced at David, whose face wore an expression of shock.

'What?' she mouthed soundlessly at him and shrugged. *That was subtle. They haven't thrown us out. We're still here, aren't we?*

Except that the DCI had expressly forbidden them to even mention Hubbard's friend who had died in a road traffic accident.

'Thank you,' said Hubbard softly, handing out plates, napkins and cutlery. 'Please help yourselves to sandwiches and coffee. There's tea in that pot.'

He poured himself a coffee before continuing, 'It's still painful, even after three months. I never got to say goodbye. His parents are absolutely devastated. And the media interest has not helped at all — not Quentin, nor his parents and especially not me or my family.'

For the past year or so, whispers and rumours had been growing about Hubbard's friendship with 28-year-old Lieutenant Quentin Sawyers. Rumours that it was more than friendship, although both men had denied it. There was nothing to substantiate the gossip, but it had clearly affected Hubbard's family, or rather, his wife's and, in particular, her father, the bombastic Earl of Seddingfold. There had been speculation that the Earl had even tried to get Quentin deployed overseas, but an injury sustained during training, although insufficient to invalid him out of the army, had been enough to thwart his transfer.

Hubbard's media strategy had been to refuse to answer questions about his personal life. He and his family had presented a strong united front. But the stress on top of his high-profile job in such a key government role must have impacted his health and could have been a contributing factor in his heart attack and consequent sojourn at St John's Hospital in Southampton.

'Anyway, that's not why you're here. Let's focus on that. What is it you wanted to ask me?'

'It's about the two doctors who were murdered, sir.'

David produced a photo of the Dwyer brothers — a copy of the one they'd found in the twins' flat, not one taken after their death — and laid it on the table.

'Yes, that was awful. They look so bright and cheerful in this. It's tragic and cruel what happened to them. Have you found out who killed them?'

'We're still investigating. They were both on duty when you were in St John's Hospital. Do you recall seeing or speaking to them, sir?'

Hubbard thought for a moment. 'No, not really. I know my consultant, of course, but not his junior doctors. When I was in recovery, he came in daily and each time, he had four or five student doctors with him. The poor victims may have been part of that group, but I'm sorry, I really didn't notice.'

*Typical politician. Too self-centred to notice anyone else.*

'We understand, sir. When you were there, did you see or hear anything that caught your attention? Anyone or anything odd?'

'No, not really. Being in a private room, I couldn't see or hear much of what was happening outside. I remember being annoyed at the number of people – nurses and doctors – who kept coming in and out, or simply popping their heads in.'

Cathy turned to Miranda. 'And you, Miss Preston, did you see either of these doctors or anyone you recognized, or notice anything that seemed unusual when you visited Sir Nicholas?'

She screwed her eyes in thought and shook her head. 'No, I don't recall seeing either of them. A couple of nurses came in to check in on Nicholas while I was there, and everything looked normal. Well, normal for a hospital, that is. To be honest, though, I wasn't really paying much attention. On top of the normal work, there were a lot of get-well cards and messages that needed replying to, and I concentrated on prioritising work, I'm afraid.'

Meanwhile, Hubbard had picked up the photo and was studying it.

'D'you know, I think one of them may have attended to me. I can't say which one as they look so alike. When my family visited, I recall a doctor coming in to do some test, but when he saw my wife and daughters, he smiled, said he'd come back later and left. I'm certain it was one of them.'

'And did he? Come back, I mean?'

'Yes, he did. A couple of hours later, with a nurse who took more blood. He listened to my heart, felt my pulse, checked the stent insertion site, and did all the usual poking and prodding. But apart from asking how I felt and telling me I was doing very well, we didn't talk much. One of them might also have come in the following night, but I was half-asleep, so either I imagined it, or it could've been another doctor altogether. I don't think I'm being very helpful, am I?'

'Every little helps, sir. Even knowing that nothing unusual happened at certain times or in certain locations helps us to narrow our field of investigation,' said Cathy.

David leaned forward. 'I hope you won't mind my asking, sir, but are you well now, after your surgery? Fully recovered?'

His tone and expression showed genuine concern, and his whole demeanour was sympathetic. *This is why he's so good at his job and especially in his role as our main family liaison officer. Dave could get the Sphinx to tell him its life story.*

Like others who met David, Hubbard also responded to his empathy. Charmed and disarmed, their host, too, leaned forward.

'Thank you. I'm fine now. I think I'm in a better shape now than before my heart attack.'

'That's good,' said David. 'The news of Quentin's death must have come as a terrible shock. Especially when you were still in hospital.'

*Now that was subtle.*

David's compassionate expression had not changed. His eyes focussed on Hubbard's were still full of understanding. He made it easy to forget that you were talking to a policeman.

Hubbard sighed. 'Miranda told me when she came to see me the following morning. She had to, otherwise I might have seen it in the press.'

He was silent for a long time, then his glance shifted to Miranda. They exchanged some sort of signal, for she shook her head sharply and when his expression grew grim, determined, her shoulders sagged. She leaned back in resignation.

'I'm sure you'll soon hear or read about it. I was hoping it'd all stay private, but apparently, it won't, and I have little choice in the matter. Quentin's parents have decided to go public with the truth. Now that he's dead, it won't affect him. They believe, or rather, hope, that it might help to bring about changes in the way people, especially staff, are treated in the forces because of their sexual orientation.'

Cathy and David sat up but said nothing.

'It's true. Quentin and I were... that we had a relationship, but we'd both agreed to keep it quiet. He'd not disclosed it to anyone in the army and I'm a family man. I didn't want to hurt my wife. By the time there were hints of it in the press and I was questioned about it, we'd already stopped seeing each other. And then I had my heart attack, and he was killed.' He looked at each detective. 'That kind of experience, of losing someone and nearly dying, changes one. It's made me re-examine my values. When Quentin's parents told me of their intentions, I decided to support them and resigned my post as Defence Secretary.'

'But why, sir?' asked Cathy. 'Surely you could help push for change if you're in a position of power?'

Hubbard's short laugh had nothing to do with amusement and everything to do with irony. 'It doesn't quite work like that, I'm afraid, Detective Inspector. I now have a vested interest in the outcome. That's not ideal, especially if one's working for the greater good. Besides, the personal nature of the issue, the questions and media coverage, were impacting my job, my health and my family. As you'll soon hear, my wife and I are separating. Whether or not it's permanent, I don't know. I truly hope not, but time will tell.'

'I'm sorry to hear that,' said Cathy. 'You've been through a lot in the last three months.'

'Yet, I'm still here. The worst of it is that I think Quentin must have heard about my heart attack and was on his way to see me when he crashed and died.'

Miranda reached out and patted his hand. At that moment, Pearson, his PR manager, walked in holding a sheaf of papers. He appeared surprised to see the police still there.

Hubbard straightened up and stood. 'If there's nothing else, I've got to prepare for another meeting.'

That was their cue to leave. The detectives too rose.

'Thank you for being so open with us, sir. You've been most helpful and hospitable.' Cathy nodded at the remnants of their lunch.

He smiled as they shook hands. 'My pleasure. And it looks like you got more than you bargained for. As I said earlier, this'll all be public soon enough, but I'd be obliged if you'd please treat this as confidential for the time being.'

'Absolutely,' Cathy assured him. 'We can be discreet.'

Discreet and subtle.

# 36

# MICK

**Thursday 19 April**

Tom leaned against the wall and shivered. Despite the thermal lining of his waterproof camouflage clothing, the chill penetrated right through to his bones. He was getting too old for this malarkey and to add to his woes, it was drizzling again. He glanced at his watch.

*What the hell is Mick doing in there? For fuck's sake, this is just a reconnaissance. All he has to do is take a dekko at the stairs and the old man.*

He knew he was being unreasonable, but he hadn't particularly enjoyed his fishing. He'd been wet all day and here he was, getting rained on again. Tom edged sideways under the overhang of the porch to shelter from the worst of the thickening rain and forced himself to relax.

Two minutes later, and another peek at his watch creased his brows in worry. Mick should have been out by now. He'd estimated five minutes, seven tops, for this job and it was nearly ten already. Something was wrong. Tom straightened, drew his gun out of its holster, screwed on a silencer, and turned towards the front door.

His earphone crackled. 'Tom?'

Eyes glued to the door and poised to move in an instant, Tom switched on his microphone. 'Yeah, you OK?'

'I think I've killed him.'

'You what?'

'Killed him. All I did was lean over to look at him.' Mick sounded distinctly annoyed. 'He sat up suddenly, his nose just inches from my face. Made me jump. Then he made a funny gurgle and simply collapsed on his back. He's not breathing and has no pulse. You're not bloody laughing, are you?'

'No, of course not,' choked Tom.

'You don't want me to do CPR on him, do you? We want him dead, right?'

'Oh my,' moaned Tom, tears running down his cheeks. 'No, don't CPR. Tuck him back in and get out of there.'

'OK.'

Tom switched off his microphone, covered his mouth and howled with laughter. A moment later, he straightened and switched it on again.

'Mick, wait. See if you can grab something personal from the old man. Something to prove that we've fulfilled our contract, and that Simon didn't die of natural causes.'

'Oh, OK. Will do. Be down soon. I'll check on the dogs too before I come out.'

Less than five minutes later, Mick was at his side.

Tom clutched his heart, groaned, and dramatically fell back against the wall.

'Ha, ha, funny. Will this do?' Mick held out a steel-strapped wristwatch in his gloved palm.

In the light of his bright LED torch, Tom turned the item over, checking the back of the watch. The inscription read:

*To Simon, Happy 70$^{th}$ Birthday, Love always, Doreen.*

'Perfect. All OK in there?'

'Yep. Old Si's still dead. Ross is still snoring, and the dogs are fine. Let's get out of here.'

# 37

## CATHY

**Thursday 19 April**

'You did well there, Dave,' Cathy said on their way back to Southampton from Hubbard's, with David taking his turn at the wheel. 'You really got him to open up.'

'Thanks.' He shot her a quick glance before turning back to the road. 'And you were quite subtle, too.' His grin quickly faded. 'But I'm not sure we got anything useful. Does this mean our theory about the crash is kaput?'

While Hubbard was recovering from surgery at St John's Hospital in Southampton, Quentin Sawyer had been killed in a motorcycle accident, at 2 a.m., on a stretch of the M4. He had been travelling from his regiment's base near Bristol, presumably on his way to Southampton.

According to the Highways CCTV, he had been riding at a speed of 110 mph when he appeared to swerve – almost jerk – along a curve and had crashed into the concrete barrier. He had died on the spot, his motorcycle smashed into pieces and scattered across the tarmac. No other vehicle was involved in the accident.

'Not at all,' she said. 'Let's wait till we see what Paul and Salim dig up.'

'I liked Hubbard. He sounded genuine.'

'Don't they all? He's a politician, remember. They know how to hide behind words, half-truths and to lie by omission.'

The look David threw her said it all.

*Since when did I come to have such a low opinion of the human race and politicians in particular?* she wondered.

B ack at the station that evening, Cathy and David briefed the team about their meeting with Sir Nicholas Hubbard. Eyebrows shot up when they recounted Hubbard's confession about his relationship with Quentin Sawyers.

'What about the motorbike crash? Anything there?' Cathy asked Paul.

DI Paul Hayes was clearly not a happy bunny.

L ast week, when they'd discovered Hubbard's name on the patients' list and uncovered the stories linking him to Quentin, Cathy had piped up with a *'What if—?'*

'What if that motorbike crash wasn't an accident? What if Hubbard engineered it to get rid of Quentin, to keep the truth of their relationship from coming out?' she'd asked.

'A contract killing, you mean?' Paul's tone had been scathing.

Cathy had stuck her heels in. 'Yes. What if Quentin decided to go public with their relationship? I see that Hubbard's always been careful in his choice of words and has never actually lied about the relationship.' She pointed to a news item. 'Look, in this one, when the journalist asks, "Are you in a relationship with Quentin Sawyer?" He said, "Quentin's a good friend, and that's our relationship." And thereafter, he has either simply ignored those questions or told the press, and anyone else who's asked, that his friendships and family relationship are none of their business and has told them categorically that he wouldn't answer any personal questions. It seems to have worked, and no one has goaded him into disclosing anything.'

'So? How d'you get from that to Hubbard arranging for Quentin to crash? At best, being outed about his relationship with Quentin would be a blip in Hubbard's political career, but I doubt it'd ruin it.'

'It might not have ruined Hubbard's career, but it would certainly affect his family life. His wife's family especially wouldn't like it.'

'So, you think because it'd affect his standing amongst the nobility and he might no longer be welcome to go shooting or riding with the Earl of Seddingfold, he'd have Quentin killed?'

'People have done so for far less. We should at least look into it.'

Paul's eyes had glinted, and Cathy still remembered his evil grin. 'You're right, Cathy. We can't ignore it. OK, you run with it. Check up on that crash. Contact the National Highways guys and follow up with the Wiltshire Police. I'll go interview Hubbard.'

Cathy had fumed. She'd been lumbered with chasing up paper, watching CCTV and treading on the toes of their colleagues in Wiltshire, while Paul would get to visit Hubbard at his home in Oxfordshire or even get to visit the Earl's stately home.

But luckily for her, the DCI had switched their roles. She'd got to interview Hubbard but had come away with nothing to substantiate her theory. Instead, she'd rather liked the man and felt sorry for him. A part of her hoped Paul wouldn't find anything, either.

Before Paul could come up with a scathing comment to Cathy's question about the motorcycle crash, the DCI joined the briefing.

'Carry on. I'll catch up while you talk,' he said.

On their drive back from Hubbard's, Cathy had updated the DCI on their meeting, reassuring him they had been subtle and had ruffled no feathers.

'So, despite my telling categorically you were *not* to mention his friend, you asked him about Quentin?' DCI Steward's quiet tone portended dire consequences.

'I'm really sorry, sir. But actually, I only said we were sorry for his loss and asked about his health. He volunteered all the personal stuff.'

'Cathy's right, sir. I think he only told us because it'll be in the news in a day or two.'

The DCI grunted, but she doubted he'd fully believed them or been entirely satisfied. She relaxed into her seat.

'Or maybe,' she said, 'he told us all that to distract us from our main enquiry. To gain our sympathy, so we wouldn't look too deeply into Quentin's accident.'

A bark of laughter. Not one of amusement, though. 'I presume you've heard about a thing called *evidence*? I hope for your sake, Paul finds some,' he'd concluded.

And now here they were, waiting for Paul to substantiate her theory.

'There's nothing to indicate that it wasn't an accident,' said Paul. 'But why he swerved when taking that curve of the M4 is not clear. The cameras show nothing. No obstruction or any animal. The officer suggested it might have been a sneeze or a bug. He was definitely going too fast. Over 110 mph at that point. When he crashed into that barrier at that speed, he had no chance. Right mess it was. Neck and multiple bones broken on impact. Dead at the scene.'

'Had he been drinking?' asked DCI Holt.

'No, he was below the alcohol limit. He'd possibly had a pint earlier in the evening, but nothing more. The toxicology report showed no drugs in his system either.'

'What about his motorbike? Any way to tell if it had been tampered with?' Cathy asked.

'Wiltshire Police said the bike was literally in pieces. I also spoke to the mechanic who said if anyone had messed with it, that crash would almost certainly have happened much sooner. I agree with their conclusion that this was a genuine accident.'

*And not one of your pie-in-the-sky theories,* she could almost hear Paul thinking.

'Let me get this straight,' said the DCI. 'After three weeks of investigation, we have nothing? Our only witness is dead. One of his assailants is also dead, and the other has vanished. And as if we don't already have enough flak from the media and aggro from up the food chain, all you lot can give me are theories involving ex-Cabinet ministers?'

He stood up and glared at each of his team. 'Get back to the flat and the hospital. Re-interview everyone. Check the CCTVs again. Stop effing around and find me the bloody killer!'

He turned on his heel and marched out.

Cathy waited until he was out of earshot before saying, 'That motorbike crash ... Maybe it wasn't Hubbard after all. What if it was his father-in-law, the Earl of Seddingfold, who engineered it?'

Nine faces turned to her in horror and disbelief.

# 38

## MICK

### Friday 20 April

For the sake of appearance and credibility, they stayed on for another day and night. Tom had wanted to stick to their original plan and stay through to Sunday, but when Mick threatened to go off without him, he gave in, and they compromised on driving straight to Southampton instead on Saturday. An idea which pleased both men.

Their morning started with Tom photographing Simon Brannick's watch before packing it up and addressing it to their client at his home address with a label printed out on his portable wireless printer. When delivered, the small parcel would shatter their client's illusion of his own anonymity yet give no clue to the sender's identity. It would also leave their client in no doubt they knew where to find him. He would also have a very hard time explaining how and why he came to possess his uncle's wristwatch.

With Mick off on a run, Tom and CJ left shortly afterwards to Inverness to post the parcel. While not totally foolproof against a determined investigator, the main post office in town was busy enough to provide him with a layer of obscurity, helped by a tartan cap over a wig of grey hair, glasses, a grey beard and a long, old but clean coat, and not least by a faultless Scottish accent.

When he returned three hours later, Mick was stretched out on the sofa, flicking through a coffee-table edition of the Cultural History Of The Scottish Highlands. The cottage was spotlessly clean and tidy. Cleaner and tidier than when they'd moved in and every item was perfectly aligned, even CJ's food and water bowls. Not a single evidence of artistic disarray in sight.

'Looks like you've been enjoying yourself,' said Tom.

Playing with CJ, Mick ignored him.

After lunch, Tom said he would give fishing another shot.

'I'll join you to check out for myself what the fuss is all about,' said Mick.

To Tom's annoyance, the younger man quickly got the hang of it and was fly-casting his line effortlessly within half an hour, and much to his disgust, had hooked three decent-sized brown trout in the next hour and a half.

Mick released the creatures back into the loch and took CJ for a long walk. When he returned two hours later carrying the exhausted puppy in his arms, Tom was still at it, but his casts were a lot smoother with no snags and, from his expression, he appeared to be enjoying the sport.

*The old man must have finally caught some,* thought Mick.

'Got four. Look at that whopper,' gloated Tom, pointing to a net semi-submerged in water with a large trout swimming around in circles. 'Almost two feet long. Isn't he a beaut?'

'Congrats. What now? You going to play at it some more?'

'Naw. Now that I've proved mine's bigger than yours, we can go.'

Mick rolled his eyes. He released the fish and watched it swish away to disappear into deeper waters.

That evening, the Fairlea was buzzing with excitement. Old Tom accosted the pair as soon as they walked in.

'Have ye heard about auld Si?'

'No, what is it?'

'He's only gone an' died.'

'I'm sorry to hear that. When?' Tom and Mick looked appropriately downcast.

'Jus' last night. Musta bin a heart attack. Nae a bad way to go, if ye ask me. Died in his bed too.'

'Let's find a table. We're leaving tomorrow morning. Business beckons, I'm afraid.'

'Right sad it is. We'll miss ye right enough.'

'We insist you join us again for dinner and you can tell us all about it.'

'Nae much to tell,' said Old Tom, and proceeded to tell them how he got the news.

Old Ross had phoned him first thing in the morning. 'Right shock it was too for poor old Ross to find his laird dead in bed like that.'

No one had known that old Si had a bad heart, but then the old bugger was never one for the doctors.

'He wasn't frightened to death, by any chance, was he?' asked Tom poker-faced, earning a glare from Mick.

'No. Why on earth would ye ask that? No, he was laying there, eyes closed, peaceful as anything.'

'That's a much better way to go than many I could think of.'

The three men nodded sagely and downed their beers.

'Sad thing though, old Si's gone and lost his wristwatch. Ross can't find it anywhere.'

'Lost his wristwatch? Was it valuable?'

'Nae, not really. It was given him by Doreen, and she were a frugal lass. Ross thought auld Si would've liked to be buried wearin' it.'

The two conspirators felt like absolute crap. But it was too late now.

'Maybe it'll turn up somewhere later,' said Tom weakly.

'Aye, mebbe.'

'What about Simon's family?'

Simon and Doreen didn't have any children, Old Tom told them. 'Nae like me an' my Maggie. We raised four of our own, and now they bless us with 11 grand kiddies. All Simon had was that nephew. A real scumbag he is too. Old Si had no time for him at all.'

That would be their client. Old Simon's nephew.

'Does he stand to inherit the Brannick House now?' The house and land must be worth it for him to go to the lengths of hiring them.

Old Tom chortled. 'If that's what he's hopin' for, he's got another think coming.' He cackled with glee.

In between bursts of gruff laughter, old Tom told them how he and the owner of the Fairlea had witnessed Simon Brannick's will two years ago when old Si had confided to him that he'd left the caretaker's cottage at the bottom of the drive to Ross.

Brannick House, with all its furniture, pictures and knick-knacks, was to go to the National Trust with the surrounding 10 acres of land. The remaining land would go to the RSPB – the Royal Society for the Protection of Birds. All his other worldly goods were to be distributed equally between Doreen's surviving siblings or their heirs.

'I thought you couldn't disinherit a close relative in Scotland,' said Tom.

'Aye, well. Seems that only applies to spouse and children, and old Si has neither. Apparently, it doesn't apply to land or buildings either. That nevvy of his will have to fight Ross and RSBP for it and reckon I know who'll win,' Old Tom chuckled.

Of his nephew, old Simon had made a special mention in his will, insisting on using his own words in an otherwise legally phrased document.

'That greedy, cheating, good-for-nothing nephew of mine, Philip Benjamin Brannick, is to get nothing. Not a penny of mine shall he have, not him nor any of his blood nor mine.'

That night, Tom made a phone call.

Four nights later, when old Simon's nephew, Philip Benjamin Brannick, went up to Scotland on hearing the news of his uncle's death, his house was burgled. As well as losing the wad of undeclared cash in his safe, his wife's jewellery and various valuables, his uncle's wristwatch also went missing.

Old Ross, the butler, found it a week later in his master's writing bureau. Luckily, it was found in time for old Simon's funeral, and he went into his grave to lie beside his wife, wearing the wristwatch she had given him on his seventieth birthday.

# 39

# CATHY

**Monday 23 April**

Despite the additional resources, the detectives hadn't got very far.

Parnell Walker, the suspect on whom they had initially pinned their hopes, was still up on the board. They'd investigated him thoroughly, put him through the grinder, searched his flat, his car, even his office, all with nothing to show for it. In her worst moments, Cathy wished they could just charge him with the Dwyer twins' murder. He was such a good fit, had even handed them a ready-made motive. But they had no actual evidence. It was far too circumstantial for the Crown Prosecution Service.

'CPS won't touch it with a bargepole,' she'd grumbled.

His arrest and release had one positive impact on Parnell Walker's family. His daughter, Phoebe, was speaking to him again. In fact, she couldn't be prouder of her father. He had elevated her standing amongst her peers. The police had thought her dad to be capable of murder just to protect her!

Ironic, considering he had sweated and panicked for 36 hours, doing everything he could to convince the police that he was incapable of hurting, let alone killing anyone.

As for the Rt. Hon. Sir Nicholas Hubbard, that was dead in the water too. Even if – and that was a gargantuan *if* – Hubbard had someone tamper with Quentin's motorcycle, there was no chance of being able to prove it. But Cathy's instincts told her he was innocent. That it'd been an accident.

Two days after their visit, the media broke the news of Hubbard and Quentin's relationship. There was a flurry of interest and interviews, but Cathy suspected it'd die down in a week, especially as Hubbard returned to his tried and tested PR strategy of saying nothing. He gave the media no grist for their mills and refused to comment or elaborate. The media, in turn, would tire of asking, and while they might continue to speculate for a while longer, the story would fizzle out and die a natural death.

Cathy wondered if he and his wife would eventually reconcile. She hoped so for their children's sake.

And of course, no one took her suspicion about the Earl of Seddingfold seriously, not even Cathy herself.

*I'm clutching at straws. Even if His Lordship had contracted out Quentin's accident, (A) We'd never be able to prove anything; (B) He wouldn't have gained anything from it. He wouldn't have been able to suppress the truth from the press, not with Quentin's parents determined to publish and be damned; and (C) What bearing could it have on the Dwyer twins' murders?*

With no new leads, they were floundering, rehashing the same lines of inquiry. Cathy was assigned to re-interview the staff at St John's Hospital. She was lucky. In Paul's case, he was reviewing CCTV footage again, so she guessed she'd bagged the better bargain. He accepted his task with surprisingly good grace and knuckled down to it. She realized that rank and hierarchy here were far more flexible than at the Met. Everyone mucked in to do whatever was required.

So, here she was, back at St John's Hospital for another round of interviews with the staff and the manager. Shari Thundé made no attempt to hide her annoyance.

'Like I already told you and the other detectives who interviewed me before, both Dwyers were rostered for the 6.00 a.m. shift on Thursday, 22 March. Neither showed up.'

Even as Cathy watched, Shari's phone and computer pinged almost constantly, demanding attention. She ignored them to respond to the DI's questions, hoping to get rid of her as quickly as possible.

White-coated doctors and blue-uniformed nurses dashed back and forth. Gurneys with patients whizzed along the corridors. Cathy had been told that the wards were full today, and they were short-staffed because a doctor and two nurses had called in sick.

They were in Shari's office, which she shared with two admin staff, both busy on the phones, with complicated multicoloured staffing rotas visible on their computer screens.

'When one of the nurses came looking for the on-duty speciality registrar, I looked up the rota and saw that Dillion Dwyer should have been on duty,' continued Shari. 'I put out a call for him, but we soon realized that he hadn't shown up. I phoned and left a voicemail and a text message. Later that afternoon, I got a call from the O&G – that's the Obstetrics and Gynaecology unit – asking me to find out from Dr Dillion

Dwyer if he knew where his brother Derek was. That's when we realized that neither of them had turned up.'

'Is that common? Does it happen a lot?'

'It's not common, no. But it happens. Doctors, nurses, technicians, assistants, etcetera, don't turn up, but they usually call in sick or let us know if they have a home emergency. Occasionally someone goes AWOL. We try to backfill with agency staff if we can, but it's not always easy.'

'What about the Dwyers? Had they gone AWOL before? Just not shown up without giving you any warning or notice?'

Shari turned to her computer and scrolled through a database. 'Derek Dwyer showed up two hours late once. Apparently, he overslept. Said he had stayed up until 3.00 a.m. completing an assignment after putting in a 14-hour shift the day before. It happens, but thankfully, not too often. It's tough here on junior doctors and trainees. Very tough. We call it trial by fire, and they have to learn to manage the stress. And then there were the two, no three times in the past 12 months, when one or both brothers called in sick. But apart from that, they'd been pretty good.'

'How did they get on with people here?'

'Okay. They joined in and got on well with everyone, but from what I saw and heard, they didn't go out of their way to make special friends. People got on better with them when they were alone. By that I mean, without the other twin.'

Cathy frowned. 'Why's that?'

'It's nothing sinister. I have twins. They're 8 and they don't need anyone else as they have each other. We, my husband and I, try hard to get them to make friends and mix with other children, but it isn't easy. I think they'll grow out of it and develop their own separate interests and lives, but I've heard that in some rare cases they don't. I suspect the Dwyer twins were one of those cases. You know how it's sometimes embarrassing to be with some couples or even close friends who have their own special body language and private jokes? Being around the Dwyer twins together felt like that.'

'What about girlfriends? How were they with the female staff?'

'Now, inspector, you're asking for gossip. I wouldn't know about their private life, and neither would my team. But, like I told DC Plummer, I've not had any complaints about their behaviour, or any accusations of sexual harassment levied against them. Frankly, the way we work trainees here, I doubt they'd have the time or inclination. They'd be too exhausted for anything other than to grab a bite to eat and crash into bed. To sleep, that is.' She laughed. After a moment's thought, she added, 'But they were quite good-looking lads, and I wouldn't be surprised if they'd paired up with some of the women staff here. But I doubt if any of those lasted very long.'

'One last question, then I'll leave you alone,' Cathy promised. 'Did they usually get rostered together?'

'We tried to accommodate them whenever we could. It made sense, as they could travel in together and their holidays would coincide. Also, on our database, with their names almost always cropping up next to each other, it just made it easier for us to tick them off together to fill in our needs. They had no problems doing nights, whereas many of the married doctors prefer not to, so that helped.'

The manager made no effort to hide her sigh of relief when Cathy finally thanked her and left her alone.

Cathy wandered off to sit in a chair in one corner of the ward to watch the surrounding activity. *The Manager was right. It's very busy.* Except for a few patients strolling the corridor, everyone else was in a hurry, striding from one task or room to the next. Even their conversations seemed to be rushed. It got her wondering what it was like at night. She decided to find out.

C athy returned at 10.00 p.m. to a totally different atmosphere. After the buzz and clamour of the daytime, it was eerie. A shiver crept up and down her spine. Not that it was dark, deserted, or unattended. On the contrary, the corridors were well lit, but the ward lights were dimmed, and the staff walked softly while going about their duties, conversing in low voices.

'This feels like a different place at night,' she said to the senior nurse on duty.

'It is quieter,' the nurse agreed. 'But we have fewer staff, so the rounds are bigger and there's a much higher patient-to-staff ratio. It works fine most of the time, but it can be challenging if something goes wrong. Say there's a cardiac crisis, we'd have to pull in several of the staff on duty, which would leave fewer to monitor the rest. God forbid multiple crises happen simultaneously.'

Something pinged and flashed on her computer screen, and with a muttered 'Excuse me,' she left in a hurry.

Unlike in the morning, all the ward doors were shut, and Cathy observed the staff pressing their identity cards against the readers on the walls. During daytime, however, with people going in and out of patients' rooms almost continuously, staff didn't use their IDs as often to gain entry through doors that were more often open than shut.

Cathy walked back to the nurse, who had returned to her desk.

'How would I get a log of all ID card-readers showing the entries and exits for the staff?'

'Our IT department would have it. They're on the fifth floor.'

Ten minutes later, Cathy was upstairs, flashing her warrant card and towering over a bewildered-looking network engineer.

'Please wait,' he said.

To her disbelief, he stepped back, drew out his mobile phone, dialled the police station number, and asked to speak to someone in charge.

It took a while but, eventually he found someone of acceptably high rank. Cathy watched and listened as he asked for the person's name, rank, and number, noting it all down. He then asked the person to describe her while his dark eyes behind his steel-rimmed glasses scanned her from head to toe. After all that, he asked the person for Cathy's warrant number, then nodded, which she assumed meant that it tallied with her card.

Finally satisfied, he allowed Cathy into his domain and led her to his desk, which looked like an air-traffic-control station with its array of monitors and gadgets.

His jaw dropped when she explained what she wanted. 'What, *all* of them? For *all* the doors?' His expression read – *are you mad?*

Cathy guessed she was asking for a lot.

'I have their schedules. It shows the dates and times they were on duty, and to which wards they were assigned. Would that help?'

'That would narrow it down. Let me think.' He sat glaring at a spot on his screen, swinging his chair in small arcs. 'How far back do you want to go?'

Cathy thought quickly. In applying for a court order for the list of patients, they'd stretched the period to the start of the year.

To be on the safe side, Cathy did the same. 'Can you get me the details from the start of the year? From 1 January?'

That'd make it just over 11 weeks before they were killed, she thought.

NK, whose full name was too complicated for her to pronounce, nodded thoughtfully. 'Can you come back in an hour? I'll have to write a little programme to extract that information from our database and test-run it to make sure it picks up all their logs. But remember, if they entered without swiping their ID – for example, if someone held the door open for them – then that entry won't show up. You'll have a more accurate log for the evenings and nights than for the day. Any data you get for the daytime, especially between 10.00 a.m. and 5.00 p.m., wouldn't be complete.'

'I understand. I've seen how it is during the day shifts. Would you be able to give me a printout, as well as send it to me by email?'

'No problem.' He nodded, already tapping at his keyboard. She turned and left.

When she returned an hour later, he handed Cathy two stacks of printout on perforated-edged continuous computer paper. *Listing paper, I think it's called,* she thought, pleased to have recalled it from a long ago memory bank. NK also gave her a floor plan for each level, identifying the individual card-readers, and explained how to crossmatch the data to the floor plan.

Cathy left him beaming at her voluble appreciation. It was an excellent piece of work, and she was grateful for his thoughtfulness, for understanding her needs and anticipating her ignorance.

*Now, all I need to do is to highlight any anomaly in the data. For example, if one or both of them spent an inordinately long time inside any particular room or went there more often than they had reason to. I would, of course, then need one of the hospital staff to check to see if there was a valid reason to explain the anomaly.*

It would be laborious and tedious, but Cathy was quite pleased to have come up with this line of inquiry. She was probably going further back than she needed to, but thought it better to be safe than sorry.

As it turned out, she should have gone even further back.

By just one more day.

# 40

## MICK

**Monday 14 May**

When the coroner released Stanley's body, the community workers and the Royal British Legion clubbed together to arrange a simple funeral service for him.

The vicar stood waiting by the podium clutching a bible. He expected only a handful of people to attend the service. All strangers or at best acquaintances of the deceased made up of one or two volunteers from the Royal British Legion, a community worker, who in turn would round up a friend or two of the dearly departed. He just prayed that they'd be sober enough to behave. Plus, a couple of people from the funeral directors to make up the numbers and, as the death had come to their attention, maybe someone from the police would be present too.

He wasn't expecting any family member and was pleasantly surprised when a woman in her sixties and a man in his late thirties or early forties showed up. He quickly amended the qualifier *pleasantly* when the dour-faced woman introduced herself as Doreen, shook his hand and made it a point to let him know that although they'd once been married, she and the deceased had not seen each other for nearly 20 years.

'But I'm not one to hold grudges and I want to do my duty. This is my son, Frank.'

*My son. Not* our *son,* noted the vicar, shaking hands with the man who looked like he would rather be elsewhere and simply wanted to get this over with.

The vicar had chosen the smallest chapel at the crematorium. He now waited with the deceased's family and the three watched in horror as more and more people filed into the chapel. Soon, all the chairs facing the podium were full. He sweated beneath his white vestments, worried that there would not be enough standing room for everyone. The thirty-plus unexpected attendees shuffled along the sides and back of the chapel, acknowledging or greeting each other with a nod, a smile and the occasional handshake.

A man, unmistakeably military from his upright bearing, the left breast of his well-cut black jacket loaded with medals, marched up to the trio.

'I'm Captain James Taylor. I'm so sorry for your loss,' he said in clipped tones, shaking hands with the widow, the son, and the vicar. 'Corporal Stanley was in my regiment and many of his old friends wanted to come and say goodbye. He was a good man.'

'Thank you for coming,' said Doreen. 'I wasn't expecting anyone to turn up, so I didn't arrange any get-together after the funeral.' Her panic-stricken eyes roved the room.

'I hope you don't mind, but we've organized a private reception at the Smithson Golf Club, just up the road from here.'

Doreen and her son's faces turned pale, and they turned horrified gazes to Captain Taylor, alarmed at the unexpected and, in their view, unjustified expense.

'Please, don't be offended,' continued the captain smoothly, 'but we'd like to pay for the reception. In fact, we've already paid for it.'

Doreen nodded graciously with barely concealed relief as the vicar herded them to their places in the front row and took his stand at the podium.

The vicar paused as two more couples slipped into the chapel and stood by the exit door. He recognized the tall, slim woman even though he had only met her once several months ago on a similar occasion. At the funeral of a young university student dead from an overdose. Detective Inspector Cathy Collins. His eyes met hers and he nodded in acknowledgement before gliding to her companions. He assumed the shorter, attractive woman with bright red hair was a friend or colleague, but he'd never seen either of the two men before. Like most others in the room, they too had the look of military personnel about them.

Mick looked around the chapel and nodded to Tom.

*So that's what the old man had been up to these past weeks, rallying the old boys around.*

A smile twitched his mouth. Stanley was getting the send-off he deserved and here they were, attending it, with no reason for anyone to question their presence.

# 41

# CATHY

**Tuesday 15 May**

C athy knuckled her tired eyes and sighed. Like a contagion, the sigh infected her nearest neighbour, DI Paul Hayes, before vaulting to the next victim, and the next, leaving slumped shoulders and figures drooping in fatigue and despondency in its wake.

Eight weeks since the Dwyer twins' murder and the team still had nothing. Despite rehashing the same theories, interviewing the same people again, adding others with only the most tenuous of links to the two men, spending days on CCTV footage, they had drawn nothing but blanks.

Cathy was convinced that Stanley had indeed seen someone that night. That his *ghost* was a real person. But Stanley was dead. He was now an urnful of ashes and a memorial plaque.

Despite the large number of detectives and support staff working on the case and the money that was draining away – as their superintendent never ceased to remind them – they didn't seem to get anywhere. Nerves frayed, tempers shortened, and frustration mounted as yet another line of inquiry fizzled out. Even the grieving parents, who had been initially supportive, were now questioning the team's competence.

It should not have been possible for someone to sneak into a building unseen and unheard, not with the surfeit of security cameras and GPS tracking via mobile phones. Yet someone had. It should not have been possible for someone to torture and kill someone in their own home, yet someone had. Killed not just one person, but two.

Marek Kováč's murder was squarely on Grozdan Horvat, and the police were not looking for anyone else. Grozdan was still missing and was proving harder to find than they expected. The UK police forces, as well as Europol, stopped and questioned several similar-looking candidates, but apart from frightening them, none of those bewildered people turned out to be Grozdan.

Cathy was positive that their flatmate, Anton Gajdoš, knew more than he'd let on, but despite repeated questioning, he had stuck to his story: *No; he had not sent the text messages to Grozdan. He knew nothing about the unregistered phone. And he was asleep in bed, not out killing anyone.*

'I think we should put a surveillance on Anton. I'm sure he's hiding something.'

'So am I,' replied Paul, 'but even with no active surveillance, he thinks we're watching him.' He grinned, 'I've already asked Uniform and community wardens to be blatantly visible two or three times a week. You know, sort of cross his path and give him a look. I've also asked traffic to pull him up occasionally and check his documents. He's going to go straight for weeks.' Paul paused and burst out laughing, almost choking on a mouthful of sandwich. He coughed, took a big gulp of water, and swallowed hard.

'Two nights ago, PC Randeep Singh hung around Anton's flat when he came home to park his taxi. Randeep made a big show of slipping into the shadows to watch him. He only stayed 20 minutes, but I bet Anton thinks he was being watched all night.'

Cathy laughed. Of all the people to use in a covert surveillance, Randeep, with his tall, lanky frame, colourful turban, and distinctive good looks, would not be a first choice. But he was brilliant and unmissable for an overt one. Anton would be jumping at shadows.

'Anton won't say anything, especially not with the risk of being an accessory to a murder hanging over him. We *will* find Grozdan. Did he strike you as the type who could live the life of a hermit? He's too obvious and easy to spot in a crowd. How long do you think he can go without a phone or a computer, or even eating out? He's young and sooner rather than later, he will surface, and we'll have him.'

'I know all that. I was wondering about the deal mentioned in those text messages Anton sent to Grozdan. It can't be anything legal.'

'What can't be anything legal?'

The two DIs jumped at the sound of DCI Matthew Holt's voice behind them.

'Sir, the secret deal that Anton mentioned in the text he sent to Grozdan.'

'You mean, *allegedly* sent to Grozdan, don't you? Or have you proof it was from Anton?'

'No, not yet, sir. Sorry, *allegedly* sent to Grozdan. It has to be illegal, and I thought it would be worth following up.'

'Do you think it's connected to the murders we're investigating? Or another murder?'

'Not necessarily. It could be drugs or trafficking or—'

'You're right, it needs following up. I assume you've passed on the details to Vice? They're equipped to deal with it. Now, get cracking on re-interviewing the hospital staff, DI Collins.'

'Yes, sir. Already on it.'

But Cathy wasn't ready to relinquish her catch to those posers in Vice. If she wanted to investigate that *secret deal* of Anton's, she would have to do it in her own time and make sure she didn't tread on the drug squad's toes.

# 42

## CATHY

**Saturday 19 May**

'What the hell am I doing here?'

This wasn't the first time Cathy had asked herself that question. Yet there she remained, on a Saturday afternoon, crouched on the edge of a grove hidden among dense shrubs and bushes, squinting at a prefabricated warehouse-type building behind a chain-link fence. In the past hour and a half, aside from the arrival and departure of the white delivery van, there seemed to be nothing going on. At least not on the outside.

As instructed by the DCI, she had passed on to Vice all the information the team had gathered relating to Anton Gajdoš and the suspicions about his involvement in possible illegal activity. One of Cathy's counterparts, DI Tony Merton, a cocky so and so, had thanked her politely enough and said they would get to it in due course. Which meant Anton was not on their radar; that he was a small fry and probably not worth their time or effort.

And so, alongside following up on the interviews and data from the hospital on the Dwyer twins' movements, she once again went through all records of Anton's phone calls, texts and logs of his taxi journeys for the past five months. Although aware that it wasn't their case, and that she shouldn't be doing any of that, something about Anton niggled at her.

DC Ian Shepherd, the team's IT whiz kid, had done a good job of identifying each of the callers, and aside from Anton's family, friends and his taxi-booking service, from where most of his calls originated, there was one regular direct call every Friday afternoon at around four. These calls from an unregistered number were very short, lasting only 15 seconds. On each Friday after receiving that call, Anton went off duty. He signed himself off-hire, picking up no more passengers after that.

Cathy wondered if these could be from a lady friend, maybe a married one, signalling the 'all-clear', but when she worked her way through the ANPR database and tracked his movements, his route terminated near a commercial dry-cleaning company in Upton, about 7 miles from the centre of Southampton.

Her curiosity piqued, she looked up the listing for Best Care Dry-Cleaning Company Limited, whose registered office was a solicitor's firm in Southampton, with their operations based in Upton. Their accounts, which were up to date and filed on time, showed a modest profit.

*So, what's Anton's interest in this company? Why was he visiting this place so regularly?*

Interestingly, she noticed that since they'd brought him in and questioned him about Marek's death, he had been nowhere near that place, nor had he clocked off on Friday afternoons.

*Curiouser and curiouser.*

After a stint in the morning at the station and the early afternoon spent cleaning and tidying the house, Cathy found herself at a loose end. She expected Mick and Tom to arrive later that evening and Andrea was coming over to her place at 5.00 that evening to help prepare a meal for the four of them.

By mid-afternoon, Cathy found herself fidgeting and checking her watch every five minutes. Unable to get her mind off Anton and the Best Care Dry-Cleaning Company, she decided to go out to the site. Just to take a look. *It can't hurt, can it? I'd still be back home in plenty of time before Andrea arrives.*

She parked her car off-road in a clearing on Upton Lane, trekked the half-mile along a worn trail through the woods, and stopped about 5 yards from the fence surrounding the building. Worried about security cameras, she dared not go any closer. Luckily, it was a clear evening with plenty of daylight still left. It would start to get dark around 7.00 p.m., but she'd be home long before that.

But now, at 4.30 p.m., she was wondering what the hell she was still doing there.

Within half an hour of arriving, fed up with staring at a building that showed no sign of activity, she had turned around to head back to her car when a white van arrived. She jotted down the registration and watched the driver jump out to unload crates of bottles and jars. He pushed a button on the wall panel and leaned in close. Cathy guessed he was speaking into a microphone. A moment later, the door buzzed open, and another man stepped out. Together, they carried the crates inside, and the door shut behind them.

*Just some chemicals for their dry-cleaning.*

She once again resumed picking her route back to her car. Halfway along the trail back, she stopped.

*They would need a lot of chemicals, usually perchloroethylene, for a dry-cleaning business. A lot. Supplied in bulk. In drums or similar large-capacity containers, not in piddly glass bottles and jars. So, what was that white van delivering? It didn't look like beverage bottles.*

Cathy returned to the spot to watch some more. The van driver and his mate were outside again, and this time, they were loading crates into the van. Within minutes, the driver waved and took off while his mate went back inside.

There was no visible security, certainly none associated with a meth lab or any type of narcotics production. Maybe because visible security would only attract unwanted attention and scrutiny. After all, what was there to steal in a legitimate laundry? Maybe some chemicals, but the machines were too big and cumbersome to move. The clothes wouldn't be profitable enough to bother. But she had no doubts that there was sophisticated electronic surveillance in that place.

Her suspicions were solely based on bottle size delivered by the white van.

*This is ridiculous. If this was a meth lab, how had Vice and the inspectors from the HSE – the Health and Safety Executive – not picked up on it? Surely, they must have inspected the site several times over the years, even made unannounced visits.*

Although there are corrupt cops and inspectors, Cathy did not for one moment believe everyone in Vice or the HSE was corrupt. Either the operation was well hidden inside, or she was totally wrong. Probably the latter.

She glanced at her watch: 4.35 p.m. *Time I went back home and forgot this venture. What a waste of an afternoon, but at least I have the evening to look forward to.*

Gingerly, she took a step back and froze.

The building's side door opened. A man stumbled forward as though someone had pushed him out. He staggered two or three paces before falling flat on his face. Two men followed. She recognized the first. It was the man who had helped the van driver with the crates. The second person was shorter, chunkier, and dressed in a suit. That must be the boss.

She heard raised voices but couldn't make out the words. The driver's mate reached out and dragged the fallen man up roughly by the back of his collar and pushed him to his knees. More shouting. The man in the suit, whom Cathy decided was the 'Boss', walked around to face the kneeling man, blocking him from view.

A few seconds later, the boss stepped aside and nodded to the driver's mate. Even at this distance, Cathy recognized the kneeling man. Anton Gajdoš.

The driver's mate held the kneeling man in place by his collar and casually reached behind to pull out a gun from the small of his back.

Cathy blinked in disbelief. This was not happening. She crossed her hands and clamped them tight over her mouth, drowning the shout that instinctively arose in her throat. She had to do something. Yet knew there was nothing she *could* do. Shouting wouldn't stop the play unfolding before her. It would only get her killed, and no one knew where she was.

Cathy stood shaking, shivering, unblinking, as her heart raced trying to outpace the thoughts whirling through her brain. Maybe they were only threatening him. She prayed they were only threatening him.

The seconds stretched as time slowed.

The driver's mate brought the gun forward and held it to the back of Anton's head.

Bang!

Although she was expecting it, knew it was inevitable, the crack of the gunshot split open the silence of the afternoon and reverberated in the still warm air. It was louder than Cathy expected. It rang inside her head and in her chest. She jumped backwards.

A million thoughts raced through her brain.

The first was incredulity: *Oh my God, they actually shot him!*

The second shamed her: *That's murder! It's now our case!*

But overlying all that was her gut and feet propelling her out of there, in no doubt whatsoever of her fate if they caught her.

*Get to the car, get out, and call for backup.*

Her gut should also have urged caution, stealth, but the flight instinct was overpowering, and Cathy was already pedalling backwards. Turning about face, she fled through the undergrowth. Her gut should also have advised her to keep running and not to look over her shoulders to see if anyone was following. She tripped over something. A root, a branch or her own big feet, she wasn't sure. With a flail of arms and a muffled cry, she crashed and landed facedown.

That's what must have attracted their attention, the unnatural movement in the bushes directly in their line of sight. They yelled.

Cathy crouched and hoped that if she stayed still, they might believe it was a fox or something and ignore it.

Foolish hope. The men were already shouting and running towards her.

Cathy pushed herself to her knees, then to her feet, and screamed in agony. Her left ankle was twisted at an unnatural angle. A wave of dizziness and nausea swamped her. She shook her head to clear it, tried to disassociate herself from the pain. It would get her killed. *Then I'll never see my daughter again, never feel Mick's arms around me, never hear my mum and dad's voices, never giggle over drinks with Andrea.*

Too late, she realized what she should have done. *I should have video-recorded the whole thing on my phone.* If she were a teenager with a phone glued to her palm, that is what she would have done. But she wasn't, and the phone was in her pocket. On silent.

Cathy also realized that she wouldn't make it to her car. The pain clamoured for attention. She could feel it sweeping over her in waves, lashing at her, crowding and shoving every logical thought out of her head. Drowning her. She heaved back, treading water, and shut it out. They'd find her soon. She had to make every moment count.

She sat back down among the bushes, drew her phone out. *Who should I call?* Not 999. By the time she was connected, explained who she was, who she wanted, those men from the dry cleaning factory would find her. Her next thought was DI Paul Hayes. Her fingers found and clicked dial on his number, then immediately clicked the red disconnect icon. *No, not him. He'll waste too much time asking questions, swearing, and shouting at me.* She hung up and dialled DCI Matthew Holt, hoping her instincts were right.

'Cathy. What is it?'

'Sir, help me, please. I'm at the Best Care Dry-Cleaning Company's factory off Upton Lane. In the bushes outside. I think it's a meth lab. I witnessed two men shoot Anton in the head and now they're coming for me. I've broken my ankle. Can't walk. I can hear them searching for me.'

'Try to hide. Stay still, don't talk. Keep this call connected. I'm recording our call. We'll get you out.'

Despite the pain, Cathy smiled. Her instincts had been right. No unnecessary questions, no berating. All that would come later.

Breathing raggedly, she continued to hold the phone to her ear. She heard his voice call to someone.

'John, give me your phone, take this, talk to Cathy. She's in trouble.'

*Who the hell is John?* Then she remembered. The DCI lived on his uncle's farm outside Winchester. She and the rest of the team had met his uncle John and aunt Susan at a BBQ last summer at their place. Lovely people.

'Cathy, it's John. You're going to be OK. Matt's calling for help. Just hold on.'

Cathy was drifting in a sea of agony. In the background, she could hear the DCI's voice. She couldn't make out the words in his curt, sharp sentences, but knew that nearby patrols would be here soon and armed police would follow. But would they be in time?

Beyond John's voice in her ear were angry male voices. The crashing sounds through the bushes grew louder as they drew nearer. They would be here soon.

Cathy reached out, grasped her left knee and dragged her leg in closer to her body, getting her ankle out of harm's way. She slipped her phone, still connected to the DCI's, into her jacket's inside breast pocket.

And suddenly they were there.

She looked up at the gun inches away from her forehead and let her pain loose. Let it free. The tidal wave swamped her, hauling a shroud of darkness behind it.

Cathy gave in and fell back into its welcoming arms.

# 43

# MICK

## Saturday 19 May

Mick slung their cases into the boot of the Land Rover and took CJ out for a walk while Tom assigned the weekend's chauffeuring duties to their drivers. A busy but successful week loaded with early starts and late finishes had, by mid Saturday afternoon, finally trickled down to jobs their junior drivers could handle, leaving them free to travel down to Southampton.

The hour and a half journey from Kingston upon Thames to Southampton took an hour longer, with bottlenecks and congestion, aggravated by roadworks at several locations along the way. Mick and Tom were still half an hour away from their destination when Tom's phone buzzed.

'Yes, gorgeous?'

Mick, who was at the wheel, rolled his eyes. He didn't need an IQ of 180-plus to guess that it was Andrea again.

'Hang on. Let me check with him.' Lowering the phone, Tom turned to Mick. 'Have you heard from Cathy?'

'No, not since I spoke to her at 13:30. Why? What's the matter?'

'Andrea says that Cathy's not home and isn't answering her calls. As arranged, she went to Cathy's just after 17:00 hours. Apparently, the ladies planned to cook dinner for us. But Cathy wasn't there, so she let herself in and has been trying to contact her ever since. Andrea's worried. She tried the station and thinks something's wrong. The person she spoke to asked her to stay put at Cathy's place but wouldn't tell her anymore.'

Mick frowned. It was unlike Cathy not to keep an appointment or to let the person know if she couldn't. Something was definitely wrong, especially if Andrea was concerned about the response from the station. Underneath her bohemian appearance, voluble character and scatter-brained behaviour, Andrea was a very sensible and sensitive person. If she was worried, it'd be with just cause.

'Tell Andrea not to worry. We'll find her.'

'Can you locate Cathy?' asked Mick after Tom briskly reassured Andrea and ended the call.

'Course,' said Tom. He booted up a tracking app on his phone.

'You've not gone and installed a tracker on her phone, have you?'

'No, of course not. Couldn't risk it. Her phone might be a police issue. It's in her car.'

Mick shook his head. *Just hope Cathy never finds out.*

Fifteen minutes later, the pair of grim-faced men were on their way to Upton.

The police had made good use of their time at the Best Care Dry-Cleaning Company. Inside a large van, three officers stooped over site plans, while another marked off information gathered using borescope inspection cameras snaked in through ventilation grills, skylights and holes drilled through side walls, the sounds of which were obscured by the machines still operating inside.

'What the f—?' barked a heavyset, black-garbed sergeant, his vest and array of accessories and gadgets adding to the girth of his upper body. 'Who the fuck let you in?'

The other three turned as Mick and Tom stepped into the already crowded van.

'Get out before I have you arrested,' barked the furious man, stepping around the others towards them.

'Just a moment.' A tall, lean man blocked the sergeant's way. 'I'm DCI Matthew Holt. You must be Mick O'Neal and Tom Cassidy.'

'Where's Cathy?' asked Mick, in no mood for pleasantries.

'Is that the floor plan? Have you identified suitable entry points? How many inside? What weapons?' Tom's eyes were glued to the blueprint on the table, his mind in full tactical mode.

'You know them, sir? They're civilians, aren't they? They can't be here.'

'I know. Just give me a minute with them,' replied Holt mildly. Dressed in a pair of old jeans, a red-and-black-checked flannel shirt over a black t-shirt and muddy green wellington boots that smelled of hay and sunshine with a faint whiff of manure, he was the epitome of a rangy farmer. He moved aside, allowing Tom to slot neatly into his vacant spot at the foldaway table and addressed Mick.

'We don't know where Cathy is. None of the cameras have sighted her. But she's inside, alive as far as we can tell.'

He turned to Tom. 'Sergeant Hockerty here is considering two entry points. The first is through the big ventilation shaft, which needs to be enlarged to fit a man. The second through one of the skylights. We don't have exact details on the people, weapons, or hostages inside. The shift officially has eight workers, but there could be more.'

'Sir, you can't tell them all that!'

Holt ignored the sergeant.

'Did the armed police shoot that man lying outside?' asked Mick.

'No. Cathy said two men from the factory did that.'

'And you've left her in there with the killers.' Mick's flat tone filled the space with menace. The air sizzled with his fury. Fists clenched, he stood stock-still, narrowed eyes fixed on the DCI.

Tom stepped between them, breaking the tension. 'Why haven't they gone in yet, Chief Inspector? It's a dry-cleaning factory, the chemicals aren't flammable, and with the ventilation still working, there should be no build-up of gas.'

'Cathy suspects there's a meth lab operating inside, which means there could be other potentially highly flammable chemicals. That could be why they brought the man outside to shoot him. They've been threatening to blow the place up with everyone inside if we try to break in.'

'What the hell was she doing here alone in the first place?'

Holt ignored Tom's implied criticism and Mick's murderous glare. 'That'll be exactly my first question to DI Collins.'

'Ah right.' Tom grinned.

'Come on, lad. We're going in. Don't let your boys shoot us, Chief Inspector.' Tom squeezed past the belligerent sergeant and headed out of the van.

'Mick,' called Holt, stopping him momentarily as he turned to follow Tom. 'Cathy's broken her ankle. You'll have to carry her out.'

Mick swung around sharply.

'No,' added the DCI hastily as Mick's eyes narrowed into mere slits and his mouth twisted in a snarl. 'It was an accident. She fell and couldn't walk. That's why they caught her.'

Nodding, Mick strode out into the night.

'Sir!' The sergeant was beside himself. 'We can't have civilians interfering with our operations.'

'Well, we're not getting anywhere fast, are we? My DI is inside with people who have no qualms about killing. These men aren't ordinary civilians. They are ex-SAS with experience in operations like this. Warn your men and order them not to shoot those two.'

But Hockerty wasn't convinced. 'It's different in the army, sir. They just go in guns blazing, killing everyone. Opposite of what we're trying to do, sir.'

'Well, if they kill anyone, you can arrest them.'

# 44

## MICK

**Saturday 19 May**

B est Care Dry-Cleaning Company's own security floodlights, as well as those set up by the police, lit up the prefab construction with its simple, open gable roof, leaving few shadows and no place to hide. Although the building itself looked solid enough, it had an air of impermanence, as if it had been airlifted and plonked down on the ground.

Police vehicles with their distinctive markings surrounded the building and officers in full tactical gear armed with carbines positioned themselves at every entry and exit point. Four black-clad figures lay flat on the roof, peering in through the skylights.

Kitted out in bulletproof vests beneath their clothes, their stun guns, knives and lock-picking tools well-hidden about their person, Mick and Tom arrived carrying a compact but profession toolbox and 20-metre lengths of climbing ropes twisted into a neat buntline coil with a carabiner at each end attached to their belts. They eyed the half a dozen more officers crouched against the factory walls and hoped that the DCI had enough clout to get the armed police to hold fire.

Their empty palms held out in clear view of the men with guns, the pair crossed the distance between the vehicles and the factory.

'Hello, lads. Major Tom Cassidy and this is Mick O'Neal,' said Tom, offering his hand to the two officers kneeling in front of a wide metal shutter.

'I thought the sarge said you guys were civilians. Have they called out the army?'

'No, sorry lads. Us two are all you get. And your sarge is right. We're bleeding civilians,' laughed Tom. He pointed to the shutter. 'Behind that is where they store the perchloroethylene drums. They've probably stacked them against the shutter, so no one can break in. That's what I'd do. We'll join your lads up on the roof. Just let them know we're coming up, would you? We'll let you in when we get inside.' Tom grinned when the officer rolled his eyes and stuck his middle finger up in the air.

An aluminium ladder leaned against the wall around the corner of the building and Mick scaled it up to the roof, almost at a run, barely making any noise. Tom followed more slowly, surprised to find himself out of breath when he reached the top. Startled by their sudden appearance, the four men turned and aimed their carbines steadily at them.

Arms up in the air, Tom said pleasantly, 'It's all right, lads. We're the rescue party. Check with your sarge. Can I sit down? The climb's done me in.'

Mick sighed. Someday soon, the man's cockiness would get them killed.

One of the officer's radio crackled. Without taking his eyes off the civilians or lowering his weapon, he answered the call. Eyebrows raised, he muttered to the others, who looked equally surprised.

'OK,' he said. 'Stay down, keep quiet and don't get in our way. If either of you gets shot, remember you are at the bottom of our rescue list.'

'Sure thing. No problem.'

After another disparaging glare at them, the four officers returned to their watch through the windows.

Tom jerked his head at Mick and pointed to a large roof cowl protecting an extractor fan sitting almost at the ridge of the roof.

'That's directly above the chemical storage area and the dry-cleaning machines.' He walked the few paces towards it and leaned in to tap the cowl casing and study the fittings before returning to Mick. 'Plastic, so it shouldn't be heavy, though the motor inside might be. Four big nuts and bolts holding it to the roof. Right, let's get them off. With luck, the cable is long enough to pull the extractor out and lay it on its side. I don't want to short the electrics if I can help it.'

They popped ear plugs in to mute the deafening whirl of the motor, but there was little they could do about the continuous blast of hot air pouring out of the unit as they squatted beside it. Uncomfortable, but luckily, not scorching. It reminded them of their time in an Iraqi desert.

Five minutes later, with the help of some machine oil from a little plastic bottle to lubricate the fixings, and an adjustable spanner, the galvanized nuts were off. With sturdy gloves protecting their hands, they grabbed the dome-shaped cowl and dragged it up slowly from beneath the roof panel. It slid out, trailing a black-sheathed cable behind it. The pair heaved a sigh of relief, grateful to the installer who had left a sufficient length of electrical cable. They pulled the unit out and toppled it on its side with the fan blades whirling away into the night sky.

The square aperture left by the removal of the extractor fan unit was not big enough to accommodate either of them through it, but they remedied this by simply levering out the remaining portion of the adjacent composite roof panel and the insulation underneath, giving them a large, rectangular-shaped opening.

Mick peered in. Tom was right. In a sectioned-off storeroom, large drums were stacked and lined up against the shutter, effectively blocking an entry or assault through that end of the building. To one side stood five enormous washing machines with large bore ducts, vents, and tanks leading from them.

No humans were visible below at this end of the building. Having effectively blocked the back and side entrances, Mick guessed the criminals and hostages were near the front of the building, watched by the four police officers peering in through the skylight. Time to go in.

At its highest point, he estimated the building was just over 10 metres tall, so one coil of rope would do the job. Mick unclipped and uncoiled the length of rope from his belt, then reached in to hitch and knot it twice around the steel ridge beam. He paused, slid a sideways glance at Tom and tied double knots, evenly spaced out every 2 metres to provide a secure hand and foothold before dropping it into the space below. The older man pretended not to notice.

A minute later, Mick disappeared into the void below. Swearing beneath his breath, Tom followed more slowly, grateful for the knots in the rope, but hating the fact that he now needed them.

**M**ick had positioned the rope so that they landed along the edge of the wall, just outside the drum storeroom. Two of the five dry-cleaning machines were still rotating, one with clothes sloshing in what looked like water, but had a strong, sweetish chemical odour, whereas the other was in its spin cycle, with the drum whirling away at high speed. Even with their earplugs, the noise this close to the machines was loud and distracting.

*Why hasn't anyone shut down the machines yet? Quietened the place down?*

Mick wondered if it was because it had been drummed into the workers that stopping the machines mid-cycle could damage the clothes, increase business costs and lose the company money. The workers were therefore following their training and instincts. Besides, everyone employed here probably wore ear defenders and was accustomed to the noise.

He had no choice but to leave them running for now and endure the racket. Anything else would alert those up front. Besides, it helped mask any sound he and Tom or the police might make in entering the building.

More gigantic washers and dryers lined the opposite wall, the central area occupied by a station of several steam-iron presses and a big oblong section filled with snaking rows of rotating carousel conveyor racks.

The two men took stock, surveyed their surroundings, then grinned in delight at the small orange-and-black, 1.4-ton Toyota electric forklift stationed along one wall, a cable connecting it to its charging point.

Tom jogged across to the vehicle, disconnected the charger, and climbed into the driver's seat while Mick unlocked the door to the storeroom. After a few false starts, Tom got the hang of it. He drove the surprisingly quiet vehicle into the room and hooked the forklift's prongs into the gap in a pallet stacked with eight drums in a double layer of four. Mick climbed on to the front of the vehicle and prised open the lids of the top four drums. Tom then reversed, clearing a pathway to the back entrance.

Mick jumped off, unlocked the metal shutter and heaved it up, beckoned the two astonished officers crouching outside to come in.

The pallet of drums firmly hooked and loaded on to the forklift, provided an excellent cover against any frontal attack. Mick and the two officers followed Tom as he manoeuvred the vehicle into the main section of the factory and drove smoothly across the concrete floor.

By now, three of the four men who had been on the roof watching the activity below through the skylight had discovered and taken advantage of the open hatchway created by Mick and Tom to scale down the rope. The three new arrivals acknowledged the two mavericks with a thumbs-up, signalled to their colleagues and spread out.

Mick slowed down to fall behind the armed officers, confident that between them and Tom, they could take care of the lot in front. No doubt more officers would soon join them.

The DCI said that none of their cameras had picked up Cathy. So where was she? Her captives could have stashed her behind or between the large machines. She was hurt and in pain, but they wouldn't care. They would have gagged and bound her.

Mick's teeth and fists clenched while the blood froze in his veins. The thought of her helpless and suffering churned his stomach. A strange sensation flooded him. It took him a moment to understand what it was. Fear. In all the situations he'd been in and all the things he'd done, fear had never played a part. Worry, yes. For his squad, for Tom, when things went wrong, but not fear and not like this. The few people he cared for had never been in such peril. That's what caring for someone did. It made you vulnerable. Made you weak. Gave your enemy the advantage. It wasn't something he could afford. Not in his line of work. Tom called them 'complications' and he had interesting ways of dealing with complications.

Mick shook his head.

*Now's not the best time for introspection or self-analysis,* his brain reminded him.

Mick quashed the fear, dredged up the anger.

His mouth stretched in a mirthless grin as he recalled Tom's repeated cajoles, instructions and reasonings during their journey here.

*'For god's sake, don't kill anyone, Mick! It will attract unwanted attention to us, give the police reason to delve further into our business,'* Tom had pleaded.

The only argument which had elicited a reluctant OK from Mick had been that he could lose Cathy. He now wished he hadn't agreed. Every fibre in him wanted to see these drug producers dead, their life wrenched from their bodies by his hands. Especially those who had captured Cathy. He might have promised not to kill, but no one mentioned he couldn't maim anyone. Anyway, all bets were off if they had harmed her. This place and everyone in it would go up in smoke.

He refocused his thoughts on the here and now.

*Where was this meth lab she'd mentioned?* He glanced around, sidling around the washing and drying machines and the steam presses. Extra-large bore plastic and shiny aluminium ducts ran up the white painted walls in sections. He tapped the empty wall spaces, but they felt and sounded solid.

Could it be underground? In a basement, perhaps? He stomped on the floor, but it too felt and sounded solid. Besides, there was no hatch or stairwell in the vicinity.

He stooped to peer beneath the rows of clear plastic-covered clothes swinging on the rails of the carousel conveyor racks. Nothing. Certainly nothing resembling a laboratory. Everything here appeared to be nothing other than a legitimate commercial laundry operation.

But Cathy wasn't given to flights of imagination. She was a detective inspector, logical and analytical, so something must have triggered her suspicions. She obviously was not among that lot up in front, which meant that somewhere in here was a special space, an area hidden out of sight. A concealed room from where the lab operated. Where Cathy was either alone or with one or more of her captors.

Mick began a systematic search for the access to the hideout.

A booming crash and thunderous bang sounded in the distance ahead, followed by a metallic clatter.

Mick swore under his breath and drew out his tactical series stun gun equipped with an LED flashlight torch.

It sounded as if Tom had not only crashed the forklift but also dropped the stack of drums, probably from a height.

Bullets would soon start flying, both from the gang and the police. Adrenaline pumping up the pace of his heartbeats, Mick hastened in his hunt for Cathy within the recesses, crannies, and shadows.

# 45

# CATHY

## Saturday 19 May

*Where am I?*

Cathy awoke to a cacophony. The noise was everywhere, hammering down on her from all directions. It was even coming through walls and ceiling. Metallic machine noises. Whirling, drums rolling. Like ten washing machines operating at the same time. And above it all, a man's voice, close by, shouting something. She couldn't make out the words, but knew he was angry and so loud it hurt her ears. Everything hurt.

An acrid smell clogged her nasal passage. Sharp, but not unpleasant. It smelled like the nail bar into which Andrea occasionally dragged her for a manicure and pedicure. Despite her protests, Cathy always enjoyed that experience. She was also secretly pleased with the results. Pampered hands and feet, pink-coated nails. Pleased for about ten days before the gel coating began chipping and peeling. Then, aided by her picking at it unconsciously, the baked paint came away, often stripping the top layers of her fingernails and toenails with it, leaving them dry and ugly for weeks.

*Why am I thinking about nail salons?* Cathy recognized the signs. Her mind was drifting. She dragged her thoughts back and breathed shallowly as she took stock. *I'm not at home with Sooty curled up beside me, nor with Mick.* The surface beneath her was cold and hard. Bright light penetrated her closed eyelids.

*Where am I? How'd I get here? How long have I been here? Where is here?*

Her eyes shot open as memory flooded in.

She was lying on her side on a smooth concrete floor. Cathy started to roll over, but instinct warned her to stay still. She flexed her fingers, looked down and realized her hands were bound with plastic ties. They hurt, but then so did everything else. Her left foot most of all. And suddenly, the pain was so overwhelming that she couldn't even scream. Levering herself up to a semi-sitting position as waves of nausea swamped her, Cathy leaned over as far as she could and retched, dry heaving as she'd had no food and only a little to drink since breakfast. Oddly, it eased the pain and cleared her head.

She wiped her mouth on her sleeve and felt her head jerk back as a hand grabbed a fistful of her hair. A thin white face with pale lips stretched in a snarl appeared just inches from hers. Bloodshot hazy blue eyes below lank dirty-blond hair glared into Cathy's. A sharp object rammed into her temple.

'You police bitch. Who told you about us? Who? Was it Anton?' An unaccented, educated voice belied the scruffy appearance. He shook her head hard, expanding her world of pain.

From a few feet away, another voice, quieter and deeper, said something in a language Cathy didn't understand but sounded Eastern European. With a growl, the thin angry face moved out of her line of sight as he straightened and released her hair, but the gun stayed firmly against her temple.

Cathy's gaze moved to the speaker, travelling upwards from the dark sharp-creased trousers to its matching jacket over a blue-striped shirt and dark-blue tie with a discreet burgundy pattern before resting on the man's grim face. Middle-aged, clean-shaven, neatly trimmed salt-and-pepper hair, he wore rimless spectacles. Her warrant card was in his hand.

'Detective Inspector Cathy Collins,' he read out, his deep voice emotionless. 'It is a real shame we don't meet under different circumstances.' An Eastern-European accent, although she couldn't place the exact origin. She suspected Slovakian, but only because of the connection to Anton. Smartly dressed, dignified-looking, she could easily imagine him at the head of a business meeting or as a gracious host at a social gathering. Cathy knew she hadn't met him before, but he looked familiar, although she couldn't place him or think of his name.

'As my son asked, did Anton tell you about this place?'

'Who are you? What is this place? Please, may I have some water?'

He nodded at the boy, who marched away in a strop.

'Please answer the question. We don't have much time.'

'No, Anton never said a word. We were questioning him about Marek Kováč's murder and Grozdan Horvat's disappearance. We did not know about this place.'

Cathy reached out with her bound hands and almost snatched the plastic cup of water out of the boy's clasp. Even as she gulped it down greedily, she didn't miss the glance between the man and his son. With his face in better focus instead of three inches from hers, Cathy realized the son was in his mid-twenties, not a teenager as he'd first appeared, although he certainly acted like one around his father.

The older man sighed and shook his head. 'See, there was no need to kill your friend. He did not betray you.' The regret was clear in his tone. 'Why're you always so hasty? Now I have more mess to clear up.'

He turned to Cathy. 'If Anton did not tell you, how did you find this place?'

'We traced Anton's calls and tracked his movements. Found an anomaly. He had calls from an unregistered phone and he came here every Friday. I presume they must have been from your son, or was it from you?'

The man barked a short, humourless laugh. 'No, not from me. Would you believe I did not know about this extra ... what's the word ... *extra-curricular* activity in my factory? Pieter here and the manager ran the place efficiently. It made money. Not a lot, but enough. I was just happy that Pieter was working. He seemed to enjoy the business. I dropped in occasionally but saw nothing. I wasn't even aware of this space.' He stopped and looked around.

'Look at it, Inspector. See how well designed it is?' He waved his hand at the long, narrow space.

The son preened at his father's words.

Cathy took a good look at the well-lit room for the first time. Approximately 18 × 7 feet, it was windowless and completely enclosed, with a sheer wall on all four sides, yet it had a good airflow. Large aluminium ducts brought in fresh air and extracted all noxious fumes. Three vinyl stools on castors flanked the long workbench lining one wall, equipped with two large double-drain stainless-steel sinks and taps, over which hung plain white kitchen cupboards. It reminded her of her school chemistry laboratory. A collection of glass beakers, flasks, reagent bottles, masks, gloves, stacks of coffee filters, goggles. Rubber tubes connected four burners to propane tanks underneath. There was even a centrifuge machine.

Her eyes stopped at the two tablet presses alongside which lay several zip-lock bags packed with white tablets.

'My son's secret laboratory. Hidden behind the dry-cleaning machines. Complete with a secret entrance that not even I knew about.' He spun to his son with a snarl, so loud it made both Pieter and Cathy jump.

'Why the fuck you look so pleased with yourself? You think I'm proud of you? It's not even your own idea. Copied from that TV show *'Breaking Bad'*. That's the life you want?' Face crimson with anger, he swung a fist at his son, but Pieter, expecting it, swayed out of his reach.

His anger was quickly spent. With a sigh, the father faced Cathy. 'What a waste,' he said. 'I thought he had talent, hoped he would be an architect, design beautiful buildings, become famous. But no, this is what he does. For money. Easy money. And he kills. Now, you are here and we're surrounded by the police. What shall we do?'

Hope blossomed within her at the genuine worry in his tone.

'No one has to get hurt. Please, let me go. They won't shoot. I'll—'

But he was already shaking his head, his eyes narrowing in thought. 'No. He's my son. I need to help him. Only you witnessed Anton's death, but you were too far to identify us, and I checked. You took no photos. Without you, there's no proof who killed Anton. We'll wipe the gun clean and lose it. Destroy this place.'

He fell silent, staring thoughtfully at Cathy. She met his gaze and her heart sank as hope crashed. She was staring into the depths of hell.

The son drew closer, licked his lips nervously and aimed his gun.

'No!' snapped his father. 'No shooting. It has to look like an accident. Pieter, put on some gloves, wipe the gun clean and then go drop it into the tank of dry-cleaning slurry. When you return, we can turn off the ventilation system, release the gas from those propane tanks, untie her and lock her in here. A lighter or matchstick will do the rest. Now go. Be quick.'

From the young man's wide grin, Cathy gathered he liked the idea, whereas her worst fear was burning to death. She had to get out. Instinctively, she struggled, trying to get to her feet.

A backhand from a fist holding the gun smashed into the side of her face and knocked her back to the floor. Her head crashed on to the concrete. An exclamation of protest from the father, a grunt of satisfaction from the son, and a cry of pain from Cathy.

She only allowed herself to lie there dazed for a few moments before struggling up to a sitting position. The room spun in bewildering circles as she watched the son do his dad's bidding. She tried to focus as the young man keyed in a PIN into a panel on the wall, watched as a section slid aside. The hidden doorway opened into a narrow passage between this room and the backs of the enormous machines.

Just as the son stepped forward, a booming crash and thunderous bang followed by metallic clatter resounded from the main part of the factory. Startled, they jumped, cast wild glances at each other and around.

The older man recovered first. 'Hurry,' he urged his offspring.

The young man disappeared outside, and Cathy turned in despair as the father stepped close.

# 46

## MICK

**Saturday 19 May**

M ick whirled at the flash of light on the edge of his vision and pressed himself flat against the wall in the dark of the narrow gap behind the row of large dry-cleaning machines. His eyes widened as a section of the wall with plastic and aluminium ducts clipped to it slid aside. Light from the room behind spilled out into the passageway.

*So that's where it is!* Top dressed with fake ducts that matched the real ones connected to the machines, it was a clever place to hide the door.

Back still tight against the wall, he sidled sideways, noiselessly covering the 5 yards to the doorway, switched the flashlight-cum-weapon on to stun mode and waited. A figure appeared silhouetted against the light, putting one foot cautiously out of the room, craning his neck to check all was well. Mick caught his breath and froze in place, his gaze dropping to the gun in the man's right hand.

'Pieter, hurry up,' called a man's voice from the hidden room.

*That's two at least,* thought Mick. *How many more inside? Is that where Cathy is?*

He watched the man called Pieter take another step forward, saw the young man's stance change as instincts kicked in warning him that danger was very close at hand. Pieter swivelled and raised his gun, but his spin brought him in contact with Mick's body, trapping his pistol arm across his chest. He tried to pull back, to straighten his arm, but Mick pushed him against the wall, leaving him no room to manoeuvre or reposition his gun.

Pieter gazed up into implacable, narrowed silvery-grey eyes and whimpered when he realized to his horror that the end of the gun's barrel was now digging into the soft flesh under his own chin.

In one smooth movement, Mick spun the man around to slam his face against the wall and twisted his arm behind his back, pushing it high and hard. Tears of pain rolled down Pieter's cheeks, his cry of pain muffled against the wall.

'Don't make a sound,' warned Mick, 'or I'll break your arm.'

He switched off and pocketed his stun gun, wrapped his free hand around Pieter's, who was still clutching his pistol. The young man tried to move his fingers, to gain control of his weapon, but they were numb, paralysed. He couldn't budge the rods of iron clamped around his hand, cutting off his blood circulation.

Mick pulled Pieter off the wall, and using his prisoner's body as a shield, pushed him back into the room. Contrary to his promise to Tom, he thumbed back the safety catch and curved his forefinger around the trigger, ready to kill or maim.

Preferably the former. Mick had always found it to be much cleaner, less complicated. Dead was dead. They could only haunt your nightmares. Whereas the latter – a maimed person – would still be around to parade their suffering. To wrap you up in guilt, haunt you both day and night.

Eyes narrowed to protect them from the onslaught of light, Mick thrust Pieter before him, his glance taking in the clinical, laboratory-like set up before landing on Cathy. She lay semi-reclined, her hands bound at the wrist, one foot swollen and twisted at an odd angle. The beast within roared, seeking release, as his gaze raked over her dishevelled appearance, matted hair, swollen, tear and dirt-streaked face, then swivelled to the man looming over her.

'No! Mick! Don't shoot!'

Her cry stopped that final squeeze of the trigger, which would have released the bullet and ended her captor's life. His nostrils flared, recognising the smell of mercaptan, the chemical added to the naturally odourless gas to give it its distinctive smell of rotten eggs. His breath caught in his throat when he saw the rubber hoses from two bottled gas tanks lying on the concrete floor, hissing like angry serpents, spitting and spewing their poison.

He'd almost killed her.

His mind computed the distance, calculated his chances of eliminating the man without risking a spark from the gun igniting the gas and engulfing Cathy in flames.

But all his calculations and permutations froze as his gaze swung to the man standing over her holding what looked like a thin, pink-handled gun, its long barrel pointing towards the hissing rubber hoses, finger firmly on the trigger. A safety gas lighter.

The man smiled, locked his eyes on Mick's. 'This is what John Wayne would call a Mexican standoff, no?'

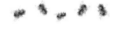

# CATHY

*S*eriously? *Did he actually intend to stand there talking about Westerns? Old Westerns at that?*

Whatever kind of the standoff this was, Cathy knew she would end up in a ball of fire. Toasted.

She stared up at Pieter's father. Although inadvertently caught up in the web of his son's deceit and bearing the brunt and burden of his sins, she'd believed he was basically a good person. She'd even sympathized with his efforts to guide his boy along the right path and had even been feeling sorry for him.

That is, until he'd disconnected the rubber tubes from the gas bottles attached to the burners, turned on the valves to release the flow of LPG close to her and picked up the lighter to set her alight.

And now, there he stood, ignoring her. His attention fully centred on Mick and Pieter.

*Mick*! Cathy still couldn't believe he was here. *He's really here, come to rescue me. Or to see me burn.* At present, the latter seemed a far more likely scenario.

No way was that going to happen. Cathy swivelled her head back to Pieter's father whose name she still couldn't recall. She scooted quietly backwards, away from the rubber snakes. His gaze didn't even flicker. It was still locked on Mick's.

Another two silent shuffles increased her distance from the gas leaks, brought her closer to Mick. She wrapped her hands around her left thigh and dragged her bad leg in. She seemed to have lost all sensation in that limb. It felt numb and cold. It didn't even hurt anymore. Somewhere in the back of her skull, on another planet, an asteroid of a thought flashed a warning that she might lose her leg. Another thought reminded her that losing a limb was not the worst thing that could happen to her right now.

Another shuffle and twist angled Cathy's body towards Pieter's dad. She drew her right leg in – the good one – and assessed the distance between them, or rather, between their limbs. Bracing herself, she pulled her right knee up, crunched her stomach muscles and, screaming at the top of her voice, kicked out with every ounce of strength she possessed.

Her whole body jarred with the impact. For once, Cathy was grateful for her long legs and her unfashionably sturdy shoes. Her friend Andrea's 4-inch stiletto heel might have done a better job and drilled into his shin, provided, of course, that it didn't miss. There was no need for that degree of subtlety or accuracy with her sensible shoe.

They all heard the crack when it connected with his shin bone, louder even than the sound of Cathy's scream or the man's bellow as he toppled over.

A microsecond later, another crack and scream followed, as Mick levered Pieter's arm up even higher and threw him bodily across to his father. The boy landed on top of his parent, both close to the orange tubes.

Cathy remembered the lighter in the father's hand. It was now trapped under his and Pieter's bodies. His finger had been on the trigger.

Had he squeezed it even as he fell?

She wasn't going to wait to find out. Cathy rolled over, pressed her palms against the concrete floor to jemmy herself and pushed up on her good leg into a semi-crouch. A startled cry burst from her as she felt a pair of powerful arms wrap around the back of her shoulders and under her knees. An instant later, she was up in the air, anchored in Mick's arms as he scooped her up.

He turned and sprinted out of the room.

Outside were half a dozen armed officers, their carbines pointing in their direction.

'Run!' shouted Mick, as he tore out of the concealed lab. 'Bomb. Get out.'

They didn't wait to be told again. They stampeded after Mick towards the exit.

Time stopped as the world drew breath and split open. The force propelled them forward as an orange glow bloomed behind them.

T hey were all there outside, her entire team, as Mick ran out of the factory building with Cathy in his arms. Everyone cheered.

She wished, not for the first time either, that she was at least half a head shorter and 15 kilos lighter. What they called *petite*. He probably looked like he was carrying a human-sized stick insect, all gangly arms and legs. Cathy urged Mick to put her down, but he ignored her and headed towards the waiting ambulance.

Even as the flames blazed behind them and the firefighters got into the act, everyone cheered as Mick drew Cathy closer and kissed her hard before laying her down on a gurney and handing her over to the medics.

That was the last cheer she got. After that, everyone got very shouty, called her names. Cathy heard *idiot*, *stupid* and even *brainless twit*. That last one was Andrea, so there wasn't much she could do about it. Actually, there wasn't much she could do about any of it, except apologize, appear contrite and promise never to do it again.

*You would think that they would be happy I'd burst a drug facility and trafficking ring wide open.* But no. Everyone was mad at her.

There was talk of disciplinary procedures, suspension and even firing her. That, of course, was from DCI Matthew Holt when he came to visit Cathy at the hospital.

One glance at his expressionless face and she grew jittery. She silently pleaded with Mick to please stay, hoping to blunt her boss's anger, but the two men exchanged a glance and Mick strode out of the room, abandoning her. *The skunk.*

'Do you appreciate the worry and trouble you've caused, DI Collins? Why didn't you pass on the information to the Drug Squad like I asked?'

'I did, sir,' Cathy protested. 'But they weren't going to do anything.'

'You took it upon yourself to presume that. They tell me otherwise. They have other priorities right now, but they would have got around to it. That facility wasn't going anywhere. It would still have been there in a month's time, and they would've arrested the gang without all this drama.'

*Ah, but they wouldn't have found the secret lab,* she thought, but only for half a second. The DCI voiced the realisation that ram-raided her smugness.

'Their K9 units which would have picked up the scent and they'd have found the hidden lab. I know the media is full of praise for you and is applauding your brilliance. But you shouldn't believe everything you hear and read. You should know that's only because we set the police PR machine in operation. We're presenting a united front and plastering smiles on our faces, but I assure you, no one is happy about what you've done.'

Cathy hung her head and picked at the threads of the hospital bedsheet.

'Several very senior people are calling for your dismissal.' She looked at him in dismay. 'I should be firing you,' he said.

*Should be, not I'm* going *to. Did that mean—?*

'But you won't, will you, sir? Please don't,' she begged.

He sighed, and a shadow crossed his face as his anger dissipated. He pulled up a chair and sat down.

'No, I won't. But you're suspended for a fortnight, and it will go on your record. I would urge you to take another couple of weeks off. Your foot will need the time to heal, anyway. But I want you to think about the consequence of your actions, Cathy. Because of your impulsive behaviour, a man is dead and many of the officers' and workers' lives were in serious danger.'

He left soon after. Left her feeling like crap, swamped with guilt and recriminations.

T hey operated on Cathy's foot the following day. Luckily for her, it was a clean break and appeared to be healing well. Her friend Andrea, who was in her element and full podiatrist mode, bombarded Cathy with information and advice, as well as a paraphernalia of equipment, and supervised her physiotherapy.

Pieter had been badly hurt. His injuries included $2^{nd}$ degree burns to his back, a broken arm and dislocated shoulder, but he'd survived the blast, as had all the factory workers. His father had not. The firefighters found the son outside the door of the meth lab. He told them that his father had physically thrown him as far as he could away from the explosion.

Cathy recalled why the father had seemed familiar. About a year ago, Tomáš Petko, a spokesman for the Slovak business community, had appeared in a TV cake baking contest to raise funds for charity. His cake had been a disaster, but his good humour had endeared him to his viewers including Cathy and her daughter who had watched the show together.

And now he was dead, and his son would go to prison for a very long time, as would most of the workers.

Pieter not only confessed to everything but also named every single person who worked for and with him, including his outside contacts, his dealers and distributors. Whether from guilt over his father's death, or a reawakened conscience, or because of the pain medication, no one knew and cared even less.

The police also questioned Mick and Tom's involvement but chose not to make a big deal out of it, especially as the pair shunned all credit. Instead, they assigned all the good work to the police's efforts.

One thing that puzzled the officers was Mick shouting out 'bomb' to them as he ran out of that room with Cathy in his arms. They asked him about it.

'Why'd you think there was a bomb in there? We found no trace of any explosive devices.'

Mick looked puzzled, and replied in all seriousness, 'Well, I was hardly going to shout "fire" at a bunch of armed police with their rifles pointed at me now, was I?'

# 47

# MICK

## Thursday 31 May

By 8.15 a.m., the flat was impeccably tidy while a load of clothes whirled around in the washing machine. Mick was showered and dressed, with nowhere to go. His clients were not due to arrive until 3.00 p.m., which left him with a whole morning free.

He whistled under his breath, a medley of melodies that somehow cohered into a haunting refrain, which was both familiar and strange.

It had been a good morning. He had shaved two whole minutes off his fastest time from his early morning half-marathons. No one had knocked on his door and he had not yet suddenly found himself confronted by uniformed police reciting his name and reading him his rights. A constant fear, given their secret profession.

Their normal business was thriving, and Tom was negotiating the hire-purchase of two more limos to add to their fleet. Last week, they had watched concrete pour out of the enormous cement mixer's rotating drum into the footings and slabs for an extension to their limousine garages.

Even his nightmares had remained locked in their strong boxes.

Mick dropped onto his settee and switched on the TV and his laptop. He thumbed the screen of his phone while it booted up. His lips stretched in a smile as he read the text message from Cathy asking if she would see him this weekend again and savoured the message's ending: *Missing u xx.*

He keyed in his response. *I hope so, but don't yet have the weekend schedule. Missing u 2.* He hesitated, then added, *V much, xx.*

It was barely ten weeks since he'd met her, and now Cathy occupied a sizeable chunk of his thoughts and emotions, of which guilt was dominant. Guilt for the life he had led and the double life he was still leading. Not so much for the killings per se. No, that didn't bother him. That was simply his job. He seldom dwelt on his assassinations or the victims, at least not during his waking hours. It was the lying. The duplicity and the act he had to maintain all the time he was with her. Having to always be on his guard.

Tom was right. She was a complication. One that was getting harder to live without.

With a growl, Mick tossed the phone on the coffee table and pulled the laptop towards him. A scan of his email inbox showed nothing interesting. The general media headlines were a repeat of the news broadcasting from the BBC channel on his TV.

He logged in to his subscription to *The Soton Times*, a low-budget local newspaper that reported, with surprising reliability and good journalistic skills, on events and newsworthy incidents in and around Southampton.

He drew in a sharp breath as the day's headlines in bold 48pt font filled the screen. It's not going to be a good day for Cathy and her team. *I hope she doesn't get a bollocking from her bosses.* He glanced at his watch. She was most likely in their morning briefing session. *I'll call her in a few minutes.*

Mick turned his attention back to the laptop screen to read the full text of the news report.

## Police still clueless 10 weeks after double murder in Southampton

Neighbours complaining of a noxious smell led to the discovery of the decomposing bodies of 29-year-old identical twins Derek and Dillion Dwyer in their 4th-floor flat in the Naylands on Harold Road, Southampton, on Saturday, 31 March. Post-mortem concluded that the two junior doctors had died of asphyxiation in the early hours of Thursday, 22 March. According to a reliable source, evidence indicates that the brothers may have been tortured prior to being killed. Investigators have so far refused to disclose any further information.

The twins were last seen on Wednesday, 21 March, when they put in a 12-hour shift at St John's University Hospital, where they were employed as speciality registrars in the General Surgery unit. Colleagues of the deceased described them as 'dedicated and hard-working', with a bright future ahead of them.

Friends, colleagues and the hospital management assumed the pair had taken a few days off when they did not show up for work over the weekend. No one from the hospital investigated the reason for their absence without leave, or their lack of response to text messages and emails from their supervisors for the ten days they were missing. Their prolonged lack of contact prompted the twin brothers' parents, who were away on a three-week Caribbean cruise, to cut their holiday short and return home early.

'We knew they had a busy schedule, but we were getting anxious when we heard nothing from them for ten days,' said the twins' mother, 54-year-old Caroline Dwyer. 'We are heart-broken; our lives are shattered and empty without our beautiful boys. They were so bright and caring. They only wanted to help people and didn't deserve this. No one does.'

Our sources revealed that there was no sign of forced entry into their flat and although the victims' phones and laptops were missing, their money and credit cards were left untouched, indicating that burglary may not have been the motive.

Speculation is rife that the two brothers might have been silenced to prevent them reporting a crime they either witnessed or overheard being planned.

*That's an interesting angle.* Mick grinned, imagining the police interviewing all the patients, particularly those with a record, who were hospitalized around the time of the murders. It was probably the only time the villains had other worries on their minds and weren't focused on plotting a crime. He chuckled and continued reading.

Despite weeks of investigations, door-to-door enquiries and interviewing almost 100 witnesses, including patients and visitors to St John's University Hospital, police have yet to charge anyone. Their only arrests to date were that of two men in their early twenties — Grozdan Horvat and Marek Kováč, both of Slovakian nationality. Less than 48 hours after their release under investigation, Marek's body was discovered in East Park by 4-year-old Oliver and his mum.

22-year-old Marek had been fatally stabbed and police have launched a search for 23-year-old Grozdan, who has been missing since the two friends left their shared flat on the night of Saturday, 7 April.

Although evidence points to a serious falling-out between the two men, and Grozdan fatally stabbing his friend before disappearing, one cannot escape the coincidence of the timing between the homicides. Is it merely happenstance, or is there something more sinister at play?

Police refuse to comment on whether there was a connection between the deaths of the two junior doctors and the Slovakian.

*Now, who made that connection?* Mick wouldn't be surprised if it had been Cathy, particularly with the link to Stanley. His eyes traced the rest of the article.

'These are complex investigations, and we are following several lines of inquiries. At this stage, we are not in a position to confirm any connection between the two cases, but we are keeping an open mind and are not ruling anything out,' said Detective Chief Inspector Matthew Holt of the Solent Constabulary.

'Our thoughts are with Derek and Dillion's parents, who are devastated by this loss. We are working around the clock to give the family the answers they deserve, and to bring their sons' killer, or killers, to justice. We are also continuing our search for Grozdan Horvat,' he added.

'We ask anyone with information to please come forward. We are following up on all enquiries. Your information, however insignificant it may seem, could be vital to our investigation. So please call us on 101 quoting Operation Silhouette, or if you do not want to give your name, please phone Crimestoppers on 0800 555 111.'

A fundraising campaign initiated by the victims' colleagues and fellow students has so far raised £93,000, with the family pledging to contribute a further £100,000 towards the cost of extending and improving the facilities in Ward 9 where the young men worked. 'We are just £7,000 short of our £200,000 target,' said Stacey Diamond, a friend and colleague of the Dwyer twins. 'Please spare a donation if you can. Your contribution, no matter how big or small, will help the hospital provide a better service to our community.'

*Very worthwhile. Their deaths had some positive outcome, after all. Few people can put that on their gravestone*, thought Mick.

Stanley's, for example, said nothing. He'd left no mark on this planet. His old regiment had paid for a memorial plaque in the Squirrel's Corner in Southampton Crematorium. Besides his name and the years of his birth and death, it simply said 'Sadly missed by family and friends'. The first, a blatant lie, added to preserve his family's dignity. And although Stanley would be missed by his friends, the truth was that they probably wouldn't think of him again once they'd returned home. Not until someone, somewhere, sometime mentioned his name again. With a sigh, Mick perused the rest of the article.

If the public or local businesses would like to donate, please go to: www.pleasegive.com/campaign/SotonStJo hn.

Prof. Chandra Mishra, Consultant at St John's University Hospital, said that the donation would augment the facilities at the hospital which has seen demand for its services triple in the last four years. 'This is a teaching hospital and the doctors we train go on to provide decades of dedicated service to the community. Which is what Derek and Dillion wanted to do, but sadly, they did not live to fulfil their dreams.

In honour of the junior doctors who lost their lives in such tragic circumstances, the trustees of the hospital have voted to rename Ward 9 as Dwyer Ward upon completion of the extension and upgrade. The renaming ceremony will take place on Wednesday, 15 August.'

Mick gasped, his eyes glued to the words. Slowly pulling the screen of his laptop down, he leaned back, the air around closing in on him as the chasm at his feet widened. The ringing inside his head amplified and the growing pressure left him struggling for breath. Just like those times when he'd been water boarded. He was drowning. This time, without any water.

With an effort, Mick dragged himself out of the panic attack, focussed on his breathing until it returned to a semblance of normalcy. In less than a minute, his whole life had changed.

A beast replaced the panic. A fiend that looked out at the world through a red mist. He needed to cage it, bind it in chains, inter it deep within.

He lurched to his feet, shuffled towards his home gym, straightening with every step, whipping his emotions to subjugation. He grabbed the suspended 60-kg leather punchbag and, ignoring the padded boxing gloves on the bench press, punched the monster until his knuckles were raw. Sweat drenched him, running down his brow into narrowed eyes, blinding him, the droplets spraying the air, but still he continued pounding the bag.

Finally, exhausted, emotions drained, the beast tamed, he collapsed on the floor, head turned towards the wall of Ayesha's photos.

*My poor, poor child.*

Mick lost track of how long he lay there but snapped alert to a sound outside his flat. A sound he had been expecting. Had been waiting for. The knock on his front door.

He peered through the peephole. Two women. One he had been awaiting. Leila.

The other took his breath away. A face he instantly recognized. It was plastered all over the wall of his gym room. Softer, kinder, infinitely more beautiful than the one that confronted him in his mirror.

His daughter, Ayesha.

In his study above his office, Tom, too, finished reading the article in *The Soton Times*. He slapped the lid of his laptop shut and banged a fist on his breakfast table, while a string of expletives escaped his clenched jaws. No one could swear quite like Major Tom Cassidy.

With a yelp, his puppy CJ turned tail and rushed out of the room, seeking refuge in Tom's bedroom. Her distressed wails quickly shut him up. He got to his feet and found her cowering in her basket, whining with her head tucked between her paws.

Tom crouched, then sat cross-legged in front of CJ, holding out a hand for her to sniff. She wagged her tail tentatively, unsure of the man he had suddenly become.

'I'm sorry, CJ. I didn't mean to frighten you. What a mess this has all become. Our lad's in trouble, you know.'

He studied the dog now curled up in his lap, her brown eyes seeking his. He smiled reassuringly, stroking her odd-coloured floppy ears, his mind already composing the long to-do list of tasks. Not the least being to organize a dog-passport.

He'd been anticipating this moment for a while now. But he hadn't expected to regret it quite so much.

# PART II

**Truth and lies**

# 48

# CATHY

## Today – Friday 27 July

1 0.00 a.m. Hindsight is supposed to be a wonderful thing. But sitting in seat 36A of South Western's 10.05 a.m. train from London Waterloo to Southampton Central, knowing what she now knew, Cathy wondered again whether she would have done anything different on that glorious, calamitous evening just over four months ago. The evening she first set eyes on Mick.

She wished she could say yes. Every instinct, every bone in her, wanted to say yes. To know that she would have turned and walked away. Not gone to Mick's hotel that night. But every ache and the unquenchable longing inside her knew otherwise.

10.05 a.m. The train's forward-motion pushed her into the springy cushion of the backrest of her seat as the tarted-up and hastily tidied South Western lurched away from London Waterloo Station. Her fellow passengers would probably frown and mutter under their breaths, but Cathy was determined to open her window to let in some fresh air as soon as they were out of London. There wasn't any point in opening it just yet and adding London's pollutants to the remnants of the sweaty mustiness mixed with the aroma of coffee and undernotes of bacon sarnie left behind by the peak-hour commuters.

Building after building flashed past the train's windows. Buildings so proudly urban, where people paid a fortune for a roof over their heads. Double or more the price for every inch of space compared to elsewhere in the country. Space where sunshine struggled to filter through the permanent haze hovering over the city and its outskirts. Even the trees and hedges, planted by determined environmentalists to offset carbon emissions, were grey as they struggled valiantly to survive.

This time last week, she had been counting the hours before she could finish work. Counting the minutes to make the journey from Southampton to London for her weekend with Mick.

Surprise, then elation had grabbed her by the throat when he phoned to ask if she would spend the weekend with him in London. A first invite. A gigantic step forward in their relationship. Or so she thought.

With hindsight, she should have known something was amiss. Mick's voice had been tight, almost curt, but she put that down to Mick simply being Mick. Reticent, shy, possibly expecting and preparing for a rejection, or her excuses to his invitation. Was hindsight causing her to imagine all that? Throwing up little clues that she ought to have picked up? Clues that she was only now re-examining, and to which she was assigning significance that she hadn't before?

Like how Mick had not stopped staring at her throughout the weekend, as if he wanted to etch her features into his memory. How close he'd held her as they climbed high on the London Eye, watching her while she drank in the spectacular views of London and basked in the summer sunshine. Their perfect dinner at the Shard, followed by cocktails, tucked into an intimate corner of the Gong Bar high up in the night sky, and the intensity of their lovemaking. Cathy had fallen into an exhausted though contented sleep, but she knew Mick had stayed awake through the night. He had not gone on his night run. Instead, he'd stayed in bed, cradling her in his arms.

Little did she know her dream weekend would finish with her crouching in a Met's prison cell. Shrinking away from the slick, over-painted walls oozing hate and fear. Cowering from the dark floor hissing accusations while the ceiling inched imperceptibly closer, determined to smother her.

But hindsight had not even been conceived that evening in March, a lifetime ago, when she'd met Andrea for drinks at the Red Lion pub.

## Four days ago – Monday 23 July

Cathy hugged her knees and scrunched down on the narrow bed in the far corner of the cell, making herself as small a target as possible. She stared at the tray of soggy sandwiches and tea. She wasn't going to eat or drink any of it. Who knew what was in it or who had spat, or worse, in it?

Despite there being no nameplate or label announcing her profession or title, it was a safe bet that everyone here knew exactly who she was, and although they might not know what her supposed crime was, they cared even less whether or not she was guilty. Cops in prison were hated the most, especially by their own lot.

Although it was over 24 hours since her last meal – the lunch with Mick on the banks of the Thames, feeding the ducks, swans, geese and pigeons – she would never be hungry enough to eat this lot. But Cathy also knew the wardens wouldn't be happy at the rejection of their offering. She had to get rid of it. The smell was making her sick.

Breathing deeply to control the nausea, she tore up the sandwich into little pieces, chucked them, along with the tea, into the steel bowl of the open seatless metal toilet and flushed the lot down.

It had taken four hours to process her through the custody suite. In that time, she had been fingerprinted, photographed, had urine and blood samples taken, for which she had signed all the consent forms they thrust at her. They had taken all her clothes away for forensic analysis, which, she thought, was a waste of time as the crime had been committed months ago. They gave Cathy a dark-blue tracksuit, t-shirt, and jumper to wear, all very shapeless and baggy. She suspected they'd simply rummaged in the menswear box when they couldn't find anything long enough in the women's lot.

But one thing she refused to do was to answer any questions without her solicitor present. She had enough self-preservation to insist on that.

The processing would have gone quicker, except that Cathy kept falling asleep, which initially annoyed the custody sergeant but then worried him enough to send for a doctor, who confirmed her suspicion that she had been drugged.

'Is it self-inflicted?' Cathy heard the sergeant ask the doctor.

'Not possible unless she can rotate her arms 360 degrees to inject herself on the back of her shoulders. I found an injection site on the right upper trapezius, the muscle that's across the tops of the shoulders. Her blood pressure is elevated, but that's to be expected, considering where she is. Other vital signs are within normal range, and she seems lucid when she's awake. I suspect it's a sedative and will just have to work its way out of her system. Since we have her consent, I have taken more blood, but won't know what's been pumped into her until the results come back.'

'Is she OK to be here? Should she be in hospital?' The sergeant looked worried. He definitely didn't want a death in custody and certainly not on his watch.

The doctor and sergeant exchanged a horror-stricken glance. Unless it was an emergency, and a dire one at that, their chances of finding a hospital bed in London for someone to sleep off the effects of a sedative were laughable.

'Can you remember when you were injected?' asked the doctor, taking Cathy's wrist and checking her pulse again.

Cathy remembered alright. Remembered every moment of the evening barely 24 hours ago.

**M**ick sat across from her, his grey eyes watching her, pitying her,

while she stared at the dark camouflage backpack on the table between them. She was numb, unbelieving, and dying with every word he uttered.

'I'm so sorry, my love.'

The words made no sense. Nothing he told her did. These were not the words she was expecting or hoping to hear.

Was it only two hours earlier that Mick had asked if they could go back home to his flat? His face was serious but carefully blank.

'We can order something in. Whatever you like. I need to tell you something important.'

Cathy's heart had raced with anticipation, joy, and worry. She hoped he didn't intend to propose. She hoped he would propose. A million emotions zipped through her veins, threatened her breath, clouded her vision as she walked on air beside him.

Back in his flat, Cathy remembered him getting up, going into the kitchen area, while she sat with her gaze fixed on the backpack, trying to absorb everything he had said during the past hour.

He returned, stood behind her, a hand on her left shoulder. Cathy exhaled, turned her head towards the warmth of his hand. She barely felt the needle slide into the muscle at the top of her right shoulder. Soon a flood of heat suffused her body, and all the lights went out. She remembered Mick's arms around her, holding her as she passed out.

'D I Collins?' prompted the doctor, giving Cathy a gentle shake.

'Sorry. I can't seem to stop dozing off. Yes, I remember being injected. Just before 7.00 p.m. on Sunday evening, I think. I remember feeling a sharp prick, then heat spreading through my whole body and everything going black. I don't remember anything after that until I woke up.'

'OK, good. That makes it almost 23 hours ago, and you've been getting more alert, even in the time I've been here. I don't think the drug was meant to harm you. Just incapacitate you temporarily. Drink lots of water, eat a light meal, maybe a sandwich if you can manage it. But you need to triple your fluid intake to flush it out of your system. You'll probably keep dozing off and on for the next 24 hours, but you should be OK after that.'

She stood up, her dark eyes full of sympathy. Cathy's flooded with tears.

'I'm on duty, so I'll call in during the night to check on you, if that's OK.'

Cathy nodded. The doctor was kind. She didn't expect or deserve kindness in this place.

'Can we question her tonight?' asked the sergeant.

'You are joking, I hope. Look at her. She's shattered and still under the influence. I would strongly recommend leaving it until tomorrow morning.'

Cathy woke up alone to the clanging of the cell door and a food tray plonked unceremoniously down on the thin mattress. She wasn't sure whether it was minutes or hours later. With a corner of the blanket, she mopped up the spilled tea and tidied up the tray.

As instructed by the doctor, they had given her six litre bottles of water. To her relief, the seals were intact. She emptied one, gulping greedily.

Thankful, yet frightened to be left alone that night, Cathy had curled up with the blanket tucked up tight around her, waiting for the nightmares.

But unlike Mick, she couldn't seek refuge on the streets to run from her bad dreams. She had nowhere to run.

# 49

# CATHY

## Today – Friday 27 July

1 0.12 a.m. The steady clacking of the train slowed as it neared Clapham Junction. The screech of wheels grinding to a halt penetrated the closed windows of the air-conditioned coach.

Cathy stared unseeingly at the passengers scurrying on and off the train, her vision filled with images of her time with Mick. Of their meeting at the pub, their first kiss outside his hotel room.

*Don't think about that night! Or any other night with Mick. What should I think about then? Definitely not the forthcoming interview with the disciplinary board this afternoon.*

That meeting would be worse than her interrogation earlier in the week at the Met's New Scotland Yard interview rooms. For a start, unlike the four Met officers, her interrogators wouldn't be strangers. They'd be people she knew, maybe even worked with. And she'd have to confront the disappointment on their faces, the contempt, the fury even, at how much she had let them all down.

Bewildering as her experience had been, her thoughts turned to her grilling by the Met and the nights in their cells. They were less painful than her loss of innocence, her sense of betrayal, but most of all, the agonising knowledge that she would never see Mick again.

## Three days ago – Tuesday 24 July

Clang! Crash! Bang!

The aggressive metallic noises overlaid with beeps, loud voices and thuds of boots on the hard floor jerked Cathy out of her sleep. For an insane moment, she thought she was in a prison cell and shot upright in bed.

Panic and realisation hit at exactly the same moment. She *was* in a prison cell. She hugged herself to stop the shivers, closed her eyes and concentrated on controlling her breathing.

*Deep breaths*, she told herself. But it wasn't the best of ideas. One inhalation through the nose had her gagging the moment the stale, fetid odours assaulted her senses.

Although she usually lived alone, she had never felt this lonely or abandoned. That's not true. This was exactly how she'd felt when she had woken up late yesterday morning, alone in Mick's apartment in London.

After that perfect weekend had ended with his disappearance and her arrest.

Warm, salty tears ran into the corners of her mouth.

*This is pathetic. Crying won't help. I have to deal with my situation, accept the fact that I'm here, in a holding cell. I'm going to be questioned. I must be careful and in control, or I could be charged and sent to a place far worse than this. I could be locked up for a long time.*

After just 19 hours in custody, most of which she had slept through, Cathy was already despairing. They would certainly hold her for the full 36 hours and were probably trying to get a magistrate to sign off an extension to 72 hours. *All the more reason to stop being pathetic and get a grip.*

Despite the stress, worry and anguish, or possibly because of them, and aided by the remnants of the sedative in her system, Cathy had slept through the night. A deep, dreamless sleep. Whatever the drug injected into her, it must have worn off, for she felt rested and refreshed. And she was starving. After washing as best as she could, she downed another bottle of water, but it did nothing to assuage her hunger. She'd have to eat whatever they gave her, close her mind to the petty satisfaction they got by spitting into her food.

*Don't think. Just drink and eat. I need the strength to beat this, to survive, to hug my daughter and my parents again. Strength to fight, to walk freely in the sunshine, meet Andrea for drinks and chat to my friends.*

This was a test, not least of her character and fortitude, but it would also show Cathy who her true friends were. Mick was lost to her. He'd betrayed her, but she still had her anchor. She just needed to hold on to that thought.

The day shift warden, while as curt as her night shift colleagues, appeared to be more human. For a start, she placed Cathy's tray down, sloshing none of the tea. She also talked, rather than barked at her.

'Eat up quickly. Your lawyer's waiting in the outer room. Your formal interviews will start at 8.00 a.m. sharp.'

*Thank you, Andrea!* Her friend had come through for her.

When she'd woken up alone in Mick's flat yesterday morning, it had taken Cathy a moment to realize where she was, another to luxuriate in the memory of the feel of his arms and a whole minute to recall what he'd told her before she had passed out from the syringe he'd emptied into her shoulder.

Hysterical, Cathy had phoned Andrea first before calling her boss, DCI Matthew Holt.

Andrea said she would ask a good friend who was an excellent lawyer to represent Cathy. 'Don't say a word. Don't say anything to anyone or answer any questions without Jim by your side.'

Her boss told her to stay put in Mick's flat while he called in the detectives from the Met to take over. She knew he would help and put in a good word for her, but although they were both originally from the Met, strangers would deal with Cathy, granting her no favours, no concessions and no reprieve.

She was guilty until proved innocent.

To give herself as much time as she could with her lawyer, Cathy crammed the cornflakes into her mouth and washed them down with the carton of milk, did a hasty toilet, changed and was ready and waiting in 20 minutes.

Her lawyer, Jim Davidson, had not been idle since Andrea's call. Cathy was surprised by how much background he already knew about the case.

'I've been in touch with DCI Holt and DI Paul Hayes. Both were very cooperative. And of course, I got a lot of information from Andrea,' he admitted.

Together they went through the disclosure presented by the Met detectives. No surprises there.

At the end of their hour and a half together, Cathy was as ready as she was going to be.

Although the cream panelled interview room was furnished with only a sturdy, utilitarian rectangular table and chairs, it boasted a large computer screen and an array of sophisticated audio and video-recording equipment. The overbright lights were angled to leave no shadows, aligned to capture every change of expression on the suspect's face. Designed to intimidate.

There were four of them. Looking at the composition of her panel of interrogators, no one could accuse the Met of being racially or sexually biased. Not during the duration of Cathy's questioning, anyway. This panel of interviewers was perfect: 50 per cent women and 50 per cent non-white.

The two men and two women sat facing Cathy and her lawyer, each with their laptops open before them.

With the introductions and preliminaries over, they asked her to go over her story.

'DI Collins, as you know, we're not investigating Operation Silhouette, the murder of the Dwyer twins. That is a case for the Solent Constabulary. You are under arrest for your part in that murder and, as an independent body, we're examining your role in the commissioning of that murder.'

'I played no part in commissioning that or any other murder. I did not conceal any evidence, nor did I knowingly aid any suspect. I am not guilty of any crime.'

*Except that of sleeping with a suspect.*

Two nights ago, Cathy had sat opposite Mick at the dining table, her heart bursting with hope, nerves tingling with anticipation. Full of expectation. Of what exactly, she still wasn't sure. Anything but what she actually got.

His confession to the murder of the two junior doctors.

He was the killer she had been hunting for these four long months.

He was Stanley's *ghost.*

The thought of Stanley scratched at another memory, something buried beneath a layer of wants, desires, trust and hope.

They had come for Cathy within half an hour of her phone call to her guvnor. Five officers, three of whom were armed, had burst through Mick's front door yesterday morning, jerking her out of the restless sleep she'd slipped into with her head on her forearms at his dining table.

So, here she was, being questioned just like any other criminal. Even though she knew the drill and had cautioned more suspects than she could count, nothing had prepared her for this. She'd never felt like this before. Bewildered, ashamed, guilty.

*Yet I've done nothing wrong, have I?*

Superintendent Alison Oleja got the ball rolling. Cathy's insides turned to jelly. The woman was not known as Super Bitch for nothing. She was formidable and ruthless, but Cathy had also heard that she could be fair. Sometimes.

'DI Collins, tell us how you first met ex-Captain Michael O'Neal.'

That Friday evening back in March would forever be etched — no, scorched in Cathy's mind. An innocent outing for a drink with a friend had led to this.

'Was that the first time you met Mr O'Neal? Are you saying you had no contact with him before?'

'That's correct. That was the first time I met Mick. I'd had no prior contact with him.'

'That was the evening of Friday, 23 March?'

'Yes, that's right.'

'And according to the pathologist's report, the Dwyer twins were murdered in the early hours of the previous morning. So, you met Mr O'Neal the day after the Dwyer twins' murder?'

*And slept with him less than 48 hours after he tortured and killed them.*

Cathy felt the blood drain to her feet. Her stomach churned. She staggered up from her seat and stood swaying.

Covering her mouth and clutching her stomach, she turned and rushed towards the toilets. Cathy made it to one of the cubicles before the female uniformed officer standing guard outside the door, and one of her interviewers, DC Amanda Dibbing, arrived at a run. They watched her retch her heart and soul into the white porcelain hole.

Exhausted, Cathy rested her cheek against the cool melamine panel wall. She was shivering, covered in a cold sweat. A cool hand pushed back her hair and a cold, damp towel wiped her forehead. She became aware of DC Dibbing crouching down beside her, helping her to stay upright, when all Cathy's inclinations were dragging her down to lie on the toilet floor.

'Thank you,' she whispered before falling into a dead faint.

Another doctor this time. Not the kind-eyed lady with her Indian accent softening her speech and soothing Cathy's anxiety. This one was in a hurry. In rapid succession, he checked her pulse, peered into her eyes, listened to her heart and lungs, took her temperature. With no blood-test results to hand, he seemed at a loss.

'All your vital signs are within normal range. Your BP's elevated, but that's hardly surprising. How do you feel?'

'I'm OK.'

'I'll recommend that you rest this afternoon, see how you are tomorrow. In the meantime, increase your fluid intake and let someone know if you feel unwell.'

Cathy's lawyer nodded in satisfaction. All this ate away at their custody time.

'You rest. I'll go tell them you're unfit to continue the interview,' said Jim Davidson smugly.

'No, Jim. I don't want to upset them. I'd like to get this over with. Not have it hanging over my head. Just ask them to give me a couple of hours. I'd like to rest for a bit and shower before I face them again.'

He looked ready to argue, but Cathy curled up on the mattress. 'Please, Jim. I'll be fine.'

Reluctantly, he went off to give the panel the news. They wouldn't be happy, but Cathy hoped that maybe the fact she was trying to cooperate would be a point in her favour.

Three hours later, teeth brushed, and hair still damp from her shower, Cathy was back in the room with her lawyer, braced for more grilling.

No sooner were the formalities of setting up the video recording, registering the date and time and identifying everyone in the room completed, than it began.

'Do you make it a habit to sleep with suspects, DI Collins?' asked DCI Nigel Roberts.

'Don't answer that!' Jim was furious. The lawyer turned to the blank-faced, cold-eyed foursome. 'DI Collins reported this as soon as she could. May I remind you she's been entirely cooperative, and may I also remind you that Mr O'Neal was never a suspect?'

Cathy saw her questioner's mouth open, ready to add another snarky remark, but she'd had enough.

'I shall answer DCI Roberts' question about my sleeping habits,' she said. 'I was totally faithful to my husband during the eight years we were together and since my divorce, Mick is only the third man I have dated. Unlike yourself, DCI Roberts, I do not make it a habit to arrange different sexual partners at every conference or overnight meeting I attend. So, no, I do not make it a habit to sleep with different partners, suspects or otherwise. I loved him. We were dating. And as Mr Davidson pointed out, Mick O'Neal was never remotely considered a suspect.'

DCI Robert's face was bright red and the expressions on the others' were priceless. After some uncomfortable shifting in their seats and embarrassed clearing of throats, Superintendent Alison Oleja spoke up.

'That was uncalled for, DI Collins, as was DCI Robert's question. You say Mr O'Neal was not a suspect. Was this because of your relationship with him?'

'No, ma'am. There was no reason or any evidence linking him to the homicide. And there was no reason to question his presence in Southampton. He and his partner were in business negotiations with a local limousine-hire company. Both firms were looking to expand their market coverage.'

'Ah, yes. His partner. Major Tom Cassidy. Have you seen Mr O'Neal's recorded confession?'

'Yes, ma'am.' Cathy and her lawyer had watched the video recording given to them as part of the disclosure. The original was with her team in Southampton, who were even now closing the case without her.

Cathy also remembered Mick holding up the pen drive as they sat facing each other across his dining table. 'My confession. I've video-recorded it,' he had said, slipping it into the backpack on the table between them.

'In his recorded confession, Mr O'Neal claims he acted alone, that his partner or boss, or whatever he is, was not involved. That he did not know of Mr O'Neal's activities,' said Superintendent Oleja. She nodded to DC Amanda Dibbing, who pressed 'play' on the remote control. Mick's face filled the big screen, expressionless, set in hard lines, grey eyes staring straight at the camera.

Cathy's jaw clenched to stop her teeth from chattering, and she dropped her hands to her lap, folded her fingers, her nails digging into her palms. They were watching her intently.

Focussing on the pain helped to control and hide the tremors juddering through her body.

'*My boss and friend, Major Tom Cassidy, is not involved in any of this. I used his business discussions in Southampton as a cover for my plans to locate and deal with the Dwyer brothers. Tom had no idea what I was doing behind his back. He would have stopped me if he'd known. I'm sorry to have deceived him, to have used him and taken advantage of his trust and friendship...*'

Another nod paused the recording, leaving Cathy with no respite. Mick's face still stared out of the big screen.

'DI Collins, would you say that's true? That Major Cassidy is an innocent pawn in Mr O'Neal's plot?'

Cathy frowned. Why were they asking her? Surely, they would, or should, know.

'I— I don't know. I only learnt the truth two days ago and have had no time or opportunity to investigate. Is there any evidence that Major Cassidy is involved? In the time I've known him, I had no reason to suspect or even consider his involvement.'

*Nor Mick's for that matter.*

'Well, if Major Cassidy is truly innocent and was unaware of his partner's activities, can you explain why he would liquidate the business and disappear? It's almost a month since anyone has seen or heard from him.'

Cathy's jaw hit the floor, and she gasped like a fish out of water.

'What? You didn't know?'

Cathy shook her head.

'Speak, please. You know the drill.'

'No, I didn't know. Are you saying that Tom sold the business and has disappeared?'

'Exactly. Did your friend, Professor Brown, not mention it?'

'Andrea? No. I knew she and Tom were no longer seeing each other. I thought their relationship had just fizzled out. It hadn't been all that serious anyway.'

Poor Andrea! No wonder she'd seemed so unhappy the last time they'd met, but Cathy had been too engrossed in her own affairs and her work. Too busy trying to solve the murders.

*Poor Andrea's going to come in for a heavy grilling. She won't have an easy time.* Cathy took some comfort from the fact that Jim Davidson would represent Andrea, too. He was bloody good. He'd put the three hours of her 'incapacity' to good use and had dug up all that interesting dirt on her interrogators.

Andrea, too, would need all the help she could get.

# 50

# CATHY

## Today – Friday 27 July

1 0.47 a.m. The rhythmic *thumpity thump* was followed by a metallic screech as the wheels battled against the brakes. Cathy watched her fellow passengers swing gently forward from the waist up and back again into their seats in a perfectly synchronized movement as the train pulled into Basingstoke Station. Several people got off, but only a couple got on before the locomotive once more squeaked and clacked its way out of the platform.

Twenty-four minutes to go before she arrived at Southampton Central in time for her 2.00 p.m. meeting, which would decide her future, her career.

*Do I still have one? Do I even want one? What's the alternative?*

## Two days ago – Wednesday 25 July

After only two nights in her cell, Cathy was already getting used to the routine. Wake up just before 6.00 a.m. and await the onslaught of the morning's din.

Last night, she'd collapsed onto the thin mattress exhausted from the day's questioning and the news that her inquisitors had been granted an extension to her detention in custody. Her lawyer had objected and tried his best, but they were determined to hold her for the full 72 hours. Cathy surprised both him and herself by accepting the news stoically.

Drained both physically and emotionally, her mind had shut down and dragged her into a deep sleep where even nightmares could not penetrate.

The interviews resumed at 8.00 a.m. with Cathy feeling more in control as she once again faced the same interrogators.

They were on a different tack today. With Cathy having nothing more to add or contribute to Tom Cassidy's disappearance, Superintendent Oleja started off the questioning.

'You would seriously have us believe that in your – what was it ... four-month relationship with Mr O'Neal – you had no suspicion of his involvement in that double homicide?'

'No, ma'am. We never talked about my work, and he never gave me any cause to consider his involvement.'

'I thought good detectives have an instinct about these things. That doesn't make you a very good detective now, does it, DI Collins?'

'Possibly not, ma'am. Not unlike yourself in the Councillor Hammond case, ma'am.'

Stunned silence greeted her words. Even Jim Davidson, who had fed Cathy the information, looked shocked.

About six years ago, the superintendent had faced a backlash when the man she had been dating for almost a year was arrested for fraud and corruption. She too had come under suspicion and questioned about her involvement in the crimes. Although she was eventually cleared, she'd gone through an extremely tough time. They'd put her through the wringer, but she had fought her way through and come out, if not exactly smelling of roses, at least being seen as an innocent victim.

Defiant, Cathy choked down the apology threatening to escape her. Her heart drummed a panic-stricken beat. She knew she shouldn't have mentioned that, but she was tired of being browbeaten and treated like a criminal.

Superintendent Oleja flushed, and her coal-black eyes held Cathy's, neither willing to be the first to blink. Suddenly, the older woman smiled. 'Fair enough. Good point. I can see where you are coming from.'

Cathy sighed in relief. She didn't want to make an enemy of the woman.

'I'm sorry. I shouldn't have said that. Please accept my apologies, ma'am.'

'Accepted. Were you aware that Mr O'Neal also had a long-term relationship with the pop star, Missy, and rumour has it he was paid for his sexual favours?'

The superintendent had meant to hurt and had unerringly found her quarry's weakest point.

A wave of dizziness hit Cathy as the blood drained to her feet. She felt her heart splinter and shatter into a million pieces. Naively, she had assumed that he was as loyal to her as she had been to him. She stared at her tormentor, the pain stark on her face, open for all to see. She had lost not just the battle, but the entire war.

The superintendent's eyes shifted. Maybe in her victory, she had found an infinitesimal speck of pity. 'Although, to be fair, the relationship seems to have ended around the time you two met and we've found no evidence of any contact between them since then. Another chauffeur appears to have replaced him both with the limousine and other services.'

Cathy's heart soared. She wanted to jump up and hug and kiss the woman, to run barefoot through the corridors and sing. But they gave her no time to enjoy the exhilaration.

'How often did you stay with Mr O'Neal in London?' DCI Nigel Roberts, the philanderer, asked.

'I've never stayed at his place before last weekend.'

Four pairs of eyebrows shot up and the four panellists exchanged glances.

'Are you saying that in the entire duration of your relationship, you had never visited Mr O'Neal's home or stayed with him in London?'

'No. He always came to Southampton. He had business there, and it just seemed to work out easier.'

'But you stayed over last weekend, so you would know what was in his flat, right?'

Where was this going? Cathy turned to Jim, who looked equally puzzled.

'Yes, I suppose so. We went out most of Saturday and Sunday, but I spent time with him in the flat.'

'So, you know what's in his wardrobe?'

Cathy frowned. 'Not really, no. His wardrobe looked like one of those modular flat packs. It's a series of double and single door partitioned units. Even though I was only staying one weekend, he'd cleared a single door section at one end for me to use. He also gave me the use of two empty drawers in a big chest of drawers.'

'Did you check the rest of the wardrobe?'

She shook her head. 'No, I didn't. Why? What was in there?'

# 51

## Monday 23 July

'Sir, you need to come and see this.'

At the shouted call from behind him, DCI Nigel Roberts whirled away from the wall of photos.

Following Cathy's arrest, he, along with a detective constable and a team of crime scene investigators, were carrying out a search of Mick's flat. He was in the suspect's home gym enviously eyeing the array of professional fitness equipment and studying the photos, wondering who the girl was.

Apart from those images, there was nothing personal in the flat. Nothing to give an insight into the man who'd lived here. No books or magazines, absolutely no knick-knacks. Even the kitchen cupboards and fridge held nothing but bog-standard items like tea, coffee, salt, pepper and cleaning material. The place was spotlessly clean. Impersonal. Like a hotel apartment.

'Where are you?'

'In the bedroom, sir. You really need to see this.'

Roberts covered the short distance from Mick's gym to the bedroom. Two blue-overall garbed officers were standing gazing into a tall white double wardrobe. They stepped aside to make room for Roberts to look at the contents beyond its wide-open doors.

'What the—,' DCI Roberts' eyes widened as his heart raced in panic. 'Don't touch anything. Move very slowly. Get out of the flat now. But don't run. Walk slowly and carefully. Don't use your phones or radios. Now, move,' he commanded.

He backed out of the room, issued the same instructions to the third CSI and his DC, who were in the kitchen and bathroom, respectively.

'What's going on, guv?'

'Stop pissing about and do as you're told,' snapped Roberts, doing his best to remain calm when every instinct was screaming at him to flee. 'Could be a bomb in there.'

That certainly got everyone moving, and within seconds, the flat was empty. Roberts waited until they were out of the building before calling for the bomb squad, who arrived in a surprisingly short time. When the DCI and the two CSIs described the contents of the wardrobe, the bomb disposal unit leader evacuated the building. Luckily, except for an elderly man on the third floor and a mum with a baby on the second, everyone else was out. All the other flats were empty.

The police and fire services set up the inner and outer cordons. They radioed in for the dog support unit, who arrived within minutes with a pair of German Shepherds specialising in explosive detection.

With two ambulances on standby, the bomb squad set to work. It was slow, meticulous, and cautious. When the DSU dogs signalled no alert for explosives, the team grew more confident.

But it still took four hours before they pronounced the 'all clear' and the bomb disposal unit leader sought DCI Nigel Roberts to give him the results.

# 52

## CATHY

**Two days ago – Wednesday 25 July**

'Well? What was in the wardrobe?' asked Cathy.

The panel of interviewers twisted their bodies away to whisper to each other before returning to Cathy and her lawyer.

'We found two strongboxes. Security safes, if you like. Each 1 metre high and each weighing 125 kilos. One safe was wrapped in a thick, solid stainless-steel anchor chain with a big padlock on it,' said DCI Roberts, his face flushing puce.

Her breath caught in her throat. Drugs, bombs or guns were the first things that sprang to mind.

*How much worse is all this going to get? An anchor chain and padlock around a safe? What was Mick storing inside that he had gone to the trouble of adding an extra barrier to an already secure storage box? It had to be explosives. With his military background, that made sense.*

'What do you think was in them?'

Beside her, Jim leaned forward in anticipation. Bewildered, Cathy shook her head.

'I don't know.' But the tumblers were already clicking in her brain as the discs lined up. And suddenly, she knew!

'Nothing,' said DCI Roberts. He looked ready to explode. 'Absolutely nothing. They were empty. We had the bomb squad out to open them. They took extra precautions because of the chain and padlock.'

He sounded aggrieved, taking it as a personal affront. Cathy couldn't blame him. He must have had to take the decision to call in the bomb squad. It must have been quite an operation and an exciting one at that. Finding explosives, ammunition or something – anything – would have been a feather in his cap. But to find nothing...

'The other safe had 14 small portable security cases stacked inside it. Again, all empty. We expected them to be filled with drugs or diamonds. Forensics checked every inch of those safes. Totally clean. Brand-new, they said. They'd never had anything inside them. What's that all about, DI Colins?'

Her thoughts flew back to a night in early May, around six weeks after they first met.

She had woken up to find Mick sitting bolt upright in bed, his torso enveloped in a sheen of perspiration.

'What is it? Are you OK?' Cathy tried to hug his cold, clammy body, but he held her off gently.

'It's nothing. Go back to sleep. I'll be fine in a minute.'

Cathy watched him get out of bed and head to the bathroom, shoulders hunched, hands clasped tightly before him. When he returned a few minutes later, he was back to his normal self, or almost normal. His eyes, haunted and lost, refused to meet hers.

'Talk to me. Was it a nightmare?'

By then, she'd learned a bit more about his captivity in Afghanistan from Tom and Andrea. Although Mick wouldn't speak about any of it, she also realized from his scars that he'd been tortured before he was rescued. His physical scars had healed. She wasn't so sure about his psychological ones.

He nodded. Cathy laid her head on his shoulder.

'I wish I could make it better for you.'

'You do, more than you realize.' He kissed the top of her head and smiled. 'Don't worry, love. I have the nightmares under control. Most of the time, anyway. They're locked away in big strong safes. I even have the safe with the worst of them bound tight with chains and a big padlock. But sometimes, bits of them somehow still manage to escape and they find me.'

He shuddered, then straightened up with a smile. 'Go back to sleep, Catherine. I'm going out for a run.'

Back then, she remembered thinking just how poetic that was and had assumed he was speaking metaphorically, but only now did she grasp just how literally he'd meant it.

None of them said anything when she explained. They probably knew more of Mick's background than she'd been able to uncover.

Maybe the MOD had been willing to release more information now that he had actually committed a crime. They had probably provided the Met with an overall picture, if not the details, of the type of missions Mick had undertaken. The things he'd seen and done. Of his captivity and rescue. Of his injuries, both physical and psychological.

Or maybe his previous employers had decided to throw him to the wolves.

And now she also understood the iron wrapping around the steel vault. It held the worst of his nightmares.

Nightmares even worse than the traumatic and degrading experiences of his captivity.

# 53

## CATHY

**Two days ago – Wednesday 25 July**

The afternoon session began much like the morning's. The big screen on the wall flickered alive, filled with an image of a backpack, just like the one Mick had showed her.

'Do you recognize this, DI Collins?' asked DI Ram Singh.

'Yes, that looks like the bag Mick showed me.'

'And do you know what's inside?'

The backpack, with the proof on the dining table, lay exactly where he'd left it after showing Cathy its contents. Two mobile phones. Two laptops. A pair of gloves. Plastic double-flex disposable cable ties. A rope, bloodied knife and the soles of Treaders boots that he'd attached to the undersides of his own.

'Yes, he told me. All the evidence we'd been looking for.'

'On the wall of his home gym are photos of a girl — a young woman. Do you know who that is?'

321

'Yes, it's his daughter. Her name's Ayesha. She's a third-year student at Southampton University. Studying Business Entrepreneurship, I understand.'

'Have you met her?'

'No, I didn't even know he had a daughter. He never mentioned her until I saw her photos on his wall.'

'What about her mother? Have you met her?'

'No, never.'

Leila. That was her name. Cathy had never met her either, yet she hated the woman. Envied her for the life she'd had with Mick, for everything she had meant to him and the bond that still connected them through their daughter.

Then Cathy thought of Emily, her own child and, at that moment, missed her more than anything in the world. And she thought of Ben, her ex-husband. Though divorced for nearly a decade, she still had a lot of affection for him, as she knew he did for her. Their daughter was a bond that still held them together and probably always would.

'DI Collins?'

The voice jerked Cathy out of her reflections. She focussed her attention on the speaker, DI Ram Singh. He wasn't so bad. Somewhere along the line, they had ceased to be monsters.

'DI Collins, did Mr O'Neal tell you why he killed those two young men?'

Yes, he had told her. The crux of it all. His reason for the murders. Mick had narrated it all in a flat, expressionless monotone, stating facts, making no excuses. And all the while, those bewitching silver-grey eyes had watched the kaleidoscope of expressions on Cathy's face. Watched while her brain rejected his words, refused to believe the sentences seeping into her ears.

# 54

# MICK

## Sunday 22 July

*M*y name is Michael Thomas O'Neal, and this is my confession to killing the two doctors, Derek and Dillion Dwyer, on Thursday 22 March. All the proof you seek is in the backpack with this memory stick.

How did it start? Isn't it strange how inconsequential things or events can spark a catastrophe?

It began when, for the first time in 22 years, I did not receive the usual innocuous text message from Leila wishing me a happy new year. At first, I thought nothing of it. She was probably busy, or maybe she forgot. But it niggled and eventually, I texted her to ask if all was well.

Leila surprised me by showing up at my flat early the following morning. She said she had a conference in central London and used the opportunity to drop by and explain. That's when I learnt that Ayesha, our daughter, had been rushed to hospital on 30 December and undergone surgery to remove her *dangerously inflamed appendix. The laparoscopy went without a hitch. She had to stay overnight, and they discharged her the following morning. Leila had been busy with Ayesha, which was why she hadn't got around to sending new year greetings to me or to anyone else.*

*'She's fine,' Leila assured me. 'There's no sign of any infection and she's recovering quickly.'*

*But I could see Leila was worried.*

*'Something's wrong, Mick,' she said. 'But Ayesha won't tell me what it is. I know it's nothing physical. But she hasn't been herself. She acts guilty and I know something's bothering her. Oh, I'm probably just being silly. I'm sure it's nothing and if it's important, Ayesha will tell me in her own time.'*

*A week later, Tom, that's Major Tom Cassidy, said he'd like to expand the business and had been exploring a partnership with a couple of limo-hire companies in Southampton, catering to the wealthier end of cruise ship passengers. He arranged a visit to Southampton, which suited me fine, as it would give me an opportunity to check on Ayesha.*

*Leila had been right. I didn't like what I saw. The girl had lost weight and looked ill. Haunted. Something was wrong. I remembered Leila telling me a few years ago that Ayesha kept a journal and wondered whether she still used it. If she did, it would be with her, in her one-bed flat on Caxton Road. I also knew she went home to Winchester on weekends. A perfect opportunity.*

*I broke in when Ayesha was away for the weekend and found her journal. Though sporadic with big gaps between the dates, it was still a repository for her secrets. I read her recent entries.*

*Ayesha wrote about the pain in her appendix, the dash to the hospital and the embarrassment of her mum creating a scene until someone attended to her. She wrote about her ride on the trolley to surgery, the anaesthetic injection and a masked doctor asking her to count backwards from 100. After surgery, she recalls telling her mum to go home, then waking up when a doctor came in. She remembers him smiling and saying, 'Shh, it's alright. Go back to sleep,' before fiddling with her anaesthetic drip line. After that, everything was hazy. She wrote she dreamed she was having sex with the doctor, but there were two of him. They were talking to each other, telling her how beautiful she was, and he or they took photos.*

*She was embarrassed and upset at how real it felt. Especially the ache and pain in a part of her body that had nothing to do with the surgery.*

*The poor child felt guilty, as if she had cheated on her boyfriend with a doctor she couldn't even remember.*

*She wrote, 'I can't tell anyone, especially not mummy. She'll create hell, insist on going to the police. How sick would I be to ruin an innocent man's life and reputation based on an erotic dream?'*

*I didn't know what to think, but mostly, I was embarrassed to read such an intimate confession. I didn't tell Leila — she'd be furious with me for invading Ayesha's privacy.*

*But what if Ayesha had not dreamt it? What if it actually happened?*

*I don't know when that thought entered my head. Or why? I wasn't even aware it had, but there it was. There was only one way to find out. If it had happened, there'd be photos. In her diary, Ayesha mentioned that the doctor had taken photos. I had to know.*

*Tom's discussions with potential partners were progressing well, and he was pleased when I asked to join him on his visits to Southampton. He thought I was finally taking* an interest in the business side of our partnership. I had to sit through boring meetings and visit umpteen sites, but it gave me plenty of opportunity to set up my plans. Finding out who was on duty on the night of 30 December was easy. All it took was a phone call to the hospital asking for names so I could send thank you cards and chocolates. The duty doctor was Derek Dwyer. Imagine my surprise when I discovered he had an identical twin. Dillion Dwyer.

So maybe Ayesha had not been dreaming after all.

In the meantime, Leila told me that Ayesha was improving. She was recovering both physically and mentally. Slowly getting back to her normal self and beginning to forget whatever had been bothering her.

But I wasn't ready to give up, not as long as there was a possibility of photos of Ayesha with those doctors.

By March, my plans were in place.

# 55

# CATHY

## Two days ago – Wednesday 25 July

DI Ram Singh clicked the remote. It was all there, in Mick's recorded confession, but they were still trying to pinpoint her involvement in the crime. Trying to get her to trip up so they could send her to hell in good conscience and throw away the key.

'Yes, he did,' said Cathy, responding to DI Singh's earlier question. 'Mick told me why he killed those two doctors. On 30 December last year, his daughter, Ayesha, was in hospital overnight for an appendix removal. She had a private room, and just after midnight, her mother left her asleep to go home, shower and change. In the two hours that her mother was gone, those two men entered the room, sedated the girl and sexually assaulted her.'

In the early hours of 31 December.

Cathy remembered her session with the hospital's IT network engineer. She had asked him to provide her with the logs of card-readers going back to the beginning of the year. From 1 January. She'd thought that would be enough, but she had missed it by one day. *One single day.*

*If only I had asked the IT engineer to pull up the earlier records. Asked him to go further back by even a month, a week, a day ... I'd have noticed the anomaly. The oddity of the twins entering Ayesha's room together.*

Even if only one brother had used his card and held the door open for the other, Cathy was convinced she would have wondered why he'd been in there for so long. Especially at that time of the night, when Ayesha had not buzzed for assistance and none of her monitors had indicated any problems.

Hindsight convinced her she would then have delved into the patient's details. Her curiosity would have driven her to dig into the patient's background, dive deeper to her birth certificate. To uncover her biological father's name.

But she hadn't gone back far enough, hadn't been thorough enough.

'Why didn't she call for help? The call button for a nurse was right beside her bed.' DI Singh's question jerked Cathy out of her self-recriminations.

'Well, you've seen and heard Mick's confession. I can only go by what he said. Ayesha was sedated and fell asleep. It sounds as if she became semi-conscious occasionally, but never enough to fully wake up or realize what was happening. She thought she'd been dreaming. When she woke up the next morning, she mistook the pain and discomfort in her groin area for the aftermath of her surgery. The strong painkillers they gave her would also have masked the pain of her attack.'

Silence greeted Cathy's words as the six people in the room thought about the crime and the punishment. She knew that at least five of them had daughters, and each one was wondering what he or she would have done in Mick's place.

But they were also the custodians of the law and, in their book, taking another's life, for whatever reason, shouldn't be condoned. Should it?

Yet it was. So often. Like in the wars that Mick had fought. The very system that punished those who killed another was the one that trained men and women to do precisely that.

# 56

## CATHY

**Today – Friday 27 July**

1 1.04 a.m. The train rolled to a stop at Winchester station and about half the remaining passengers got off, replaced by a scant ten.

Cathy's daughter, her parents, Andrea, her ex, even DI Paul Hayes, had wanted to pick her up when she arrived at Southampton Central, but she had begged them not to. She wanted to do this alone, brace herself, prepare to face her future.

That is what she had intended to do during the hour and seventeen minutes of her journey from London Waterloo to Southampton. Prepare her answers to the disciplinary board.

Yet here she was, reliving her last day in the Met's cell.

# Yesterday morning – Thursday 26 July

S he woke up with an overwhelming feeling of dread. Despite her lawyer's assurances, Cathy was unsure of the outcome.

The 72 hours that they could hold her would expire at noon. They would either have to charge or release her. Her lawyer was confident that it would be the latter, that there was no evidence of her collusion in the crime, but Cathy remained convinced that they would ask her to stand up while they chanted the condemnation and the arrest caution. They would charge her and send her to prison.

*I deserve it for my stupidity. My naivety at trusting a man I'd known for just a few months.*

All those lies, the continuous deception. His mantle of truth was woven from a thousand lies.

His betrayal was all that she could think about. It was drowning her, feeding the root of hatred within.

She could forgive him for his crimes. Many a parent would avenge their child.

She could even forgive him for her arrest and for putting her through the past few days.

But not for lying to her. For making a fool of her.

She'd loved him and believed that he loved her. Was that a lie, too?

Cathy frowned as she went about completing her morning routine.

*What else had he lied about? He was a killer who'd tortured his victims before murdering them. He was Stanley's ghost.*

That's when it clicked. The memory buried beneath her gullibility. Stanley's death. Mick's midnight run on the night of Marek's death. Grozdan's disappearance.

The arrival of the warden and the clang of her cell door interrupted Cathy's thoughts. This would have to wait. She had to be alert and on her toes for the next few hours. Make sure she gave them no reason to keep her.

She parked her musings for review later and followed the warden to the interview room.

The four interrogators looked tired. Hollow-eyed. Their work would have continued late into the night as they analysed every word, action and nuance of the interviews, hunting for evidence of their colleague's wrongdoing. They already had plenty of evidence of her stupidity and her ineptitude as a detective.

'How did Mr O'Neal get into the Dwyers' flat with no one seeing him? We understand that you and your team found no CCTV footage of anyone in the vicinity and that Mr O'Neal left no DNA or any evidence leading to him?'

'Mick had nine or ten weeks to plan the murders. Plenty of time to pinpoint every camera along the route and work out how to avoid them. He's SAS-trained and knows all about stealth. He's trained to kill.'

From the sharp glances directed at her, Cathy guessed the bitterness was evident in her voice.

At a nod from DCI Roberts, DC Dibbing clicked the remote and fast forwarded the recording of Mick's confession.

His face once again stared at them out of the big screen.

'—*I didn't go there to kill, only to recover the photos and videos. If necessary, I was prepared to torture them to get their passwords and make them take down anything they may have posted online. The twins were reluctant at first, but they soon saw I wasn't making idle threats when I sliced off one of their little fingers at the first joint and threatened to chop off the whole hand if they didn't cooperate. The choke rope restraints helped in convincing them I meant business.*

*And then I watched part of the video.*'

He paused, narrowed eyes glinting and mouth twisting in a snarl. His rage was palpable. It reached out and touched everyone in the room. And just as quickly, it was gone. A sharp intake of breath and he was back in control, his face and voice expressionless once again.

'*Don't doctors take an oath?*' he asked his audience. '*The Hippocratic Oath? To do no intentional harm? Yet those bastards entered Ayesha's room while her mother was away, and they violated her.*

*I remember little after that. The next thing I recall is looking down at their bodies on the bed.*

*I am truly sorry. Not for killing them. They deserved to die. But for the way I killed them. I regret that. I'm a soldier, not a butcher.*'

'O'Neal claims that he did not break into the Dwyer twins' flat to kill them. His intention was only to recover the phones and laptops. Do you believe that?'

Cathy nodded. 'I do. He told me he was only checking the recording to make sure that the Dwyers had given him the right one. He said that right until then, he wasn't even certain whether Ayesha had imagined the assault.'

'Have you seen the contents of the victims' mobile phones?' asked DCI Roberts.

Victims. Interesting. There were many in this case, but Cathy guessed they meant the Dwyer twins.

'No,' said Cathy. 'I've not seen the contents of the mobile phone or laptops.'

But Mick had. He'd seen what they'd done to his daughter.

The interview reconvened after a short break. Jim kept glancing at his watch until Cathy told him to stop it, to stop antagonising them. He was even more unhappy when she said that even if they released her at noon, she'd offer to stay on to continue the interview for however long they wanted.

'DI Collins? You said you hadn't seen the contents of the victims' mobile phones,' said DCI Roberts. 'Why not?'

She remembered the haunted expression on Mick's face as he pointed to the phones and laptops inside the backpack on his dining table.

'I didn't need to. Mick had already given me all the evidence we needed. But he had seen the photos and videos, and they led to the murders.'

'DI Collins, so you believe the Dwyer twins' murders were not pre-meditated?'

'Yes ma'am, I do. I'm sure that if Mick had not watched the video, had not seen what they did to his daughter, those two brothers would still be alive.'

Superintendent Oleja leaned forward, her unblinking gaze focussed on Cathy. A serpent preparing to strike.

'You've heard Mr O'Neal accuse the Dwyer twins of violating his daughter and the proof should be on their phones or laptops, or both. Shouldn't it?'

'Yes,' nodded Cathy, a puzzled frown creasing her forehead.

'Would it surprise you to learn that there is not a shred of evidence in either of the twins' laptops or phones of the assault on Ayesha? They've been deleted. No, actually, they've been destroyed. Even our tech team hasn't been able to rebuild or recover them. There's no record of it on any of their cloud storage drives, either.'

Cathy shook her head. Beside her, Jim looked equally blank.

'I—I don't understand,' stammered Cathy eventually. 'I don't know why Mick would delete them. They would at least explain the murders, even if they don't justify them.'

DC Dibbing picked up the remote and pressed play on the recording of Mick's confession.

'—*The holdall has all the evidence you need. The ropes will match the fibres that forensics recovers from their ligatures.*

*The plastic restraints are in there too. They may still hold the twins' DNA. Likewise with the knife.*

*Sorry for the misdirection with the soles of the Treaders boots. I bet Andrea's furious about that.'*

For a second, his eyes crinkled, and a smile lifted the corners of his mouth.

*'I was careful whenever I handled the Dwyers' phones and laptops, so you should still find their fingerprints and DNA on them. But you won't find any photos or videos of the assault on Ayesha. I've deleted them and I hope your IT experts can't recover them. I don't want anyone to see those.'*

The audience in the interview room watched the colour leech away from Mick's face, the hollows in his cheeks deepen and eyes darken to a dead grey.

*'I wish I hadn't seen those. Wish I hadn't looked. It isn't something any father should see. But you can't unsee something, can you?'*

Cathy's heart clenched in pity. *Poor Mick. No vault in the world could constrain those memories.*

A few seconds of unbroken silence later, Mick continued. *'You won't find anything in Ayesha's journal either. I tore those pages out and destroyed them. But there's still enough evidence in those doctors' phones and laptops to prove I'm telling the truth. At the very least, the Dwyers' ID cards should show that one or both of them spent an inordinately long time in Ayesha's room when they had no reason to be there at all.'*

The video paused.

'That's a line of inquiry you were following, wasn't it, DI Collins?'

*Was that a hint of admiration in the superintendent's tone?*

'Yes, but I hadn't gone back far enough,' said Cathy.

# 57

## MICK

**Seven months earlier – Wednesday 03 January**

*E* leven weeks before the Dwyer twins' murder.

Mick jogged in place and twisted his head 180 degrees to scan the deserted streets tinged yellow under the streetlights in the early morning mist. He checked the hedges and shrubs for any subtle change in shape. Satisfied, he turned to unlock the main door to Inglewood Mansions and stopped, sniffing the air. His entire body clenched and the pounding of his heart deafened him.

He recognized the subtle perfume in the air. Leila.

*What was she doing here, so early in the morning?*

His back to the wall, Mick opened an app on his phone to check the videos recorded by the three cameras in the entrance hall. Cameras that none of the other residents were aware of. He'd checked them before going out on his run and knew that no one else had entered or left the building between midnight and 4.00 a.m.

The footage captured while he was on his half-marathon run showed a slim, petite woman, her dark hair twisted up in a French roll, dressed in tight black jeans, a black blazer over a cream roll-neck sweater, carrying a cream raincoat over an arm, a shoulder bag and wearing black high-heeled boots. *Beautiful and elegant.*

Mick watched as she hesitated between the lift and the stairs and chose the stairs. He waited a full five minutes before turning off the app. She was alone.

Satisfied, he unlocked the door and entered the spacious, carpeted hallway. He didn't bother to check his mailbox. At 5.30 a.m., it was still too early for the postman.

He ran up the stairs to his flat on the fourth floor, taking two steps with each stride. Although he trod lightly, Leila must have been alert and listening for him. She waited at the front of his door. He stopped at the top of the landing and stared. Her face was an unhealthy shade of pale, her large brown eyes red-rimmed, and she was trembling.

'Leila?'

With a wail, she launched herself at him, her slim body shaking with sobs. Mick held her tight until her sobs subsided, then unlocked his door, led her inside and sat beside her with an arm still around her.

'What is it? Why didn't you phone to say you were coming?'

'Phone? I— I didn't think... I— I couldn't think ...'

'What's wrong? Is it Ayesha? Is she OK?'

A vigorous shake of her head and a fresh outburst of sobs. Taking her by both shoulders, he turned her to face him, bracing himself for the worst.

'Tell me. Is she OK? Did her operation go wrong? You said it went well, that she was fine.'

'It's all my fault, Mick! I shouldn't have left her. I didn't know. I didn't think anything could happen.' Her wails bounced off the walls.

'Leila, you need to calm down. I'll get you a glass of water.'

When he returned a minute later, she grabbed the glass and gulped most of it in one go. Mick went back to the kitchen area, poured out two mugs of hot coffee from the insulated pot of his pre-programmed coffee machine, and topped one up with milk.

Leila was no longer on the settee when he returned to the living-room area. He found her in his home gym, standing in front of the wall of Ayesha's photos. He tensed and braced himself for the worst.

'Is she dead?'

'What? No!' Leila turned to him, her face white with shock. 'No, of course not!'

Leila turned to stand in front of Ayesha's most recent photograph: the full-facial portrait. Her present to Mick on their daughter's twenty-first birthday.

'An accident? A complication from the operation?' Automatically, he bit his tongue to ward off evil — a superstitious action Leila had foisted on him over two decades ago and one he unconsciously performed to this day. But Leila shook her head without turning around. She huddled into herself, and her shoulders shook.

'What is it then?'

She drew a shuddering breath but wouldn't look at him.

'The laparoscopy went well, and they removed her appendix with no problems. Ayesha's surgery was late in the afternoon under general anaesthetic, and she had to stay in the hospital overnight. She had a private room. I was with her the whole time, but after dinner, when the nurse gave her a sedative, Ayesha told me to go home and get some proper rest instead of trying to sleep in a chair. I knew she would be asleep for several hours, so I left her to go home for a shower, change of clothes, and to let the dog out for a few minutes. I was only home for an hour and with the drive back and forth, I was gone for less than two hours.'

'She's been abducted?'

'No, Mick. She was raped.'

Mick knew what it was like to be punched in the solar plexus. He'd experienced it hundreds of times, but he had never felt such a body blow before. He had no breath left. His mouth opened and closed, but he couldn't breathe. He doubled over, not realising that the keening filling the room was coming from him.

When he was breathing again, Leila sat down beside him.

'Tell me.' His voice was quiet and even, his face a blank.

'When I got back to her room at the hospital, everything looked fine. Nothing looked disturbed, and she was still fast asleep. In the morning, she was uncomfortable, but that was to be expected after the surgery. Her stitches looked fine, so I took her home. That afternoon, she told me.' Leila stopped, unable to continue.

'Go on,' said Mick in the same expressionless monotone.

'Ayesha thought it'd been a bad dream, but she remembered it. She said she couldn't move, couldn't speak or call for help. Could barely open her eyes. She tried but couldn't push them away. She thought there were two of them, but she's not sure. Maybe it was the same person attacking her twice, or maybe she was seeing double. But she's convinced that she heard two voices talking to each other even though they sounded very similar. She remembers their voices. And she's sure she heard the clicks of mobile phone cameras.'

'Where is Ayesha now?'

'At home, with her father — I mean, with Amir. He was on a business trip to Shanghai and caught the first flight back when I told him about her surgery. He got back late last evening. But he doesn't know. Ayesha didn't want me to tell him. She doesn't want anyone else to know.'

'Did the police—?'

Leila shook her head vehemently. 'No, she's adamant she won't tell the police. She doesn't want them caught, tried and convicted, Mick. She wants them dead.'

# 58

# CATHY

**Today – Friday 27 July**

1.13 a.m. The train sped through the countryside and approached Southampton Airport Parkway Station. Fields with trees and hedges marking off their boundaries presented a green-hued palette on one side of the train. On the other side lay acres of parking and tarmacked spaces, large warehouse-type buildings, hotels and businesses. Several small planes, both commercial and private parked in their bays, gleamed in the summer sunshine. Cathy and Andrea had often talked about taking a trip to one of over 40 European destinations served by the airport, but their schedules had never worked out. Cathy envied the people escaping the grind of their daily lives, quarantining their troubles, at least for a while.

She would reach her destination in another eight minutes and would have no choice but to face her future. But she parked that prospect for now and thought about that last afternoon of her interview at the Met.

## Yesterday afternoon – Thursday 26 July

S he should have been elated. Just before noon, they'd released her without charge. They found no evidence of her involvement and appeared satisfied that she hadn't helped to cover up the crime. But emotionally drained and frozen, Cathy had simply nodded when Superintendent Oleja announced their decision.

'Thank you. I know you still have questions, and I'm willing to stay on here as long as you need me to answer any queries you have,' she offered, ignoring her lawyer's scowl.

'We would appreciate that. It would also save us from having to recall you. We can close this matter, send off our report to your superiors and get back to our jobs.'

They seemed more relaxed, less aggressive during that last session. Although they still maintained poker faces and watchful eyes, both Cathy and Jim felt an easing of the tension.

Superintendent Oleja leaned forward. 'You told us you hadn't viewed the contents of the Dwyers' mobile phone or laptops. So, presumably you don't know what else is on there?'

*Now what? What else were they going to bring up? More reasons to keep me here? Maybe even re-arrest and charge me?* Her heart racing, Cathy looked to Jim for help, but he was equally puzzled.

'The Dwyer twins had done this before. At least three times that we know of. And they video-recorded it. It's on their laptops.'

Cathy gasped.

After a long silence, Superintendent Oleja continued. 'We won't keep you much longer. But can you tell us ... No one suspected Mr O'Neal. There was absolutely no evidence pointing to him. He left no trace that would lead the police to him. In other words, he may never have been caught. So why did he confess? Why risk everything after going to such lengths to commit what could have been the perfect crime?'

Memory of the pain and anger in Mick's voice reverberated in Cathy's head.

*Every time I saw their smiling faces plastered on the news, every time I read about how good, how kind they were, I wished they were still alive so I could kill them all over again. Every time I thought about Ayesha and the other patients – people whom those bastards were supposed to help – I wanted to smash them to a pulp. They betrayed their oath and their patients' trust. They caused intentional harm. I could've lived with their virtues being touted in the press and social media. I could even endure the crowdfunding to raise money for a charity in their name. After all, it'd help others and something good would come of those creeps' existence. But the announcement that the hospital proposed to rename the ward after them—. To think that they'd be remembered forever as heroes. No, that was a step too far—.*

'Mick couldn't take that. Not a permanent memorial to them, in the very ward where they assaulted his daughter,' said Cathy.

She jerked her head up as the realisation of the consequences of Mick's confession struck her. 'But that also meant exposing his daughter's role in all this. I don't understand why'd he'd do that.'

'Apparently, Mr O'Neal sent Leila a copy of his confession a few hours after he told you. Just before he disappeared. When she failed to get hold of him, she rushed to her daughter's flat and a couple of hours later, they contacted the police.' For the first time, the superintendent's smile held genuine amusement. 'I'm told that DCI Matthew Holt spent most last Monday dealing with two very hysterical women. And I'm also told he blames you for that.'

Cathy groaned. There was a whole truckload of pain awaiting her when she returned home. *Maybe the Met's cells aren't that bad after all.*

'What's going to happen to Ayesha?'

'Nothing really, apart from being questioned and your team going through their phones and emails. There's no evidence Ayesha even knew about her biological father – although it's a safe bet she does now – let alone what he was up to. There's nothing linking her or her mother to those murders and no proof of the assault on the Dwyers' phones or laptops. Besides, they can afford to hire the best legal services in England, which I understand from DCI Matt Holt they've already done.'

*I'm glad. Mick'll be too. The poor girl will have more than enough to deal with when the media picks up on all this. And they will...* But Cathy did not voice her thoughts.

'What about the hospital? Their plan to rename the ward?'

'That's definitely not going to happen. Your boss already had a word with the hospital board.'

# 59

## MICK

**Thursday 22 March**

Mick leaned in, using all his weight and strength to thrust the men apart. With one knee pressed into the bed for leverage, he stretched the already taut rope linking the twin brothers by their necks. He watched the tremors twitching their bodies fighting for life even as it ebbed away. He held on long after their last throes ceased. Held on until resuscitation was impossible.

Eventually satisfied, he straightened. Expressionless, he stared at the purple hued visages, the bulging eyes and protruding tongues before leaning over to unfasten the noose from around each corpse's neck. He stood back to assess the scene before him. All looked well. Other than the bodies themselves, he'd touched nothing in the bedroom.

*Wonder how long before they find these two. Not for a few days, I hope.*

A flicker of movement on the outermost edge of his field of vision caught his attention. His gaze landed on the fly high up on the wall, well beyond his reach, its large reddish compound eyes fixed on him. Alert, it twitched and in anticipation, rubbed its hind legs together.

Mick coiled the blue-and-white polyester washing line around his fist and elbow like a sleeping viper and went into the Dwyer brothers' living room. He picked the snipped pieces of cable ties and the lengths of rope he'd used as neck restraints off the floor and shoved the lot into his backpack. In went the two laptops and mobile phones. From the dining table, he gathered up the strips of duct tape, empty syringes, needles, stun gun and bloodied knife. His gaze landed on the sliced off fingertip. He hesitated, shrugged, left it lying there.

A final measured walk around the room reassured him. He'd missed nothing. Left no trace. He hoisted the heavy backpack across his shoulders. Time to go.

Mick peered through the peephole. The landing was clear. He edged down the stairs and out of the building.

Keeping to the shadows and avoiding CCTV cameras, he sidled through unlit, deserted alleys. The rats, cats and foxes rummaging in bins ignored him as he slipped through the gloom on the three-mile trek back to the car park where Tom waited. In an alleyway, he peeled off the undersole of his boots and stashed them into the backpack.

'High bloody time,' grumbled Tom when Mick tapped on the window of his car. 'All OK?'

'Yep. Uh, well, maybe.'

Despite the darkness of their surroundings, Mick felt the ferocity of Tom's glare.

'You'll never guess who I ran into at the Naylands.'

'I'm not in the mood for guessing games.'

'Stanley. Corporal James Stanley. Remember him? From our mission in Iraq?'

'Woah. He lives in the Naylands?'

'Well, you could kind of say that. He certainly sleeps there. In the bin store. He's homeless.'

Silence while Tom pondered. 'Did he recognize you?'

'Yes, I'm sure he did.'

'And you left him alive?'

'Yes. Even after he asked me to kill him.'

Another long silence while they considered their options. Tom sighed. 'That's a complication we could've done without. Let's wait and see what happens.'

'Have you told Leila yet?' asked Tom a minute later.

'Just doing it,' said Mick, tapping into his phone. He hit the 'send' icon.

*Am in Soton. R u free for dinner tonight?*

Her answer would be no. But Leila would know what he meant.

# 60

# CATHY

**Yesterday evening – Thursday 26 July**

It was almost 6.00 p.m. when they finally let her go. Cathy checked into a nearby hotel and showered three times before she felt clean. The king sized bed with its crisp clean white sheets was the most inviting thing in the room.

However, before collapsing into it, she had one more task. She phoned her boss, DCI Matthew Holt.

'Are you OK, Cathy? Superintendent Oleja phoned to say that they released you without charge.'

'I'm fine, sir. I'll be OK. I'm calling about Marek Kováč's murder and Grozdan Horvat's disappearance.'

'What about it? It's not your case anymore, Cathy.'

'I know, sir. I understand from Superintendent Oleja that Major Tom Cassidy has sold his business, liquidated his assets, and disappeared. Have you found him?'

'No, not yet. Not that it's any of your business.'

'Have you searched his place? He lives on his business premises. His flat's above the offices. Have you searched it, sir?'

'Again, not your concern.' His tone grew colder, curter.

'Please, sir, tell me.'

'What's this about, Cathy?'

'I think I know what happened to Grozdan ... where he is.'

Silence. But he hadn't hung up on her yet. She waited, then heard the hiss of a sigh in her ear.

'We searched Tom Cassidy's premises. It now belongs to another company, Premier Limo Services, who bought it lock, stock and barrel. There was nothing left of Major Cassidy's personal belongings anywhere on site. Apparently, the new owners had been looking to buy him out for some time, so they jumped at the chance. Paid cash. All of which have disappeared into one or more offshore accounts. Even though we've no evidence he was involved in the Dwyer twins' murder, there's an alert out for him. Just like there is for Michael O'Neal.'

That last part was meant to sting. Cathy guessed the stigma of her relationship would haunt her for a long time, but right now, she had more important matters to discuss.

'Was there any sign of any building or construction work in his garden?'

'In his garden? No, none. Why? What's that got to do with Grozdan? Oh, wait a minute.'

She heard the clicking of his computer keys.

'He was building an extension to his garages at the back. He already had the concrete slab laid and was waiting for planning permission to complete the build. The new owners have the approval now and are going ahead with it.'

'I think Grozdan Horvat is buried beneath that concrete, sir.'

Another silence. Cathy expected him to tell her to stop being ridiculous and start worrying about herself, begin preparing for her disciplinary hearing tomorrow. But she should have known better. DCI Holt was good at connecting dots.

'You think that Tom Cassidy and Mick O'Neil killed Marek and Grozdan, took Grozdan's body back to Kingston and buried him there?'

'Yes, sir.'

'Why?'

'Because they believed Marek and Grozdan killed Stanley. Or at least, they were responsible for his death. Stanley was one of theirs and they look after their own.'

'Hmm...'

Cathy waited out the long pause.

'You'd better be right. I'll have to sell this to the Super and to the Court as the premises are outside our jurisdiction. The new owners will not be happy.'

DCI Holt sighed. 'I should have listened to my instincts and not hired you. You realize you are nothing but trouble, don't you?'

'Yes, sir. Sorry, sir.'

For the first time in a very long time, Cathy smiled.

# 61

## GROZDAN

**Four months ago – Monday 9 April**

On the night following their encounter with Stanley and his subsequent death, Grozdan and Marek pushed their way into the little patch of clearing behind the shrubs a few metres beyond the Titanic Engineers' Memorial in East Park, Southampton.

They had not expected him to die. Their intention had been to teach him a lesson, to make an example of him for the others they preyed on, and to anyone who proposed to betray them. They thought of old Stanley with regret. They'd just lost an easy source of income.

But right now, their focus was on the shadowy figure in the bushes, dimly illuminated by the glow of a mobile phone. To the hand beckoning them further into the depths of the hedges.

They thrust aside the branches, heads bent, their forearms raised protectively in front of their faces to ward off sharp twigs.

'Ticho!' *Quietly!* Ordered the silhouette leading the way.

The faint glow of the phone torch clicked off. After the lights at the Titanic Engineers' Memorial, the blanket of darkness was like a bucket of ink poured over their heads.

Grozdan swore. 'What the fuck, Anton?'

'Shut up,' ordered the voice, moving further into a blackness that consumed their irises. With sight now a worthless accessory, they followed the voice.

A sharp tug on the back of his jacket stopped Grozdan in his tracks. His legs continued their forward momentum while the centre of gravity of his upper body shifted, tilting him backwards, causing him to lose his balance. He opened his mouth to cry out, but an arm wrapped tight around his neck choked off all sound. Even as he felt himself tip and fall backwards, his hands reached out to pull off the stranglehold of the arm across his throat, but he clutched empty air. With a whoosh, his lungs emptied the breath it had drawn to cry out.

Grozdan tried to correct the backward momentum and break his fall by dropping on one knee, his arms whirling, trying to grasp something. Anything. They grasped sharp, spiky twigs. With a hoarse cry, he let go.

A weight thrust down on his shoulder, forcing him down on both knees while the stranglehold around his throat tightened. Grozdan opened his mouth, trying to suck in air. He was blacking out. Suddenly, the throttlehold eased, freeing him. Head tilted to the night sky, he wheezed, drawing in an enormous lungful of precious air.

A pair of hard, metal-like vices clamped on either side of his face. No, not metal. He knew they weren't metal because he could feel the warmth of human hands through the rubbery gloves. His fingers hooked onto his assailant's, tried to claw them away, but those warm rods of steel held on. He couldn't budge them.

The vice tightened. He felt his head lifted upwards, his neck stretched to its fullest length. After that chokehold, it felt heavenly, not unlike the physiotherapy he'd had a few years before when he'd strained his trapezius, his neck and shoulder muscles. It felt good. For a millisecond, it felt wonderful.

The palms clinching his face turned his head to his right as far as it would go and held it there. So soothing, relaxing. Grozdan felt a knee against the middle of his shoulder blades as the man braced himself. Then, in a lightning-fast move, his captor twisted Grozdan's neck sharply to the left in completely the opposite direction. That sudden rotation to the left continued and continued.

*Crack!*

Grozdan's head now faced backwards, far beyond the natural capability of any human neck.

The crack as his cervical vertebrae snapped and his brainstem severed rang deafeningly in Grozdan's ears. It reverberated within his skull and stayed with him as he continued his journey into eternity.

After several paces of blindly following the shadow within the shadows, the odd noises behind him alerted Marek that his friend was no longer beside him. He turned round, squinted, then shut his eyes tight to adjust them to the darkness. He opened them again and gasped. For a heartbeat, the sight of his big friend on his knees with a shadow stooping over him took predominance over the chokehold that rendered him immobile and cut off his own oxygen supply.

But his survival instinct quickly reasserted itself. Scrabbling desperately at the arm around his throat and despite the strength of that hold, Marek dragged himself forward. His reflex to escape overcame the urge to help Grozdan.

The elbow digging into his back and the kick to the back of his knees sent him towards the ground, but the stranglehold around his throat didn't ease off. Rigid bars pressed into the sides of his neck. Despite their inflexibility and strength, he knew they were fingers. He didn't realize those digits were seeking his carotid artery, cutting off blood supply to his brain.

A hollow ringing sounded inside his head as he lost consciousness. A white haze swamped him. Someone continued to stuff and cram wool into his skull, but it was no longer soft or fluffy. The haze turned pitch-black.

Marek's arms flopped at his side, and his legs turned to jelly. He no longer seemed able to coordinate any of his motor functions.

Though semi-conscious and no longer in control of himself, he still retained awareness, knew there was someone behind him, holding him up. He was aware of the hard, unyielding body against his back, manoeuvring and manipulating his movements like a puppet master.

He felt himself propelled forward, his feet skimming the ground, almost floating towards his friend until he was close enough to touch him.

Or rather, to be punched by him. Hard. Right on the mouth.

*How odd*, he thought, the pain barely registering as his lips split against his teeth. *Why is Grozdan's head flopping like that?*

But the strike re-engaged his brain, even sharpened his vision. There was another shadowy figure behind Grozdan, smaller than his tall, bulky friend, but holding him upright as easily as though he were a 5-year-old child. Marek watched as the lithe shadow clasped Grozdan's wrist and drew his arm back. He registered the pain and shock as the clenched fist lashed out again to sock him hard against his jaw.

Marek's head snapped sharply sideways as a black cloud descended, this time enveloping him in oblivion.

Had he been awake and cognisant, Marek would have been shocked at the knife that suddenly appeared in Grozdan's fist. Stunned to see the shadow grasp Grozdan's arm, draw it back, and thrust it forward. Watched unbelievingly as his friend's fist plunged the knife between Marek's ribs, straight through his heart.

He did not hear a thing and felt little. Although still upstanding propped up by the stranger behind him, Marek did not hear the sucking sound of his sparse flesh trying to hold on to the blade as it was pulled out. But he definitely felt the knife strike again, this time into his stomach. He wheezed as the shadow behind Grozdan manipulating his friend's fist, wrenched the blade out and tossed it aside.

The arms holding him let go and the body behind him moved away. Marek crumpled to the ground in a foetal position, as his heart slowed and finally stopped.

He stared sightlessly as one of the assailants scuffed the earth all around him. The second hoisted Grozdan up and over his shoulders in a fireman's lift and melted into the bushes.

The man who stayed behind switched on his mobile torch, checked for a pulse in Marek's throat, grunted in satisfaction when he found none. His torch swept the surroundings. He dragged a fallen branch over the arena where the drama had played out. Then he, too, vanished into the darkness.

Centre stage, Marek lay curled up on the cold earth without a ghost-light left on for him or the other spirits haunting this small open air theatre to illuminate their ghostly performance.

# 62

## MICK

### Tuesday 10 April

*Less than 24 hours* after Grozdan and Marek's death, a sturdy marquee erected alongside the garages sheltered their killers and shielded their labour from the cold April showers, as well as from prying eyes – human and those of any satellites or drones passing overhead. Naturally paranoid, they made certain it concealed them from any spectators, even accidental ones. The only light within the dark tarpaulin-walled tent came from the headlamps the men had strapped around their foreheads and a spike-mounted floodlight, its glare directed downwards into a rectangular pit with the edges marked out by stakes and string.

Mick and Tom had begun digging at 9.00 p.m., and now three hours later, the trench was almost 5 feet deep. Another foot to go. Tom pulled the ladder down into the pit and climbed out. He staggered a few paces to collapse breathlessly on the bare ground, well away from the heaped-up earth.

'Take a break, lad,' he called.

Mick vaulted out of the pit, squatted beside the older man and handed him a bottle of water.

'You're getting too old for this. Isn't it time you retired and got yourself an allotment?'

Tom groaned. 'What? And do more digging? No way! Fishing. That's going to be my thing. I'll sit on the banks of a lake or a river and watch the world go by. What about you?'

'I don't think I'll live that long.'

'Don't be ridiculous. You really are morbid tonight. Of course, you will. I'll make sure you do. I need someone to take care of me when I go gaga.'

'You already are, and I already do,' said Mick.

'Hey!'

Mick laughed, rose and leapt back into the hole.

'Your ankle seems to have miraculously healed,' said Tom.

'Those bandages were itching.'

'You'll need to keep them on for another couple of days, at least. Your sprain was supposedly serious enough to have got me out of bed in the middle of the night to fetch you.'

Mick grunted and rammed the shovel into the earth. Tom joined him reluctantly.

The next two hours were harder than either of them had envisaged. The earth grew tighter packed, and the deeper they dug, the further they had to toss the soil. Although Mick fared better, he too had to stop more often as his shoulders screamed in agony. They took turns. One digging while the other pitched the loose mud out of the pit.

Eventually, it was done. The rectangular pit was deep enough at over 6 feet to satisfy Tom. They needn't have dug it so deep. They could have got away with a 4-foot hole, especially with all the hardcore and concrete that would be poured over it in the next few days. But Tom had insisted that they did it right. A full 6 feet deep.

Drooping with fatigue, they climbed out and stood at its edge, staring into its dark depths.

Mick fished out another couple of water bottles and tossed one to Tom, frowning as the older man's shaky hands fumbled the catch.

'Give me the keys,' he said.

'I'm fine. I just need a minute.'

'Keys,' he repeated.

Too tired to argue, Tom shuffled across to a plastic crate in the marquee's corner, reached into his jacket pocket and handed over his car keys.

Mick slipped on a raincoat, pocketed the keys and grabbed the handles of a wheelbarrow.

'Give me a minute and I'll give you a hand. It won't be easy getting it out of the car.'

'I'll be fine. I know what to expect.'

Mick flicked on the switch of his headlamp and strode off into the night, while Tom slid down on his haunches, leaned against the wall of the garage adjoining the marquee, and closed his eyes.

He jerked awake when Mick returned half an hour later, wheeling the barrow laden with an enormous bundle wrapped in a woollen blanket.

'Isn't that my—?' outraged, he pointed an indignant finger at the blanket.

'Yep. You'll need a new one unless you want to wash this.'

'No way! Why'd you have to use my blanket? There are plastic sheets in the garden shed.'

'Not thick enough. It was bloody difficult getting it out of the car, you know. I needed something thick to help protect it from the edges of the boot.'

Tom grunted his irritation.

'C'mon. Let's get it over with.'

Between them, they unwrapped the bundle and stripped Grozdan's body. Everyone knew a nude body decomposed faster than a clothed one, especially buried in bare earth. Pity there were no wounds on the corpse. The cuts would have provided entry points for insects and bacteria to accelerate decomposition. But Grozdan's death had been clean and quick.

*Better than he deserved,* thought Mick.

Even with the two of them coordinating their actions, stripping the corpse proved to be more difficult and took longer than they expected. The body was in full rigor mortis, and they couldn't manoeuvre the clothes past his limbs. Added to which, Grozdan was a big, bulky man. In the end, they had to cut off most of his clothing.

Despite the cold in the air, Mick and Tom were sweating and panting by the time they finished undressing the body. Finally, there he lay in the barrow, as naked as the day he was born, still curled up in a foetal position.

With a glance at each other, they pushed the wheelbarrow to the edge of the pit and tipped the body into its grave, wincing at the loud thump when it hit bottom.

'You know, we should've staged it differently and reversed their roles,' said Tom. 'We should've had Marek stab

Grozdan and left this big fella in the park, then brought Marek back here with us. He was only a weedy guy. We could have got away with a smaller grave and a lot less digging.'

'Now he tells me!' In disgust, Mick jammed his shovel into the piled up earth and tossed a spadeful into the pit.

# 63

# CATHY

## Today – Friday 27 July

1 1.22 a.m. The voice over the train's PA system announcing that they were approaching Southampton Central station jerked Cathy back to the present. They'd arrived.

Like her, everyone shuffled around, collecting their belongings. Many had their phones out and were speaking into them or texting. She would make her way to her meeting by taxi.

Cathy's hands sought and drew out the folded note from her pocket and smoothed out the creases. She'd already read it a gazillion times, but it still broke her heart.

*My beautiful Catherine,*

*I am so very sorry for so many things, but most of all for lying to you, for betraying your trust. There is much that I regret and wish I could undo, but not my time with you. Every moment with you was precious to me.*

*I love you.*
*Mick*

Cathy carefully refolded the note along the creases and tucked it into her pocket.

I love you too, she thought. 'I hate you,' she whispered.

Would she ever see him again?

Did she want to?

The police had already launched a search for both Tom and Mick but had so far found no one by those names or description travelling out of the UK. The search was now global. Their departure seemed to have been meticulously planned, but Cathy also knew that it meant a lifetime of hiding for them.

She suspected, hoped, that the three of them – Mick, Tom and their puppy CJ, Calamity Jane – were together somewhere.

She hoped they would be caught and thrown into prison for a long time.

She prayed they would remain free.

*I've no idea what'll happen to me. Will I still have my job after my meeting with the Disciplinary Board? Did I still want it?*

All Cathy knew was that whatever her future, it would be a bleak one without Mick.

# EPILOGUE

## Saturday morning

C athy jerked awake from the fitful sleep she'd fallen into barely two hours ago. Confused and disoriented, she lay still, curled up in a foetal position with the bedcover tangled around her, awaiting the onslaught of the clamour she'd become accustomed to during the past week.

The silence that greeted her felt alien. She sniffed and the stench of open toilets pervaded her nostrils. The reek had permeated through her pores into her core. A corruption that no number of showers or soaks in the bath could erase.

She lay motionless, suspended between reverie and reality.

*Am I still in prison and dreaming I'm at home? Or am I at home reliving my nightmare?*

Realisation dawned, relief followed, and her heartbeats steadied. The assault on her senses was a memory, a nightmare. She was home. In her own bed. With her daughter and parents asleep in the adjoining rooms.

The reunion with her family had been emotional with 14-year-old Emily glued to her side all evening. Her daughter had even reverted to calling Cathy *mummy* instead of *mum* as she'd been doing for the past two years. Her parents too had remained within touching distance.

*I'd come so close to losing them.* Cathy shuddered at the thought, trying not to think of the man who'd wreaked such havoc on her life.

*I'm here. I'm OK, or I will be...*

She breathed in deeply and stretched, relishing the crisp, clean smell and luxuriating in the softness of her bed.

Eventually, she rose and crept downstairs.

Her disciplinary hearing had been far more brutal than she expected. Yesterday afternoon, she had faced a panel of senior officers whom she only knew by name, led by the Chief Superintendent with whom she had never exchanged more than a greeting.

'We'll let you know our decision in 24 hours,' they told her at the end of the meeting.

24 hours waiting for the axe to fall, for fall it would. Of that, she had no doubt.

After all, she deserved it. Her bosses had borne the brunt of the media fallout. But a segment of the press had been sympathetic to the motive behind the crimes. A few even hailed Mick as a hero. The police, however, spoke out strongly against vigilante justice.

'I bet Mick would kill anyone who hurt you, mum,' her daughter Emily had said last night with ghoulish relish.

*He probably would*, thought Cathy. But in the eyes of law, he was unequivocally a criminal. He would be arrested and prosecuted as soon as they found him.

Curled up on the settee with her fingers wrapped around a steaming mug of tea, Cathy tried to squelch the pain in her heart and the vacuum consuming her like a black hole.

The rumble of a vehicle outside distracted her. She glanced at her watch. Almost 7.00 a.m., still too early for the post and most deliveries.

*Probably one of the neighbours.* She couldn't be bothered to get up and check.

But a knock on her front door a minute later forced her up. She glanced from the delivery man on her threshold to the white van with a colourful logo 'Solent Florists' emblazoned on its side parked on the street.

She accepted the long, slim box and scrawled her signature on the tablet he held out.

'Thank you,' she smiled.

With a grunt, the man waved and jogged back to his van.

Mystified, Cathy laid the elegant white and gold box on the coffee table. She glanced around the room at the bouquets from friends and colleagues. A bouquet was the norm, this single rose a puzzle.

She undid the red silk ribbon and lifted the lid off the package from Solent Florists.

A perfect red rose, nestled in a bed of white silk. It was beautiful.

Eyes closed, she smiled and inhaled the sweet, delicate scent of roses wafting across the room.

*Who—?*

Mystified, Cathy picked up the simple but elegant gold-edged card.

The message read:

*Ever yours,*
*M.*

# THANK YOU FOR READING

**Please help by leaving a review.**

Reviews and recommendations are crucial for independent authors like me. Even a short, one sentence review can make a big difference.

I'd be grateful if you would post a brief review on Amazon today. A few sentences to say you enjoyed this book would be brilliant.

And if you enjoyed this book, it would be great if you would consider recommending it to your family and friends.

Thank you for reading my book.

With best wishes,

*Jay*

# ACKNOWLEDGEMENTS

The idea for this book began with an assignment for my Writing Crime course with Faber Academy where we had to create a police detective. For me, that was Detective Inspector Cathy Collins. Another assignment to write an action scene, and ex-SAS Captain Mick O'Neal was born.

Turning an idea into a book was fun, but the real work begins after that. Honing it into a publishable novel requires critical but encouraging feedback. Luckily, I have two people I can rely on for honest and constructive advice.

Firstly, my brother, Rajan. I am forever grateful for the countless hours you so generously continue to give me. Thank you for your endless patience and for suffering through my first drafts, followed by—I've lost count of how many—subsequent revisions and numerous edits. You've been there for me literally from cover to cover.

I am so blessed to also have my son, Gavin's enduring support. Despite the pressure of work and a busy family life, you still make the time and space for me. I couldn't have done it without your insight and advice. And I love your design concept for my front cover.

Without you both, this book would have remained yet another manuscript cluttering up my computer.

And to my delight, my novel won the 2022 Page Turner Award in the Crime Genre under its then working title *The Assassin Who Loved Me*.

I would also like to give a big thanks to my editor, Gale Winskill and to my beta readers, James Robertson, Jenny Walters and my sister, Manju for their valuable feedback. You gave me the courage to publish this book.

While the city of Southampton located in Hampshire in England is a real place, many of the street names and sites are fictional, such as St John's Hospital, the Solent Constabulary, the Southampton City Police, their headquarters. Bertling, Seddingfold (and the Earl of Seddingfold), Greengage Barracks amongst others in this book are also imaginary and any resemblance to actual places or people are purely coincidental.

Although it is possible to do much of the research over the internet, there are some questions that only people in the field can answer. The logistics of delivering mail to apartment blocks, for example. My thanks to the lovely Kirsty for explaining how it all works. Kirsty delivers our mail *'come rain, snow or gloom'* (to paraphrase Terry Pratchett's words in Going Postal), and she does so with a cheerfulness that brightens our day.

A penultimate and very special thanks to my husband, George, to whom this book is dedicated, for his unstinting support, encouragement and patience.

And finally, a gigantic thank you to all my readers. It has been a joy writing for you, and I hope you enjoyed this book.

# AUTHOR NEWSLETTER

**Want to know when my next book is released?**

Sign up to my website and you'll be among the first to know!
**www.jayjonesbooks.com**
It is spam-free, and I promise not to share your email address
with anyone else and I will only contact you about my books.
And if you enjoyed this book, please tell your family and
friends about it.
Thank you,
Jay

www.jayjonesbooks.com

# About the Author

Winner of 2022 Page Turner Crime Genre Award, **Jay Jones** has always been an avid reader. If it has words, she'll read it.

As a child with limited access to bookshops and libraries, she'd even read her next year's textbooks for fun.

And she wrote. Filled cheap notebooks with stories, essays and poems.

With a background in accounting, finance and law, spreadsheets rather than words dominated her working career and Jay didn't realise how much she missed writing until she took it up again a few years ago.

Jay now lives in Worcester with her husband and a very pampered cat. A seasoned traveller, she has also lived, worked and studied in India, China and France. Jay's writings reflect her appreciation of the varied cultures, customs and beliefs gained from her experiences abroad.

When not writing or reading, Jay enjoys painting, cooking and slow walks – slow because of the numerous stops to rescue suicidal earthworms and snails along the way.

www.jayjonesbooks.com

Printed in Great Britain
by Amazon